AURORA: A CHILD OF TWO WORLDS

AURORA: A CHILD OF TWO WORLDS

DAVID A. HARDY

COSMOS

AURORA: A CHILD OF TWO WORLDS

Published in the US by **Cosmos Books, an imprint of Wildside Press**
PO Box 301, Holicong, PA 18928-0301
www.cosmos-books.com
www.wildsidepress.com

ISBN: 1-59224-201-4

ACKNOWLEDGEMENTS

I am indebted to the late Dr Anthony T. Lawton, one-time President of the British Interplanetary Society, for checking and supplying data on star evolution and the mechanism of novae and supernovae. To Michael J. Guest, Secretary of the Midland Dowsing Association, for checking the description of dowsing. The interpretation of this information is entirely mine! To Paul Barnett for his encouragement and for editing the final MS. And not least to my wife, Ruth (a non-SF reader, normally) for painstakingly reading and re-reading this story and offering many valuable comments, suggestions and corrections.

ACT ONE

Any Port in a Storm

Any Port in a Storm

The darkened land lay swathed in bandages of cloud which, pallidly reflecting the light of a full Moon, hid fresh wounds and old scars alike.

The horizon flattened as he levelled the craft out at five thousand metres. When the clouds parted, not a glimmer appeared below except a glint of moonlight on water in the distance. To his unaided eyes, the city spread out beneath him might be totally lifeless. His instruments said otherwise, though; they showed he was passing through a lattice of powerful radio beams. Reaching forward slightly, he touched a button. Just a regular pulse throbbed in his ears: no voices.

With a reflex that startled even himself, he swooped upward, narrowly missing the black-coated craft which had suddenly appeared before him, diving across his own line of flight. Only its four sets of flickering exhausts had picked it out to his keen eyes. Increasing the sensitivity of his screen (and mentally cursing himself for relying on his own vision until then), he saw it drawing away from him; but others were approaching. Five ... ten ... twenty ... All were roughly at his own level, but losing height.

He eased his craft into their line, following them down to about three thousand metres. Above, a few stars shone coldly.

Below and ahead of him, a cluster of brilliant new stars appeared as though sprinkled by a giant hand. The coils of the great river he had seen earlier shone like molten silver in the brightening glow. The blue-white flares were joined by more—and more. Now there were hundreds, dripping from the sky beneath plumes of white vapour until they drowned out the moonlight.

It seemed, at first, a beautiful sight, reminiscent of the pyrotechnics at a carnival. But soon it became obvious that this incandescent snow had an evil intent. Alighting upon buildings, it transformed itself swiftly into orange and red flames which licked hungrily at roofs and windows. In the fitful light of the flames he could see thick black smoke begin to billow upward. Now great gouts of fire started to leap into the air at various points along the sides of the river, then further into the city. He could envisage bricks, tiles and chunks of concrete flying in all directions.

The river turned from silver into blood. Pale beams of light sprang from the ground and probed at the clouds, sweeping slowly back and forth.

His craft rocked, buffeted by a blast of hot air from below. Spiralling slowly downwards he headed further south, away from the worst of the destruction, and began to descend.

He had no option. His fuel was almost exhausted.

#

The Heinkel was "riding the beam" above the English coastline, the strong and regular pulse in the wireless operator's earphones showing that his receiver was keeping them on course for their target, ignoring the decoy beams laid by other German stations to bluff the British. Hauptmann Herman Schirmer, the pilot, knew exactly where to deliver his package that night: Waterloo Station. In just about thirty minutes the bomb-doors would open and eight incendiaries would be followed by two 250-kilo high explosives.

The thought gave Schirmer no pleasure. Ten years earlier, when he'd been seventeen, he had visited Britain and made many friends. Quite possibly he was now about to destroy some of those friends . . . but he had been trained to obey orders without question, so he would drop his deadly load and then return for more. The most he could do was to try to ensure that his aim was accurate and would not senselessly destroy the homes of innocent Londoners.

As midnight approached, his aircraft flew steadily at 290 kilometres per hour and five kilometres high, following in line on the tails of a dozen identical Heinkels. Some of their pilots, he knew only too well, would not be so scrupulous about where their loads landed. Just drop them and get back to base, that was their attitude. He sighed and rubbed his cramped neck.

There was no need now for the intersecting beams to guide them to their target. As he drew closer, Schirmer could clearly see that London was ablaze, burning like a bonfire on the horizon.

The sight appalled him.

The misty-white pencils of the searchlights quested to and fro, but he felt fairly confident that the coating of lamp-black on the Heinkels would absorb the light.

He certainly hoped so . . .

There was a sudden hellish racket in the cockpit, and he saw the unmistakable glowing red lines of tracer drawing a dotted line through the thin metal skin to his right.

A sharp stab of pain in his calf, and he could see, through a windscreen now streaming with black oil from the starboard engine, the familiar shape of a Spitfire pulling away for a second attack. A yellow tongue of flame burst from the Heinkel's engine.

He hauled on the stick—the craft was yawing to starboard—but it would not respond.

"Get rid of the bombs!" he gasped.

His aircraft must be lightened. He felt a perverse pleasure, despite his Luftwaffe training, as he imagined the bombs falling harmlessly on the open countryside below. Then he realized with a shock that the Heinkel was already well over the capital.

"Bail out!" he barked into his intercom.

No reply.

"Hans? Wernher?"

He glanced behind him. All four of his crew were slumped across their controls.

Through a jagged hole in the floor he glimpsed a broad, shining curve of the Thames reflecting burning warehouses and factories. Frantically he searched for somewhere to crash the Heinkel; not, as he knew he should, where it would do maximum damage, but where it would do as little as possible.

But where? The river was behind him. There was nowhere else . . .

As the plane began to spin it struck him forcibly that he did not want to die. He struggled desperately with the escape hatch. It finally burst open and he was choked by the acrid smell of the thick, oily smoke that blinded him before it swirled away in the slipstream.

He leapt into emptiness.

Moon. Clouds. Black buildings silhouetted against flames. Each whirled past time and again. He was falling, falling.

Schirmer jerked frantically at the ripcord. Too late—he had left it too late.

Then the parachute fluttered above him with a jolt that almost pulled his arms out of their sockets.

He knew he was travelling too fast, too close to the ground.

He had not called upon God in years, but now, eyes closed, he muttered a silent prayer.

#

When he opened his eyes again there was a shape beside him. For a moment he thought he was about to collide with another parachutist. But this figure had no 'chute—and he had the strangest feeling that it had risen *towards* him, not fallen. As it reached out its arms to him, a mere thirty metres above dark rooftops, it seemed not to touch him but to engulf him in a firm yet pliable web. Together they drifted relatively gently to the ground.

#

"Jerries! Two of 'em on one flamin' parachute!"

"Come on—let's give 'em wot for!"

Within seconds they were surrounded by men in Home Guard uniforms and helmets, rifle butts raised, heavy boots poised for kicking. Half-unconscious already, Schirmer tensed for the blows to fall.

When he opened his eyes the next time, the guardian angel responsible for saving his life had vanished. Around him lay Home Guard men in strangely stiff postures: arms still raised as though to pummel, legs outstretched to kick.

Then one of them stirred, moaned. Another sat up slowly, cursing. Herman edged away from them, but at that moment he saw the dim, cowled lights of a vehicle bearing down, jolting on the rubble-strewn street. It screeched to a halt, and in the brief glare of light from a distant explosion he saw the red cross on its side.

Two women ran out of the cab. One examined and questioned the rapidly recovering Home Guard men. The other bent over Schirmer. He saw the look of distaste which flickered across her homely face as she took in his Luftwaffe flying suit and harness, but she quickly became professional and turned her attention to his bleeding leg. Minutes later he was being thrust on a stretcher into the back of the ambulance.

Herman Schirmer knew that now he had at least a chance of surviving the war and seeing his family again. If only his fellow airmen would allow it, he thought wryly, as yet another wave of bombers thundered overhead.

Already, his mysterious saviour was being dismissed by the Home Guard stalwarts—and by himself—as a combination of shock, hallucination, imagination and optical illusion.

#

Old Annie Wimbush didn't hold with air raid shelters, and she told the warden so, vociferously.

"I've 'ad a good life, and I've lived in this 'ouse for the last fifty years. So did my Fred, till he died in 'is bed, Gawd bless 'im. 'Ere I've lived, and 'ere I'll die, and if some Jerry bomb's goin' to blow me 'ouse up it can take me with it, and that's that."

Seeing that she was not to be persuaded, Warden Bill Bramley pulled the blackout curtains closer together, then went outside to ensure that the chink of light that had first attracted his attention no longer showed.

"Good night, then," he called round the door, and he meant it sincerely.

Camberwell was peaceful so far, but further north, beyond the Thames, the skyline was an angry, shifting red glow. From time to time a vortex of hot air and smoke would boil up to meet the lowering cloud, which gave back the ruddy glare. With luck, he thought, the raid would not come any further south tonight.

Even as he completed the thought, he heard a high-pitched whine . . . which rapidly became a rushing roar. Then everything went black.

Warden Bill Bramley's war was over.

#

The house adjoining Mrs Wimbush's semi seemed to burst apart, yet hers was left standing, incongruously tall and narrow, apparently intact.

The appearance was deceptive. The connecting wall had fallen in upon the widow, leaving her half-buried. Both her legs were broken, and she had suffered smashed ribs and many other internal injuries.

Yet she remained conscious and alert; in shock and not yet aware of the pain.

She pushed weakly at the bricks all around her.

"Throwin' ruddy bricks now, they are. Joey?—are you all right, Joey?"

A domed cage lay on its side in the rubble, its bars bent and its door sprung open. There was a fluttering of tiny wings and a green shape landed on her shoulder. The budgerigar started nibbling at her ear.

"Oh, Joey, love, *there* you are! I'd rather they got me than you."

A spasm of further pain creased Annie's lined face, and again she scrabbled feebly at the bricks.

A new sound made her turn her head. She winced again. Had it just been more falling rubble?

"Help!" she cried. "Is anybody there?"

Then, with a flash of the humour for which she had been known in the neighbourhood for many years, she muttered, "It's a pity you ain't a pigeon, Joey. Then you could carry a message for me . . . Oooh, I wish somebody'd take this pain away."

A pale, insubstantial figure drifted into her field of view. All the lights had gone out when the bomb struck, but a broken gas main next door burnt with a harsh hiss, its yellow-white pillar of fire casting fugitive shadows. The glare limned the figure with gold, and for a moment she thought of an angel.

"Is that you, Mr Bramley? Can you give me an 'and? I'm stuck!"

The flames that had been licking tentatively at the rafters protruding from the open roof-space suddenly blossomed into a roaring, crackling ball of fire. Beams shifted and, with a groaning creak, began to topple.

The stranger placed a hand gently on the old lady's temple, then slipped away quickly. There was nothing more he could do here, and his time was short.

As her house began to collapse around her, Annie Wimbush's wish of a few minutes before was granted.

There was no more pain.

#

"Go to sleep, my baby . . . " crooned Dorothy Petrie drowsily, regretting for the thousandth time that she had ever let her husband, Rory, persuade her to leave Scotland for London when he was offered a better-paid job. Now he was away in the trenches, Lord knew where, up to his eyes in mud or worse, while she, instead of being safely asleep in their old, stone-built cottage tucked snugly into the hillside, tried to doze on a horse-hair sofa while her eight-year-old son Stephen waved his toy guns, assiduously shooting down the aeroplanes droning endlessly overhead, and her baby daughter, Aurora, tossed restlessly in her cot, whimpering, about to cry again.

Aurora. The imaginative name had been Dorothy's idea. The Northern Lights had been draping their ethereal multicoloured banners above the cottage on the night Dorothy and the kids had left for the south, for London.

Stephen had been dangerously ill with pneumonia—she put it down to his having to be taken through the cold air night after night to the shelters—but was now well on the mend. He had qualified for a Morrison indoor shelter: chocolate-brown metal plates bolted to a girder frame, with metal-grid sides. The Morrison was supposed to double as a table during the day, but the boy played inside it almost constantly, sticking cut-out models of Hurricanes, Spitfires, Lancasters, Messerschmitts and Heinkels to its "sky" with black cotton and Plasticine, spotlighting them with battery-powered searchlights and aiming wooden shells at them from model guns, complaining because caps were no longer available to supply sound effects.

The house shook as the *crump!* of a nearby explosion seemed to flatten the air.

That was too close for comfort!

Darting across the room, Dorothy grabbed the baby up from the cot and dived for the Morrison.

An eerie whistling sound grew louder, louder, louder. A cloud of soot burst from the fireplace. There was clatter from the roof.

For a moment there was silence, apart from a spattering rain of plaster.

Then the ceiling fell in.

"Stevie! Get back!" she cried in horror, lying on her side with a leg twisted beneath her, trapped under a heavy joist. The baby lay on the ground, just beyond her reach, but was bawling lustily, apparently more frightened than hurt. Through the clouds of choking dust she watched as her son, as though in slow motion, tried to crawl towards her from the shelter, wailing, terrified. Above her the roof gaped open to the sky. She could see showers of sparks streaming upwards from a burning building nearby. Water gushed out the end of a lead pipe that protruded from the hole, spreading in a dark stain down the wallpaper.

But these horrors were as nothing compared to another. Right above her, swinging from the rafters by the cords of its parachute, hung a dull metal cylinder.

A mine!

Her wartime conditioning was profound: even in her fright she found part of her brain thinking of the underwear she could make from the parachute's green silken folds.

But only for a second. Then the fear came surging back through her.

The tall chimney of Dobson & Dart's paint factory next door, which should have towered above her, was missing—absent from the patch of livid night sky framed by the shattered ceiling above her. And now she could see a solid fountain of flame gushing up from the factory, its roar like a blowtorch trying to sear the clouds. Tins of paint and varnish rocketed into the sky—at any moment one could splash its blazing contents around this room.

We're trapped! Oh, God, take me *but spare the kids . . .*

Stephen had crawled out of the Morrison. She watched, powerless, frozen, as the rest of the ceiling and a section of the Dobson & Dart chimney collapsed, covering Stevie and Aurora in dust, grit and stones. The baby disappeared completely, the sound of her crying cut off abruptly. Stevie, ominously silent now, was only partially hidden by the rubble and the rising shrouds of dust, his open eyes upon her.

She screamed wildly.

"Help! Oh, for God's sake, somebody, help!"

Silhouetted against the flames and sparks which filled the frame of sky overhead there came into view something bulbous, metallic and balloon-like. It slid slowly out of sight, sinking downwards, its underbelly orange in the reflected glare. There was a haze around it which seemed not entirely smoke—almost as though the smoke and sparks were deflected around it as it sank onto the blazing factory.

The ceiling of flame reddened and dimmed, reminding her of a candle in church being smothered by a brass snuffer. The roar and crackle diminished as though someone were turning down the volume of a wireless set. The sky, so fiery moments before, became dark. A few wisps of pink cloud drifted overhead, and a star winked.

Stevie moaned faintly.

"Stevie! Are you all right, love?" At least he was alive.

But what about the baby?

"I—I think so, Mummy." He started to sob again. "But I can't move." Then the natural curiosity of the child kicked in. "What was that funny thing up there?"

Several timbers crashed down between them, one narrowly missing his head. The mine hanging above them, the Sword of Damocles, shifted.

It's going to fall right on top of us.

Something moved above the mine. Refocusing her eyes, she saw the balloon-like object appear again, now hovering, almost motionless. It was smaller than she had thought. She felt rather than heard a low, throbbing hum.

The mine moved again. Her scream filled her mind until that was all there was.

Then, between her fingers she saw the mine *rise*, drawn upwards as though by a magnet. Bomb and balloon slid out of view.

As did the rest of the world . . .

#

The weight had gone from her legs, and someone was shining a bright, un-shielded torch on Stephen.

"Put that light out!" she cried automatically, then: "Oh, sorry, sorry, sorry! Thank you, thank you for helping—but won't they see your light?"

Dorothy glanced up at the sky. The drone of aircraft, which had seemed continuous for hours, was gone. The heavens were paling with the dawn—*or is it just the light of the city burning?*

She remembered the baby, and looked around frantically. A pathetic white bundle lay on a dust-covered chair.

Grunting with pain, she struggled to get to her feet—and succeeded, surprised she wasn't more badly injured.

The man in the wrecked room put out his hand to stop her.

He set down his lamp, a globe without obvious battery-pack. He had been scrabbling in the mound of plaster, bricks and mortar that had almost buried the boy. He had said nothing in reply to her. She frowned as she took in his tight, grey uniform and close-fitting helmet. There was something wrong about him, but she didn't know what it was.

Then realization dawned.

A German parachutist!

Her fingers closed around a length of broken rafter, but then she dropped it. German or not, he was human—and he had helped her, and he was now trying to help her son.

The man stood up, then clutched his side as if in pain.

"Are you hurt? Are—are you—German?" she babbled. "Er—Deutsch? What is your name?" She pointed at her own chest. "Dorothy."

The man looked at her, still without a word. She thought he smiled.

17

Dorothy made another effort to reach her baby, but at that moment the stranger pulled Stevie from under the pile of debris. Laying the small form down gently, he ran his hands over the boy's body and legs.

Stevie jerked and stiffened, and Dorothy took a half-pace towards him with a cry, but the man waved her back almost savagely. In the shadows she couldn't see what he was doing.

Retreating, she bumped into the chair where baby Aurora lay.

Stevie stirred and sat up. "Hello. Who are you?" he asked in an incongruously calm voice, as if he had just woken from a peaceful sleep.

The stranger helped the boy to his feet. Stevie swayed unsteadily for a moment, like a new-born faun, then walked stiffly to his mother.

Dorothy clutched the body of her little daughter tightly to her, tears streaming down her cheeks. Her gaze flicked back and forth from her lifeless baby to her son. It was too much. Hysterically, she laughed and cried, then slipped once more into oblivion.

#

A loud battering sound beat against her. She opened her eyes to see two men bursting through the front door. Both wore the uniform of Air Raid Wardens.

"Are you all right, Mrs Petrie?" yelled one, his gaze roving the shattered room warily, obviously terrified there would be a further fall of rubble. She knew him—Mr Hicks, the greengrocer. The other was unknown to her.

Dorothy spared them barely a glance, for from the chair came the plaintive wail of a hungry baby.

Aurora's alive? Yet I was so sure . . .

Mr Hicks went off for help after a while, and Dorothy tried to explain to the other man.

"If there was a German, madam," said the warden, "we'll get him, don't you worry. He may have been a Good Samaritan, but he can't go running around loose in London for long. For his own good, apart from anything else."

"You don't understand . . . " she shouted in exasperation.

"Mummy, what was that silvery thing we saw?" interrupted Stevie.

"What? Oh . . . it must have been a . . . a barrage balloon that got shot and drifted down, dear. Yes, that's it, a barrage balloon. Now, will you listen, Mr . . . ?"

"Thompson. Just calm down, ducks. We'll have to find you somewhere to live for the time being, but your roof can be fixed. You're lucky you can all walk out of here."

"Lucky? To *walk*? That's what I've been trying to tell you! Stephen hasn't walked since he fell off a swing when he was two. He's been paralysed from the waist down ever since."

Thompson stared, speechless. He had just opened his mouth to speak when a movement above caught his eye.

They both looked up in time to see a metallic spheroid drifting upward. It shrank to the size of a full Moon, then vanished in a brilliant blue, soundless explosion.

"Hydrogen, you know. It does that," said Thompson.

#

It was some time later that Dorothy Petrie realized in horror that the baby girl she held in her arms was not Aurora.

She was quite sure.

After all, a mother knows her own child.

Yet it was ridiculous. Of course the baby was Aurora! It had to be!

Over the years that followed, Dorothy never dared mention her knowledge to anyone, and after a while she convinced herself that the shock of all those strange and violent events must have done something to her mind.

The baby *had* to be Aurora.

Didn't she?

ACT TWO
The Musician

The Musician

"Spare us a couple a bob, mate? Just enough for a cup of coffee?"

The girl couldn't have been more than fifteen. Her face was thin and drawn—and dirty—yet she was pretty in a pale, elfin kind of way.

"You mean ten new pence, don't you?" grinned Lefty. "Well, I was just going to the pub, as it happens. I'll buy you a Coke, if you like, if we can get to the bar before they close."

"Coke? Oh, wow! Yeah, all right, then. Why not?"

Five minutes later Lefty was gazing in awe as she downed a large gin and tonic in one swig.

"You'll get me arrested," he said. "Buying alcoholic drinks for minors."

"I'm not a minor. Don't you worry—I'm old enough."

"Yeah, yeah, and I'm the Duke of Edinburgh. I just hope you can prove it if the Law comes snooping around." He stuffed a wad of banknotes into his inside pocket.

"You're a bit flush, aren't you?" she asked, cocking her head.

"Just been paid for a job."

"Oh yeah? What do you do then, this time of night? Burgle houses?"

"Ha, ha. No. During the day I'm self-unemployed. But I'm in a band—the Gas Giants, heard of us? We've been getting quite a few gigs in the evenings."

"Funny name. No, I never heard of them. Why're you called that?"

"Oh, some of the outer planets are called gas giants 'cause, well, they're just big balls of gas. That's us!" His white teeth shone. "No, it just sorta sounded right—we play "spacey" sort of music—one day we'll show Pink Floyd and Hawkwind how it's done—and 'it's a gas.' You know?"

"Not really. What do *you* play?"

"Bass guitar. I'm left-handed—they call me Lefty—and just to be really different I tune it E, B, G, D, like the top four strings on an ordinary guitar, only back to front. I can really leap around on it though!"

"If you say so. That stuff's all Greek to me. I don't know anything about music. Pop all sounds the same, and the stuff they play on Radio Three's boring. Mind you, a boy took me to the Last Night of the Proms once." Her face, which had been almost sullen, brightened. "Now *that* was great. Not the music so much—it didn't mean much to me, really—but all those people, enjoying it together. I've never known anything like that. Except . . . "

"Except what?"

"I dunno. Something I seem to remember. But I can never seem to get a handle on it. You know what I mean?"

"I suppose. Well you must come to one of our gigs, then you'll see what it's all about."

"Maybe. Can I have another drink?"

"Eh? Oh, right, sure." He sneaked a glance at her unusually pale, almost violet eyes, set in dark hollows. He couldn't quite figure her out. Under the grime she was really very good-looking, with her long, very blonde hair, but sort of remote. And she was so slim as to be almost twiggy. *Perhaps she's been ill?* he wondered.

As he got up the barman shouted, "Last orders please, ladies and gents!" It was already 10.40pm.

"Better make it a double then," said the girl with a grin.

"Do you think you oughta drink so much?"

"Habit," she replied without apparent offence. "It doesn't help, though. Neither does anything else I've tried. Once I thought acid was the answer, but . . . "

"What are you trying to find? Drugs aren't the way, you know. Oh, yeah, I tried them too—took me two years to kick them for good. Cold turkey . . . ugh." Lefty shuddered. "If it'll help you to talk about it, though, go ahead. I'm a good listener, they tell me. Hey, listen, I don't even know your name . . . ?"

She put her hands behind her neck and piled her hair on top of her head. It suited her, thought Lefty. Made her look older.

"It's Aurora. Don't you dare laugh."

He raised an eyebrow but said nothing.

"Oh, I don't know myself what's wrong with me. I always feel there's something missing, that's all. Whatever I do, I don't seem to belong."

She paused for a long moment, eyes closed, until Lefty thought she had fallen asleep. Then she continued, drowsily.

"My dad died in the war. I almost did too, so my mother told me—in the Blitz. We moved back up to Scotland after the war—near Inverness."

"Inverness? Wow—Swingsville! So what brings you back here?" asked Lefty. Then he frowned. "Hang on! What do you mean, you were in the Blitz? That'd make you over thirty! Come on, there's no way you're more than sixteen. Eighteen, tops. What's your game?"

The girl–woman called Aurora gave him an enigmatic smile. "No game. I don't tell many people, and to be honest I don't know why I'm telling you, but I'm thirty-two. Yes, on the level."

Lefty gave her a long, hard look, then shook his head as if pestered by a fly. "Yeah, right. Go on, then. You were saying—?"

"Mum died when I was ten, in a car crash. I got out without a scratch. But I didn't have any other living relatives except my older brother, Steve. We were in and out of children's homes until I was fifteen. I kept running away. I was good at school, or I was whenever I bothered to go. The problem was, I found lessons too easy. The other kids thought I was a swot, and the teachers couldn't handle me. So I used to bunk off. Except for science—I liked that. I was good at art too. Of course, even that threw them into a tizzy, 'cause you weren't supposed to be good at both. Steve would have been OK if it hadn't been for me. He's a worker. He's settled down with his own family now—haven't seen him for years.

"Anyway, after that I could never seem to hold down a job for more than a week or two." Then, in a sudden rush, she added: "I always seem to cause trouble, wherever I go. You'll see—you won't want me around for long, either."

She started to rise, ready to leave, but Lefty gripped her arm. "Where're you going? You got a place to stay?"

"Oh, sure, I've got a nice comfy cardboard box on the Embankment. As long as somebody hasn't beaten me to it . . . "

"Come on, I'll take you to my pad. You could do with somethin' to eat, anyway. It's all right—I'll sleep on the couch."

She looked at him doubtfully for a moment, then came to a decision.

"Sure. Why not? Thanks."

Outside, it was raining heavily. Lefty hailed a passing cab but it sailed on past, its wake drenching them.

"Come on, it's not far," he yelled, grabbing Aurora's hand, his head down.

"We can walk. Run."

Minutes later they were scampering up half-a-dozen worn, chipped concrete steps and passing through a door still boasting a few shreds of brown paint. Then up four flights of twisting, lino-covered stairs, then another door, which Lefty kicked just below the handle. It flew open.

"It's not much, but it's home, to coin a phrase," Lefty said with a grin. He reached for a box of matches on the cast-iron mantelpiece and shook it, then bent down and lit the gas fire.

"Look, you really oughta get out of those clothes. They're as wet as if you'd jumped into the Thames. If you . . . "

He stopped in surprise as, with a few deft movements, Aurora shrugged out of her clothes and draped them over a chair near the fire. That done, she flopped naked into another chair in front of it. Against the segment of dark sky framed by the dirty, rain-streaked window her face and body reflected the warm orange glow of the gas fire.

Lefty hastily looked in the other direction, pointing. "That's—er—that's the piano where we do most of our songwriting. The rest of the guys have got flats in this dump, or just down the road. There's the bathroom; you have to pull the chain twice to make it flush. No shower, but there should be hot water if you want a bath. The bedroom's through there. I can probably find you a pair of pyjamas if you . . ."

"No, thanks. I never bother, not when I've got a proper bed."

"Oh, man!" Lefty raised his eyes heavenwards. He reached inside the bedroom door and pulled a string which hung there. An unshaded orange bulb clicked on over the bed, and he picked up his pyjamas from a heap on the floor.

"Sleep well," he said through a yawn as Aurora passed him on her way in.

#

He raised his head groggily and prised open his bleary eyes. What had woken him? Someone must have turned on the radio, for there was tinkling music coming from behind him. Something on Radio Three? Classical, yet a bit avant-garde? Normally the dial was never moved from Radio One. It seemed a bit loud and clear for the old trannie, though. He levered himself up and peered over the back of the sofa.

Aurora, wearing only briefs and bra—but at least she'd got *something* on—was sitting at the piano, her fingers flickering over the yellowed keys, her face trancelike.

"Hey—you never told me *you* could play!" Lefty yelled, louder than he had intended. "You said you didn't like music much! So where'd you learn to do that?"

The girl started violently and drew back her hands as though the keys had suddenly become red-hot. "I said I didn't like the music I've *heard*. I've never had a chance to play an instrument myself before."

"Oh, sure. Now pull the other one—got bells on it!"

"It's true." She looked at him blankly. "Why not? You just find out where the notes are and then play them, don't you?"

"Yeah, right on. Except that most people take weeks just to learn the basics—and some have lessons for years and still never get further than Jingle Bells . . . "

"Well, p'raps I'm just a natural, then. Some people are, aren't they?"

"So the story goes," said Lefty dubiously. A moment later the door sprang open with the inevitable crash and four men, all aged between twenty and thirty, burst into the room. They screeched to a halt on spotting Aurora and began making exaggerated motions of backing out of the door again.

One of them, who sported an Afro hairstyle in bright red hair, said with a grin, "Hey, sorry to break in on your scene, man!"

"Like, we didn't know you'd got company!" added the one with a droopy Mexican-style moustache.

Lefty glowered, but before he could speak Aurora snapped: "I don't know what you're all staring at. But, if you're embarrassed, I'll go and get dressed."

She left the room with a histrionic sigh. The five young men exchanged guilty looks, wondering what it was they should be feeling guilty about.

A minute or two later she reappeared wearing her jeans, now dry and stiff.

"Perhaps I can do the introductions now," said Lefty with a flourish, as the door opened and a youth with shoulder-length dark hair strolled in. "The latecomer, as usual, is Synth. The rest of this mob"—he pointed—"are Ginge, Doug, Acker and Herbie. Herbie's our road manager, but he doubles on guitar as well. Guys, this is Aurora."

He didn't explain further. The others seemed immediately to accept her presence as one of the gang.

"Hey, the new synth's arrived," burst out the newcomer. "It's just got to be stacks better than that old thing I cobbled together."

"It better be," grunted Acker, "after we've sold all our worldly goods to pay for it." He grimaced at Aurora. "Just to put a deposit on it, even."

"Synthesizer? Oh—is *that* why you call him Synth?" Aurora whispered to Lefty. "I thought perhaps he was—you know . . . "

Lefty smiled. "Don't let him hear you say that!" He continued more loudly: "This one's polyphonic—not like the old Moogs." He pronounced the name to rhyme with "rogues."

Aurora looked totally blank. "Sorry, mate, but I haven't a clue what you're talking about."

"Oh, yeah, I forgot—you aren't into our kind of music, are you? Well, on the old Moog synthesizers you could only play single notes. If you wanted to record something like Walter Carlos's album *Switched-On Bach* you had to keep overdubbing—re-recording from one tape to another—to get the harmonies and so on. But we've just got hold of one that plays chords. And it's really compact, as well."

The group fell to discussing their gig that night and Aurora roamed around the room, taking science-fiction paperbacks and magazines from the shelves that lined the walls and staring with a puzzled expression at the star-charts and maps of the Moon and Mars, and at the big art print of a planetary landscape with a huge red sun looming in its sky, bearing the title *Stellar Radiance*, that filled the rest of the wall-space along with faded posters of rock bands in concert. Someone had turned on the old radio, and they took a brief interest as a news bulletin announced that Apollo 16 had landed safely at Descartes. Lefty bemoaned the fact that the next Moon landing could well be the last manned space mission for decades if not forever. "We should be going on to Mars—*that's* where it's at," he stated decisively.

Aurora blinked, as if coming out of a reverie, as Ginge called: "See you in the grotty club—sorry, Grotto Club—tonight, then."

"Who, me?" she said.

"Well you want to see what we can do, don't you?" said Lefty.

"Oh, well, s'pose so. Why not? I've got nothing better to do."

"Cor, such enthusiasm! You'll see—one of these fine days you'll be boasting about knowing us when we were just starting out!"

Rock

No doubt, if the light of day were ever admitted, the Grotto Club's decor would have looked cheap and shoddy; but in the pulsing shadows cast by concealed blue, green and ultraviolet tubes it seemed an ideal setting for the Gas Giants. Boulder-shaped tables and chairs crouched beneath papier-mâché arches; stalactites hung from the ceiling. Aurora hesitated as she entered through the skull-shaped doorway, almost as though afraid to step inside. Then she threaded her way to a table near the stage, along the front of which was draped plastic ivy, glowing a vivid green in the hidden lighting.

The club was only half-full so early—it was barely ten o'clock. At the side of the stage an elderly man in evening dress was playing Top Twenty tunes from six months before on an electric organ. Lefty had told her that the guy had used to own the club when it was a much more respectable and staid affair, and had been allowed to stay on as "resident organist" as part of the deal when he was forced to sell it. The rest of the clientele secretly laughed at him, but it didn't matter. He was almost completely deaf.

On the darkened stage itself, her new friends were busily setting up their equipment, of which there seemed to be a great deal. The organist looked round in annoyance as a loudspeaker gave a loud *pop!* which even he could hear, and a sibilant, echoing voice chanted: "Testing. Testing. One-two. One-two." The synthesizer emitted a sound that Aurora mentally likened to a constipated duck; then, as Synth moved what looked like pegs on a complicated Solitaire board, it gave forth a piercing shriek, this time more reminiscent of a cat whose tail had been yanked. This was too much for the organist, who got up and left, scowling.

The tables filled up. For a while the only sounds were the hubbub of voices and the clinking of glasses. The air became smoky, and Aurora noticed a strange, sweetish aroma which was not tobacco, but which she recognized only too well. Someone lit joss sticks near the front of the stage. Then, without warning, came a whispered "One, two—one, two, three, four!", followed this time by a staccato rattle of snare drums and a wall of sound which drowned out all conversation.

Or should have done. Looking about her, Aurora noticed that somehow most people seemed to manage to keep talking to each other as if nothing had changed.

She sat forward expectantly, but soon sank back into her seat. This was nothing but noise to her. The bass boomed, and occasionally an interesting little phrase from the lead guitar would break through, but when the synthesizer could be picked out at all it sounded like a fairground organ. The piece ground to a ragged close and received a few desultory claps from the audience. Next came a slow, turgid and apparently endless composition, throughout which the synthesizer made sounds like rushing winds or waves, but with no obvious relationship to whatever else was going on. When this dirge finally stuttered to an uncertain finish there was no applause.

And so it went on. Her mind began to wander. Lefty had remarked to her that they had started out as "pretty much your standard heavyish rock band," and the description appeared all too accurate. He seemed certain that, when they could afford all the equipment they needed and time in a recording studio, they would take the charts by storm with a single, followed up closely by an album. "Of course, the single's only for the publicity—Top of the Pops and all that, you know. And the money, of course. We'll be an albums band really." She had gathered that he was a bit worried about Synth, who "fancies himself as a dab hand at the old electronics, but he's a pretty ordinary keyboards player really. Maybe he'll improve with practice. I hope."

Aurora was actually leaving her seat to go when Lefty caught her eye and jerked his head back in a "come here" gesture. She walked forward and, still playing, he squatted at the front of the stage, putting his mouth close to her ear.

"It's not going too well tonight—there's just no feedback from the audience. It's like that sometimes." She had to strain to hear his voice. "... and Synth hasn't really got the hang of his new toy, though he's been playing with it all day. It's not helped, of course, that he's got himself half-stoned on a bottle of the old vino while we were setting up. Feel like having a go?"

"What d'you mean? Play up there? *Me?* I couldn't!" Aurora whispered, then shouted above the racket: "There's no *way* I could play that thing! Especially in front of an audience."

"Come on," ordered Lefty, grabbing her hand and abruptly standing up, so drawing her up onto the stage whether she wanted to be there or not.

"Just do what you did on the old joanna this morning. Let's face it, you couldn't make it any worse, could you?"

Synth allowed himself to be dispossessed with less objection than might have been expected, and went off to find more wine. Aurora stood in a pool of blue light, surrounded on all sides by humped black shapes with glowing, winking red eyes, some emitting, at this close range, baleful hisses or throaty hums. She wanted nothing more than to fly out of the gaping door and lose herself again, wandering as she had wandered for half her aimless life.

"I don't know what to play—I don't *know* any of your bloody tunes!" she wailed.

"Just play anything, but *do* it," hissed Doug from behind his mountain of drums and cymbals. "'Baa Baa Black Sheep', if you like. We'll jam around it."

Ginge played a couple of rapid scales on his guitar, establishing a key, and Acker followed him on saxophone. She tried an experimental note or two, a chord, and almost reeled at the blast of sound from the PA system around her. Herbie leaned over and touched a knob. "That's the gain control. Volume, OK? This"—he rotated a miniature joystick—"is for the quad effect. Quadraphonic? And this slider's the note-bender."

Volume she understood; the other terms might as well have been Arabic. She turned down the knob, gave herself a quick private recital, then fiddled with the miniature jack-plugs on the Solitaire board for a moment. Finally she turned the knob back up, sighed resignedly, and announced: "OK. Here goes nothing." The audience ignored her.

Within three bars not a word was being spoken in the crowded room. Glasses paused motionless on their way to lips; chicken nuggets lay congealing in baskets. The room was filled with the sound of clear, ice-cold crystals being struck by an elfin hammer in some subterranean cavern. Suddenly the tawdry artificial surroundings were real, glistening rock.

Aurora's left hand moved to the control board as if of its own volition, and the sound of a faery choir joined in, swelling and soaring.

At first the electronic notes rose alone, shivering and cascading from the fake icicles hanging from the roof. Then, tentatively, the snare drums struck up a rhythm. At first it sounded crude, clumsy and out of place, but soon Doug was weaving an intricate tattoo with brushes and cymbals. He beamed with pleasure as he became aware of Lefty's electric bass tracing a lattice pattern of sound in and out of his own. Ginge's foot rose and fell on his wah-wah pedal as his old Fender made soft, plaintive sighs such as his fingers had never evoked before. Acker had switched to a flute, producing birdlike trills and arpeggios. As for Herbie, he stood stock-still, mouth wide open, his acoustic guitar trailing from one hand.

As the last few notes dripped from the speakers there was silence. Several women and one or two men were openly crying. Then someone began to clap, hesitantly, and the applause grew into a storm. Aurora blinked, seeming to emerge from a daze, and managed a wan smile. She looked drained.

Lefty seized a microphone and said, stumblingly: "Er—thanks. This is, um, Aurora. Give her a big hand, folks—she's only been sittin' in with us tonight. First time in public. But we hope it won't be the last. Don't we?" He looked over at her pleadingly, his words drowned in cries of "More!"

The next melody started like a toccata, but as it progressed and the other musicians joined in it became ever more lively and happy. The audience began to participate, clapping and swaying. A few couples began to dance, until the whole room was in motion. Aurora discovered that the quad lever sent her notes swooping and circling around the room from strategically placed speakers. Herbie vanished backstage, and soon two strobe-lights began to flash, one at each side, so that the dancers' movements seemed jerky and spasmodic, as if they were stiff-jointed puppets or part of a film shown at the wrong speed.

Then, just as the music seemed about to reach a crescendo of joy, there came several jarring discords and Aurora slumped lifeless across the keyboard.

#

Thousands of white-gowned people sat around the huge amphitheatre, some with eyes closed, just listening, others watching entranced as the musicians played. Each musician wore his or her instrument lightly, from a cord around the neck or a belt at the waist; yet the sound filled the vast natural crater with its carved seats, and overflowed and spilled into the surrounding countryside.

In the Old People's village, those who no longer wished to travel beyond their own homes sat outside their domed houses, nodding and smiling with memories of many past MusicFests.

The sky deepened to a beautiful, transparent violet. A golden disc rose. At first it seemed like a moon, but then it evolved into a floating craft. As it rose higher it passed into shadow and darkened, as if in eclipse. On the northern horizon a glow appeared. A bright spark detached itself and ascended into the darkling sky. As Aurora watched, it dimmed to red, brightened briefly, and was obscured by vapour. From the dark disc, anxious eyes stared down at her . . .

#

Aurora coughed slightly as Lefty exhaled smoke from his cigarette in a sigh of relief. He stubbed out its red glow in a saucer. "Cripes, we really thought we'd lost you too there for a minute," he said.

She gazed around her. She lay on a spotlessly clean white bed. Beyond the circle of pale, anxious faces—and Lefty's dark anxious face, though even that looked pale—was only a further white circle that she recognized after a moment or two as a hospital screen. Lefty, Ginge, Herbie, Doug, Acker. Plus a nurse and a tall man in a white coat.

"Where's Synth?" she asked, struggling to sit up. "What do you mean, lost me *too*?"

"Nothing. Nothing." Lefty made a move to light another cigarette, but the nurse caught his eye and frowned.

"If you don't mind, Mr Clemson, I think now that you know she's all right . . . In fact"—she looked questioningly at the doctor, who nodded—"it would be best if you all left now and let Miss—erm—Aurora rest."

"No!" cried Aurora sharply, "Where *is* Synth? I want to know—right now—or I won't rest. Something's happened to him, hasn't it?"

"No, he's fine," said Lefty. "But he's left the band—walked out while you were still playing last night, tell you the truth. He's stripped his flat. The manager at the Grotto says Synth told him . . . well, that you made him look like an idiot. But that wasn't your fault—he *is* an idiot."

Aurora hid her face in her hands. "Yes, it *was* my fault," she sobbed. "I warned you, didn't I? I told you I'm always trouble and you wouldn't want me around . . . "

Ginge stepped forward before anyone else could speak. "You couldn't be more wrong there, gal. Something good happened while you were around us.

Real good. We all played better than we ever knew we could." The circle of heads nodded vigorously. "And as for you, you were fuckin' amazing on that synthesizer, pardon my French. Jeez, we *need* you in the band now. Don't we, guys?" More nods. "You *will* join us, won't you . . .?"

But Aurora's eyes were flickering shut again.

"I never even got to tell her about the manager of Yes being in the audience, and wanting to book us as support band on their next tour," complained Ginge.

#

There was nothing wrong with Aurora, the doctor told Lefty when he collected her from the hospital two days later, apart from the life she had been leading. Nothing that rest, good food and vitamins couldn't fix.

She was installed in her own room in part of what had been Synth's flat. Ginge and Lefty had moved into the rest of it, since it was so much better than their previous places.

There they were all able to work out new numbers. It was almost always Aurora who took the lead in their compositions; but they quickly discovered that she found it almost impossible to play the same piece twice. This hardly seemed to matter, though, and instead they evolved a sort of code by which they knew what type of number they would play next, whether fast, slow, happy, plaintive, heavy rock, vocal or instrumental.

They also found that, while they all enjoyed playing together and almost every piece proved an emotional experience of some kind, they never reached in practice the heights they had in the Grotto Club. Even so, they deliberately avoided any further public appearances. They wanted to save themselves for the tour with Yes.

Two weeks before the first scheduled gig of the tour, in London, Herbie rushed into the flat, obviously highly excited.

"I've fixed it! A whole day in the UROK Studios! The way we've been playing lately, we should be able to record a whole album, no problem, and pick the best two tracks for our single. We can have the single into the shops while the tour's still on—and just watch it go up the charts!"

Days later Aurora found herself being pushed out of a battered, psychedelically painted minibus and helping to carry boxes, amplifiers and guitar-cases through an ordinary-looking green door, past the dusty and flyblown window of a small office from which an elderly uniformed man peered at them suspiciously, and down a long corridor lined with doors. Through another door and down some rickety wooden steps into a litter-strewn open courtyard between high buildings; up more steps into what looked like the warehouse it had once been.

The inside of the warehouse was a revelation, though. Emerging from a short corridor, Aurora found herself surrounded by glass booths, some containing stand microphones, others chairs and music stands. Fluorescent tubes hung from the high ceiling, while thick black electrical cables snaked in all directions across the wooden boarded floor, on which stood several huge speaker cabinets. In a gallery right across one end of the room, with a metal stairway leading up to it, were more glass windows, behind which brightly lit figures moved about.

The band, with other helpers and hangers-on, rapidly set up their equipment. Aurora noticed that the drum kit was placed in a booth of its own, and saw Doug fitting a pair of headphones over his bushy hair. When she found that she was expected to do the same, she became agitated.

"No!" she cried. "If I can't have everyone *with* me, I don't play."

The studio engineers tried hard to get her to change her mind, but she was adamant. So the rest of the band were clustered around the synthesizer, microphones were rearranged, and, after the usual twangs and toots of tuning up, the recording session began for real.

The first number lasted twenty minutes. Although as soon as she began playing Aurora fell into her trancelike state, she did see one of the figures in the control booth pick up a telephone several times. Shortly afterwards, people began to file silently into the studio. All but a couple of red lights in the actual studio were dimmed, leaving the control room a bright oasis.

The second piece was also over fifteen minutes long and, when it finished, after a respectful silence of a few seconds in deference to the tape machines, spontaneous applause broke out.

A tinny voice spoke from nowhere. "*Far out!* We don't even need any overdubs. But you'll have to do some shorter numbers—three, four minutes, five max—if you want to put out a single." Aurora saw that one of the men behind the long control panel in the glasshouse was speaking into a microphone with a long flexible neck. It looked like a goose, she thought.

"Let's do the vocal?" suggested Ginge, hopefully. He had written the lyric, and was rather proud of it. Another batch of onlookers surged through the door while the red RECORDING light was out.

"OK, the vocal. Then *The Seagull*—and let's keep it short," said Herbie.

Lefty sang the lead vocal; he had a good blues voice, hoarse yet tuneful. Doug, with a mike slung over his drums, joined in the chorus line. To everyone's surprise, for she had never done this before, Aurora pulled over a nearby live microphone and began to sing, wordlessly. Or was she singing in some foreign language? It didn't seem to matter. Her voice, while not strong, was pure and clear. She sang a strange harmony to the middle-eight bars, playing the melody line on single, gliding notes. The result was ethereal.

Once again there was wild applause at the end, and it was obvious from comments she heard that these studios had never witnessed such scenes before. Or such music. The effort was taking its toll, but Aurora couldn't recall ever feeling so happy.

At the close of the next piece, though, Lefty looked concerned, for she was white and strained. "Can we call it a day?" he asked the control room.

The recording engineers were bemused. The Gas Giants had been in the studio for less than two hours. Yet there was certainly enough material in the can for an album, and for the A and B sides of a single. A double-sided number one single, too, or they'd trade in their headphones for brooms and go street-sweeping, as one engineer put it.

From the crowd came cries of "No, more—more!" and "Keep it going while it's hot!"

Lefty scowled at them and pointed to Aurora. "Look at her, can't you? She's about all in."

He unplugged his bass and put it into its battered case. This signalled the rest of the group to follow his lead. Aurora revived enough to help a little, though she still looked shaken.

She spoke once. "Thanks, Lefty. You're a real rock."

When they had left, the studio seemed even emptier than usual. Little groups of people stood around aimlessly for a while, discussing what they had just heard and the rosy future of the band, then drifted away.

#

"Ladies and Gentlemen . . . Guys and Gals . . . Let's have a big hand for . . . the Gas Giants!"

The curtains rolled back and there was a scatter of clapping as sound began to fill the auditorium. Most of the audience had never heard of the band. It was only the support group, after all. The bar remained full to bursting. Latecomers straggled in and stumbled along the rows of seats, forcing grumbling sitters to stand.

The stage was bathed in ripples of violet, blue, green, yellow light which changed and pulsed with the music. Herbie had proved to have no mean talent with electronics now that Synth no longer monopolised the equipment, and his second guitar seemed no longer needed. He operated a kind of keyboard which produced changes of light instead of sound. The band had broken with the convention of patched jeans and T-shirts, and all wore close-fitting black, including Aurora; though her costume was more in the nature of a cat-suit, against which her bright hair shone.

The audience hardly noticed. At first this was because they were talking among themselves, as they normally did during support acts. But very shortly there was a chorus of "Ssshhhh!" and the late arrivals started getting angry glares. In no time the listeners were being carried away on wave after wave of soaring sound, lifting every one of them out of their humdrum, everyday existence, making them forget troubles, ills, quarrels petty or serious, and at the same time welding them into one great corporate entity which was part of the music.

There were no separate pieces of music or songs this time, nor need for applause. For the two thousand people in the theatre, each in his or her own way, gave back as much as they received. But the music changed and flowed, so that at times everyone present was silent and sad, at others joyous, bright-eyed. Management, usherettes and bouncers stood at the sides, relaxed; for, despite the electric, emotion-charged atmosphere, there was no hint of rowdiness. A BBC television crew, setting up cameras for the headline group, hastily started filming.

Not everyone agreed on what happened next. To some, it remained a really great concert, the best music they had ever heard, with an unusually good rapport between musicians and audience. And even those who saw the "visions" did not all agree on what they saw. But to most of the latter:

The music was a mighty silver waterfall, leaping and cascading down, down, amongst the crags of a tall volcanic mountain whose peak was lost in the clouds. It crashed, it rushed, it roared, and then it split into myriad streams which splashed, gurgled, tinkled between moss-covered rocks.

The stream which was the music entered a dark cave, where it flowed in echoing darkness for a while, then light reappeared, emanating from globular shapes—fungi?—on the walls of the cavern: blue, green, purple. As the light brightened, the rivulet widened and figures became visible, bathing naked in the now-warm water. Other tributaries swirled in, half-seen through wisps of steam, from gulleys among the rocks. Strange, fern-like plants sprang from the banks.

In a sudden glare of sound the torrent sluiced straight down a hillside in the full light of day; yet this daylight had an unearthly quality. The stream broadened, and meandered through open countryside. Trees lined its banks, trailing yellow-green leaves in its swirling surface. On the left, the land rose to a huge, flat-topped hill. Many white-robed people were making their way up its slopes. Among them ran nude and bronzed pale-eyed children, youths and girls, laughing and dancing. The music seemed to swell as though joined by an orchestra and choir from outside itself, rolling down from the rim of the hill . . .

The people in the auditorium blinked, collectively, as the music seemed to falter. The scene blurred. There were low metal buildings, an interminable flat expanse of sand. Some of the audience felt they were being carried in strong arms. Then the view tilted upward, up over curved metal plates.

Confusion.

Noise.

Pressure.

Red darkness.

Black darkness.

For a long time, total lack of sensation.

Sudden shock, pain. A surge of movement, forward; then falling. Somewhere far off, as though seen through crystal, violent blasts of light: red, yellow, white, red again. Darkness. Falling, falling. Gentle hands lifting, lowering. A jolt, a hard surface below.

Noise!

Fear!

There was a startling crackle and a shower of sparks, and the music stopped abruptly. Aurora reeled back from her instrument, fell into the drums and was caught by Doug, as limp as though she were a rag doll. The curtains were hurriedly lowered. There was a cursory announcement that someone had been taken ill.

After a long and uneasy pause the main band came on and played their usual set. It was one of their best performances, but they played to an apathetic and unresponsive house.

Next day the critics in the musical and national press virtually ignored them. They wrote of the incredibly talented debut performance of this un-known support group, and of the unfortunate collapse of their beautiful young female keyboards player (whose age was given as sixteen). A few mentioned the almost psychical effect upon the audience; others, practical men and women at heart, wrote of the effective pre-recorded orchestral and choral tapes which had augmented the live performance, and of what must surely be a breakthrough in back-projection, suggesting a new holographic laser process producing lifelike and three-dimensional moving images of scenes and people.

The rest of the Gas Giants' tour had to be cancelled, of course, but, thanks to all the publicity, both the single and the LP, rush-released within the week, were immediate hits, remaining in the charts for months. Even so, everyone who had been present at the concert—or at the recording studio, or at the Grotto Club—agreed that, fine though the records were, they failed to capture the intensely personal atmosphere of the live performances. Something indefinable was missing.

Aurora was missing, too. The Gas Giants brought in Herbie's younger sister, her hair bleached blonde, and mimed to their tapes on *Top of the Pops*. But without Aurora they seemed like insensate marionettes.

A few months later, they dissolved the band.

#

Lefty often relived that night in his dreams. He saw Aurora reach into the electronics-filled innards of the synthesizer, seeking . . . seeking *what*? Some new sound? Who knew?

He had shouted uselessly: "Aurora—DON'T!"

The shock from the full mains voltage had sent her flying backwards. As Doug had carried her inert body into the dressing room, he'd known for sure she was dead.

But she wasn't. After they had loosened her clothes and, in lieu of brandy, poured a measure of scotch from Ginge's hipflask down her throat, she had revived quickly, and sat up. It seemed to Lefty that something had gone from her face. As she changed into her street clothes and walked to the door her expression was blank, reminding him of the first time he had seen her.

Little girl lost.

"Where do you think you're going?" he asked.

"Back up to Inverness, perhaps. I think maybe I'll study for a while; try to get into university. I'm wasting my time here."

"Wasting your time? But what about the band! We're gonna make it big, can't you dig that? You can't just walk out on the rock scene now, just like that."

"Rock?" she said. A faraway look flickered in her eyes and then was gone. "Oh, yes, rock," she'd said coldly as she'd closed the door behind her. "That's all that matters, isn't it?

"Rock . . . "

ACT THREE
Arsia Mons

Arsia Mons

Rock. Rock and more rock. Black rock, ochre rock, amber rock. Nothing but rock everywhere you looked. Anne Pryor chipped at the flank of Arsia Mons with her geologist's hammer and carefully placed the latest fragment in her sample case. She spoke the identifying data into her helmet mike, tonguing on the recorder; writing was difficult wearing the gloves of the Mars environment suit. That said, the flexible and almost skin-tight Mars suit was a big improvement on the bulky Apollo suits. For a while it had looked as though the type of "hard suit" produced by ILC Dover with Hamilton Sundstrand, as used on the International Space Station, would be pressed into service here too. But, although in space legs are almost superfluous, here on the surface of Mars mobility and freedom of movement were paramount.

The colours around here, she mused for the umpteenth time, were surprisingly drab. Despite her training, she had still expected rich reds, oranges and yellows—the colours that appeared in just about all the photographs and space art she had seen. But the reality—at least in this locality—was mainly pale brown, with variations into buff, yellow and tan. The scenery in the central area of Iceland, where she had spent some weeks on a field trip, had been very similar. And almost as cold . . .

That was an exaggeration, she acknowledged wryly. Tharsis was *cold*, even for Mars.

That was one of the reasons why the area had been chosen for the expedition. The strange parallel ridges on the lee side of Arsia Mons, looking curiously like ploughed fields, had turned out to be a recessional moraine; that is, dirt and rubble left behind by a glacier. It had been known for many years that clouds often blew over the volcano; these precipitated as storms of ice crystals. And the ice stayed where it fell on these high slopes. It had been building up for a long time . . . She had seen similar layered glaciers in Iceland, too; those had been caused by the ash from repeated eruptions. One of her tasks here was to see if these layers on Arsia Mons could have the same cause.

Apart from that, Arsia Mons was the southernmost of a set of triplets, three shield volcanoes of very similar size, the other two being Pavonis and Ascraeus. To the northwest stood the far mightier Olympus Mons, which towered above the plain to a height ten times that of Earth's Mount Everest. Olympus Mons was *too* big, really, for it was impossible to take it all in, except from out in space. Earth's largest shield volcano—Mauna Loa on the big island of Hawaii—provided a similar visual effect, dominating the landscape only as a long, low hill. But the volume of Olympus Mons was over fifty times even that of Mauna Loa. There was evidence that there could have been thermal activity in this area, millions or possibly just thousands of years ago. Ever since the highly controversial discovery in the mid-1990s of "fossil life" in a Martian rock—ALH 84001—found in the Antarctic and the *Pathfinder* and other unmanned missions that had followed, scientists had hoped for The Big One: the unequivocal discovery of life on Mars.

It might seem hard to believe, but even working on an alien world like Mars could become commonplace after a while. Not boring, precisely, but, even so, as Anne Pryor worked her mind kept drifting back to the events that had led her here.

#

After leaving London, Aurora had gone back up to Scotland, as she'd said she probably would. For a while she had stayed with her brother Stephen; but he was now forty, and looked it, with his receding hairline, greying hair and bifocal spectacles, while she still seemed like a teenager. It was bound to cause comment, especially as Steve's wife, Brenda, was hardly any older than Aurora and yet looked nearly as old as her husband.

So she didn't stay there for long; just long enough to recuperate and re-view her plans for the future. She decided to go back to school and try to make up for all her wasted years.

With her artistic talents it hadn't been difficult to doctor her birth certificate; she wanted to avoid questions about the disparity between her real and her apparent age. Looking at her, no one would think to query her new age of seventeen.

Many times, as the years passed, Aurora did puzzle over her own appearance. (When anyone commented on her youthfulness, she would quip: "Ah, but you should see the portrait in my attic!") There was nothing she could do about it, and nor could she explain it; so she supposed she should just be grateful.

And she was never ill. Oh, her body protested when she abused it, as she had done back in the late Sixties, but she had never caught even the usual childhood diseases like mumps, measles or chickenpox, let alone anything more serious. What should she do? Tell a doctor that "I look too young and I'm never ill"? At best she would become a guinea pig for medical research, at worst a freak for the media to parade before a sensation-hungry public. No, best to keep a low profile, and, when necessary, keep moving on . . .

Sometimes, though, she did feel very lonely. Was there really nobody else in all the world like her? More: her brief time with the Gas Giants seemed to have left her almost drained of emotion. It was as if she had packed a lifetime of what most people would regard as normal, personal feelings into that short period, but that her near-death experience had then wiped these from her brain.

As she had once told Lefty, she was clever at scholastic matters as long as she put her mind to them. And this she did. Within a few years she had a crop of O- and A-levels to her credit, and she followed these up by applying for and obtaining a place at Birmingham's redbrick university, which her enquiries showed to be one of the best for scientific subjects.

Aurora's appetite for education was insatiable now, and the more she crammed into her brain the more her ability to learn seemed to expand. But she would stay with one subject for long periods, often sighing with frustration at the amounts of data available, impossible to assimilate in one lifetime. On the other hand she did not let this deter her; if her appearance and her physical and mental abilities were any guide, she could well have a very long lifetime ahead of her in which to absorb it all. She studied chemistry and physics, finally obtaining her doctorate in astrophysics, specializing in asteroids, comets and impact craters.

She also took a course in computing, and spent many hours in the evenings doing her own private work, much of it on the internet. Linked to computer networks all over the world, she could hack into the files of record offices and create a succession of new identities for herself, at the same time planting a virus program that destroyed all traces of her previous identities and then of itself, as and when it became necessary.

For another five years Aurora stayed around universities, largely cocooned from the realities of life, doing research and some lecturing. At last she decided that it was once again time to experience the real world. By now she had been forty-eight, but looked perhaps twenty-two. During all this time she had formed no strong personal relationships, though generally she seemed to be well liked. Some men, spurned, put about a rumour that she had lesbian tendencies, but she laughed these off. The plain fact was that she simply was not interested.

Unable to find a fulfilling job in Britain—or, for a while, any job at all for which she was not "overqualified"—she left for the United States. There she found the climate—cultural, scientific and atmospheric—much more to her liking. She had flirted with NASA but found it lacking, dogged by problems as it had been since the *Challenger* shuttle tragedy, and moved on to the California Institute of Technology. In the academic atmosphere of CalTech she seemed to be in line for a professorship, only to find that this time her declared and apparent youth worked against her, despite her obviously superior experience and qualifications. She had left in high dudgeon and found a position as a geologist in a California oil company, GeoTek. The job mainly involved using advanced computer techniques and high-definition satellite imagery, but there were enough field trips to keep her interested and satisfied.

The personnel at GeoTek consisted mainly of bright young men and women, and she fitted in well. For a while. Whether it was real or imagined she couldn't tell, but after a time she began to feel that her colleagues were looking at her strangely, and so she left. A number of similar positions followed. She worked on an ocean-floor mining project; then for an environmental organization doing research on the hole in the ozone layer over the Antarctic; then there was a spell among the observatories on Mauna Kea on Hawaii . . .

Her stay in the Pacific Islands sparked an interest in vulcanology, and for some years she visited the Earth's wildest places, researching plate tectonics and continental drift. She gradually found she preferred these desolate and rugged areas to the more populated areas of Planet Earth.

She took up painting again, as a hobby, and produced some spectacular canvases of volcanoes, rift valleys and glaciers; accurate yet romantic, some of them were almost worthy of comparison with nineteenth-century American "field" artists of the Hudson River School, like Frederic Church and Thomas Moran, who had travelled to the Grand Canyon, Yellowstone or Antarctica and exhibited their massive canvases to an awed and sometimes disbelieving public. They had been responsible for these areas becoming National Parks.

Always Aurora kept half an eye on what was happening in the field of space research, hoping for a resurgence in interest in manned missions, such as had fired mankind in the 1960s and 1970s, but the picture was dismal. Still, she was at JPL when the Voyager images came in from Jupiter, Saturn, Uranus and Neptune, becoming excited by the volcanoes and geysers on Io and Triton.

Several times she had to call upon her secret computer program in order to explain away her appearance and start a new life, but it was difficult, and she lived in constant fear of meeting someone who had known her twenty or more years ago. She had become an expert forger, with the help of computers and high-definition printers. She changed her appearance, too, more than once, growing and cutting or even dying her hair, sometimes wearing glasses, other tricks . . . Also, in order for her to get work, each new self needed qualifications. Really, though, this was only a matter of altering the name and dates on the genuine ones she possessed—no one would be likely to query her abilities once they saw her results.

Increasingly she experienced that feeling, which she had once mentioned to Lefty, of "searching for something." The problem was, she had no idea what it was she was searching *for*.

Meanwhile, the world changed.

There were upheavals in Eastern Europe; the Berlin Wall came down, Communism was all but banished from the Soviet Union, and the Soviet Union itself fragmented into a loose confederation of independent republics. To those space buffs who had seen a collaboration between the USSR and the USA as the only hope of a manned mission to Mars, it seemed that their dream was shattered. The "fossil life" controversy and the astounding high-resolution images from Mars Global Surveyor, which in 1999 provided indisputable evidence of water on Mars, briefly gave hope that the USA would go it alone with a manned mission, but the public—and thus the government—was divided on whether it was worth the expense.

For a while it had seemed that NASA's much-vaunted "faster, cheaper, better" policy of using small, unmanned probes would win the day. But the arrival and prompt disappearance of both the Polar Lander and the Climate Orbiter—switched off by little green men, jeered the media—showed clearly that, while perhaps faster and cheaper, this method was certainly not *better*. The losses proved a blessing in disguise for those who had always wanted humans, not machines, to be the ones to explore the red world.

Eventually a sort of stability returned to the Soviet Republics. East–West trade flourished in an open-market economy, and somehow the European Community also settled most of its differences. The year 2001 became famous—infamous—not for bases on the Moon but for the horrific events of September 11th, and for a while all governments were side-tracked by the so-called War on Terrorism. At best it seemed that an uneasy truce existed between the nations, but eventually governments turned to the idea of an international space extravaganza to divert the eyes of the world from their own problems, to boost investment and employment in technological areas, and (the official line) to foster goodwill and cooperation among nations. Fortunately the latest Russian leader, Vladimir Putin, was in favour of space travel; the spectacular demise of the space station Mir in 2001 had left his country with an unrivalled amount of experience of living in space, but no way to use it. Putin did not like his country's demotion from a leading power in space to an also-ran.

A joint project was announced, involving the USA, Japan, the former Soviet States, Europe (from which the leading partner was France) and Canada, which latter, early in the twenty-first century, had tripled its spending on space research—in other words, basically the same countries as had been involved in the building of the ISS. Britain, of course, was not a partner this time around, since its governments had stubbornly refused to invest in the adventure of space—and had thus allowed some of the country's best brains to depart abroad.

In 2001 Aurora joined the Mars Society which, under its dynamic leader Robert Zubrin, seemed to have the requisite drive and the best ideas for a manned mission. Such was the groundswell of interest that NASA was eventually persuaded to allow some collaboration with such organizations, and even industry; multinationals became involved, noting the plethora of opportunities for sponsorship and commercial endorsements of products to be used on the first mission. For *all* contributions, expertise and experience were valuable; and the Mars mission was going to be expensive—though this aspect could be put into perspective by comparing it with the twelve billion spent every year in the USA and Europe on perfume, almost the amount of NASA's budget . . .

NASA, true to form, insisted on a launch date of 2018, meaning that humans would be on Mars to celebrate the fiftieth anniversary of the Apollo 11 landing.

Attempts had already been made to convert the formerly Soviet military–industrial complex to more peaceful ends, but it is not always easy to beat swords into ploughshares. There were many stories about what had happened when manufacturers of military rockets turned to making bathroom fittings and suchlike; the results had been disastrous, with poor-quality equipment being made by workers with low morale and no real interest in the product. How much better to put such expertise into making the power-plants for the motors of a Mars mission.

Yes, Mars was the answer. But this time, to satisfy the world, the mission had to be no mere Apollo-like landing—pick up a few rocks and return to Earth within a few days. That would in any case have been impossible, due to the orbital dynamics of such a mission—though, thanks to the development, mainly by the Johnson Space Center, of a new plasma drive that achieved a temperature of one million degrees Celsius contained by a magnetic bottle, the journey could take three months instead of the six or more that years earlier had been envisaged by planners whose horizons had been limited to chemical propellants. Chemical propellants would still be needed to take the ships above the Earth's atmosphere and to land on Mars, but the plasma drive would be effective for the journey in between. The higher acceleration possible with the plasma drive also solved the very serious zero-gravity problem. The crew would be constantly under one-third gravity, since they would be under power all the way. And neither would they need to depend upon solar panels for electricity.

Even the first flight would be a long-stay mission of over two years. Also, a commitment had to be made to establish a permanent base, small at first but eventually self-supporting. Robot landers would be sent ahead to set up a base, and to deposit supplies. Another incentive was that Mars could then become a staging post for the asteroids, where Earth's industry would find mountains of minerals, such as almost pure nickel–iron, there for the taking. Further valuable materials would be available from Mars's two moons and from the surface of Mars itself. Martian soil contains forty per cent oxygen chemically bound up with iron (hence the rusty colour of much of Mars), plus magnesium, sodium, sulphur and chlorine, while the atmosphere contains nitrogen. Carbon is available aplenty from the asteroids and from Phobos, the nearer satellite.

Aurora had found the whole prospect completely exciting, and impossible to resist. It was as if there were something—something stronger than herself—dictating to her that she must take part in the great Martian adventure, and doing so became her obsession. She had had little difficulty in obtaining a position back at NASA, and quickly she got to know all the right people . . . She had made sure she passed all the fitness and aptitude tests—which she did with no problems—and ended up as a member of the geology team. Not as a British member, of course; she had become an American citizen years ago. She wasn't the only one in this situation: the Canadian member, Dr Bryan Beaumont, a vulcanologist as well as co-pilot of the Lander, was also of English descent, his parents having emigrated just before he was born.

So here she was, on Mars. Now known as Dr Anne Pryor, she was seventy-eight and looked perhaps thirty-five.

She had come up with the theory that she must be one of a new breed of human, resistant to both time and disease. What other answer could there be? She took to scanning the media and the more specialist journals for reports or even hints that others of her kind existed, but with increasing disappointment and puzzlement. If they did, they were keeping as quiet as herself. Sometimes she felt a deep loneliness, but she knew no way to relieve it.

#

Anne Pryor, Aurora, came out of her reverie, suddenly dazzled by low evening sunlight blazing through a cleft between two lava outcrops. Near the shrunken Sun the sky was a washed-out blue, but the colour shaded through deep pink to a deep indigo only a few degrees higher.

It must be time to return to the Hut—an empty propellant tank which had been parachuted down and landed on small retro-rockets and inflation bags. Sectioned into two halves, the Hut contained living and sleeping quarters plus a laboratory and an admin and communications centre.

A rising plume of ochre dust showed that the rover was approaching on its daily round to pick up crew-members who'd been left at various locations.

Aurora packed up her equipment and walked a few metres to where she would be easily visible to the driver.

#

The next day was a rest day for Aurora. Recreational activities were very important on such a long mission, to avoid boredom and the stress of working continuously in close proximity with the same people day after day. Some of the crew spent hours recording on videodiscs messages that were squirted in one short burst on the radio link to their loved ones on Earth, or composing a type of e-mail. Others read, watched video films, wrote, played chess, listened to or played music, or engaged in various games—the physical ones being made more interesting by the low gravity and, when played out of doors, by the thin atmosphere.

Golf was a favourite, out on the desert. Players used a ball which was less massive than its Earth equivalent and made of a plastic material full of holes, like a sponge, so that in the one-third gravity it travelled about the same distance as a normal ball back home. The Martian golfball was fluorescent green so it would show up against the reddish terrain. Even so, lost balls were common. Since the supply of balls was not inexhaustible, each also contained a microminiaturized radio transmitter, similar to those sometimes used on Earth to tag birds and small animals.

Aurora enjoyed a game of golf herself, but had decided to become the first artist on Mars. (Not the first in *space*, for Alexei Leonov and Alan Bean had long ago beaten her to that landmark.) Before leaving Earth she had tried to inveigle a friend who worked in the laboratories of a paint company (had she but known it, a distant, multinational descendant of Dobson & Dart, next door to which she had lived as a small child) to produce pigments and a medium which would work in sub-zero temperatures and a carbon dioxide/nitrogen atmosphere with a pressure only one per cent of Earth's. All attempts had failed. A polymeric paint with an electrically heated palette and "brush" had been the most likely contender, but even with it the results had been lumpy and unsatisfactory. Chalks or pastels could be made to work, but she never felt that they produced "real" art.

So instead she used a device which had become popular with avant-garde artists on Earth: a "canvas" which combined computer graphics and the latest flat-screen technology. It was less than a centimetre thick. The brush was a type of light-pen which could be adjusted by touching a key-pad to produce wide, flat strokes, thin pen-like lines, or gradated airbrush effects—or anything in between. With a virtually infinite range of colours, the resulting image could be saved and its crystal matrix finally fixed so that no further changes could be made, accidentally or even deliberately. Once the key-pad unit was unplugged and detached, the image became a one-off, permanent work of art, ready for hanging.

So now she was back on the southern flank of Arsia, sitting on a light metal stool just inside the entrance to a lava tube, the tube's opening serving as a natural frame for the terrain which she was attempting to capture. As she had done many times before, she marvelled at the *realness* of the scene before her. At times it was easy to forget that she was on an alien world and to find herself thinking that she was back in Iceland or Kamchatka. Then, with an overwhelming wave of emotion, she would realize where she actually was. She had seen space art back on Earth, of course—had even tried her hand at imaginary planetary scenes herself—and of course she had seen the photographs taken by the unmanned rovers and aeroprobes which had preceded the manned mission. But observing the landscape for hours made her see minute details—textures, veins, cracks, colour differences, qualities of light and shadow, reflections—which would otherwise have gone unobserved. No artist based back on Earth, and no photograph, could hope to capture these in the way that she could. *Yet some scientists wanted to send only robots to this world,* she thought. *How absurd! Those scientists must be as soulless as the robots they thought we should send. And as lacking in imagination . . .*

Against the dark cave entrance the sky was a luminous lavender. Below it an intersecting network of small crevasses was proving difficult to sketch. She had already blocked in some weird formations of twisted. lava that formed the foreground.

To the east, against the slope of the volcano, a pale plume rose. She glanced at the watch built into the sleeve of her silvered suit. Surely it was too early for the rover? Yes, of course it was. The angle of sunlight was telling her that it was only early afternoon. And surely, anyway, that plume was too white to be dust?

Intrigued, she got up and, in an astronaut's slow-motion steps, picked her way across the rugged ground to where the haze was still visible, over a kilometre away. By the time she was within a few metres from the spot her pulse was racing. From a deep pit surrounded by a rough cone of tumbled lava, a nebulous mist rose, dissipating quickly in the thin air.

Aurora tongued her radio-mike on. "Pryor to Base. Pryor to Base? I think

I have an anomaly here."

"Anomaly!" The unemotional language of science.

"Roger, Pryor, Base here—Vitali speaking. What do you have, Anne?"

She was glad that it was Vitali Orlov who was on duty, as she had formed quite a friendship with the bluff but genial Russian engineer. Of course, like the rest of the team she was grateful to him, too, for having got them down to the surface safely: he had been the pilot of the conical Lander. A genuine democracy existed among the crew, since each was an expert in at least two fields, and took his or her responsibility to the rest very seriously, but Orlov was nominally in command of the landing party, having seniority because of his much greater experience of space travel. He had helped build and had served in the International Space Station, and had flown many Soyuz flights to and from that.

"I suggest that you get some of the geology team out here asap, Vitali. I've got some sort of activity coming from what looks like a hornito."

"Activity? Have you got your water-bottle filled with vodka—or is it bourbon?"

"If it wasn't full of water, which it is, it would be a good single malt whisky! No, listen, I'm quite sober, and dead serious. Now move your ass and get someone out here right away with instruments and cameras—especially video."

There was a beep and a second voice broke in: "Rover 1 here, Claude speaking. We're already on our way over in your direction, Anne. Our seismometers picked up a small 'quake—only about 2 on the Richter Scale—about an hour ago, but we hadn't been able to pinpoint it. So, thanks for your input; you can go back to your daubing now!"

"Anne here. You have to be joking! I'm not about to miss this, rest day or not!"

Twenty minutes later the rover appeared over a low scarp, bouncing across the uneven lava on its metal-mesh "tyres." But, by the time it had drawn up and its own dust cloud had dispersed, the white mist had disappeared apart from a few fitful puffs. The funnel-like walls of the little cone were crusted with a rime of ice crystals, glittering like tiny diamonds.

French geologist Claude Verdet was the first to give his opinion. His choice as a crew member had been a masterpiece of political diplomacy. To be sure, France had a big stake in the mission, but so had Germany, and the Germans had provided much of its ground support. Claude, although French, had been on attachment via ESA to the Sänger company in Germany for some years, and was thought of as part of their establishment. In addition, he was of Creole ancestry and black enough to satisfy the vociferous organizations on Earth who insisted on the inclusion of minorities in just about every undertaking. Such political considerations might have had to be overruled on the Mars mission, where everyone's lives might at any moment depend on one or other individual crew-member; fortunately Verdet would have been the natural choice anyway.

Aurora grinned wryly. Up here on Mars such concerns as race, nationality and skin-colour seemed a very long way away—which of course in a very literal sense was true. Distance made them seem even more ludicrous than they already were, which took some doing. The lucky—politically speaking—coincidence of Verdet's blackness had never crossed her mind until he'd mentioned it himself.

"The way I see it," he was saying, "a slab of rock down below gave way under stress, and allowed an underground cache of ice to come into contact with a heat source. Maybe radioactivity—could be it even released a pocket of magma. The ice flashed into steam—*et voila!*"

As usual, not everyone agreed, and the discussion became heated, turned into an argument that continued on through the afternoon. The most exciting aspect of the discovery of this heat source, and underground water, was the possibility of *life*—their main reason for being on Mars, after all. So far only microscopic worm-like fossils, similar to those found on the meteorite on Earth, had been discovered, and these were certainly not the sort of conclusive evidence they'd been hoping for.

What was needed was proof of indigenous Martian life, preferably still alive! As Viking had discovered, the surface of Mars, its regolith, had been thoroughly sterilized by the presence of peroxides. But the discovery, also in the late 1970s, that weird forms of life thrive in the absence of sunlight and oxygen around sulphurous undersea volcanic vents called black smokers had expanded the parameters considerably. Life exists in rocks a kilometre under Earth's surface, and can lie dormant for up to forty thousand years until water arrives to reactivate it. Indeed, Earth has a greater amount of biomass beneath than on the surface. So hope was still high that some form of life would be found on or beneath Mars.

Naturally, Aurora played a full part in the debate, and did no more sketching that day.

As the Sun sank, the crew-members piled into the cylindrical rover and drove back towards their base.

The going was tricky, especially in the low sunlight, which cast long, slanting violet–black shadows. The slightest depression looked like a deep crater. Hayashi Minako switched on the powerful headlight as she edged her way cautiously along a ledge formed by a lava tube, her rather pudgy face, framed by dark hair, intent as she concentrated on driving, peering through the plexiglass bubble of the cabin.

Suddenly, with no warning apart from a crunching sound heard through the chassis of the vehicle, the roof of the tube beneath them collapsed. The rover teetered along for a few metres at an alarming angle, then rolled over completely. It clanged against scattered boulders, overturned again and came to rest on its side in soft dust.

The crew picked themselves up.

"Is everyone OK?" asked Verdet.

There were cries of "I think so" and "Just bruises, I guess."

Then they became aware of the fact that Aurora lay deathly pale. The right sleeve of her spacesuit had been ripped open on a buckled and jagged piece of bulkhead. Blood gushed from her shoulder, and white bone protruded. Someone grabbed the First Aid box, and before long was applying a tourniquet and pad. Fortunately, the cab of the rover was pressurized, and, although badly dented, its outer skin did not seem to have been fractured.

With difficulty, they winched the rover upright, and in a purple twilight the vehicle limped back to base.

#

At first it seemed that Aurora was back in that strange yet familiar dream she had known before. It had reappeared several times since her brief yet spectacular sortie into the world of rock music—nearly always when she was for some reason at best semiconscious. She had come to call the experiences her "flashes." But this time the white-gowned figures stood around looking down at her gravely. There was no music or gaiety. Behind them, the slopes of the volcano (could it be Olympus Mons? No, surely it was too small—and it was clad in green for more than two-thirds of its height) were wreathed in clouds. Suddenly the view was blotted out. Brilliant violet–white light flared, too painful to look at. She tried to cover her eyes, but her arm would not move . . .

#

She screamed, and opened her eyes to see the tiny sick bay, partitioned off from the rest of the Hut. Robert Lundquist, the mission's only qualified physician, leaned over and pushed her back into her pillow.

Much later, he gave his patient the news. "Anne, my dear, I don't know how else to break this to you. If we were back on Earth a surgeon might just be able to help you. But there was nothing else I could do. Your arm was severed at the shoulder. I—I've had to amputate it. I am so, so sorry."

Memories

Aurora sat up on her cot, trying to eat breakfast with her left hand. She was determined to play as full a part as possible, even with only one arm, and had already made a start on learning how to write, use a computer keyboard and perform other everyday tasks one-handed. If only it hadn't been her right arm! Reflexively, she wriggled phantom fingers. She had heard of this phenomenon, but still was surprised by it each time it happened.

Lundquist pushed aside the plastic curtain and entered the makeshift sick quarters. "And how are we this morning?" he asked with a rather forced smile. He looked typically Swedish, Aurora thought. His wavy yellow hair was thinning at the temples. He was pleasant, but spoke only when necessary. His family had been American for several generations; had his wife been here she could probably have sewn the arm back on and connected the necessary nerves and blood vessels, for she was a leading surgeon.

"Well, I don't know how *you* are, but my shoulder's giving me hell," said Aurora. "I guess I'll live, though. Won't I?"

"Oh, yes. You're fit and healthy, and you didn't lose too much blood. There's no infection—it's just the muscles and nerves knitting."

She tried to lighten the mood. "Hmmm. That's neat. I never did learn to knit even when I had two hands."

Lundquist looked relieved. "I don't see why you shouldn't get dressed today, and perhaps have a go at getting the database up to date. That's if you feel like it."

#

She began to make herself useful to the team by performing tasks which, if they were honest, the other members would rather were left to someone else anyway. But she itched to get out onto the surface again—itched as much as her shoulder did—and began to pester the physician.

Finally he announced that it was time to remove the special dressing that had been in place for the last couple of weeks.

As he examined the pink stub at her shoulder he frowned.

"What's the matter, Doc?" asked Aurora worriedly. She didn't like Lundquist's expression.

"Oh, nothing, probably. It's healed remarkably well in such a short time. It just doesn't look how I expected, somehow."

"What do you mean? What's wrong with it? Don't keep me in suspense!"

Lundquist peered closer. With a look of relief, he said: "No, it's nothing. Just my imagination, I guess. The scar tissue's formed an unusual pattern, that's all. Sorry to scare you . . . "

#

Two more weeks went by, and Aurora persuaded Claude Verdet, who was also their life-support officer, to modify her spacesuit, removing the right sleeve and sealing the shoulder, preparatory to her first venture back out into the open.

First, though, Lundquist had to make a final examination to be sure that the newly healed flesh would not be irritated by the wearing of a suit. This time his frown did not go away.

"There's something very strange here, Anne. I thought it was my imagination that first time. But it wasn't."

Aurora looked down at her exposed shoulder. "Come on, Doc. It feels fine now; just twitches a bit now and then, that's all. And it looks OK to me. What could be wrong?"

"I didn't say anything was *wrong*, exactly. But what I thought were odd-shaped wrinkles in the scar tissue definitely look like five little . . . buds, now. I can't believe I'm saying this, but . . . Oh, hell, it looks as if, impossible though this seems, you're growing a new arm."

Aurora laughed nervously, and looked uncertainly from Lundquist to Verdet and back. "Come on, you two! Is this supposed to be some kind of joke?"

"No, it's not. I don't know what to make of it. All we can do is see how you go on. I certainly don't think you should worry about it."

Then Lundquist turned to the other man. "But I don't think you should take the sleeve off that spacesuit yet—just in case."

#

Naturally, the story of the new arm became the main subject of conversation, with many theories being put forward to account for the strange phenomenon. Robert Lundquist favoured the idea that it was something to do with the low gravity, or even that the long period of weightlessness during the voyage out had had some effect on the metabolism, somehow causing stem-cell regeneration. The problem with this theory was that it was in no way borne out by the zero-gee experiments that had been carried out in Earth orbit over many years.

Bryan Beaumont, who tended to have a mystical streak, thought it must be due to some property of Mars. "Could be there's something in the magnetic field; or maybe she's ingested some Martian minerals—you all know how that dust gets everywhere, despite our precautions. Or the air itself, maybe?"

His theories grew wilder. "Hey, perhaps there are micro-organisms in the air? Tiny little alien doctors! Or—what do they call them?—nanobots? Whatever it is, it just has to be to do with Mars itself. New limbs don't grow, back on Earth. Well, not on people, anyway—only on lizards and things."

Lundquist, whose main role on the mission was as biologist, scoffed at the idea that some sort of microscopic form of Martian life could be responsible. But he had to admit that he was as baffled as everyone else.

As for Aurora herself, she watched, bemused, as day after day the stump of her shoulder elongated and grew. At first it was soft and quite flexible, but as time passed it became more rigid and developed an obvious elbow joint. Tiny nails, like those of a newborn baby, appeared on the ends of the stubby fingers. It was weird, incredible, mind-boggling . . . impossible!

Yet, knowing what the others did not know about herself, Aurora saw it as an extension of her own "strangeness." As if in daydreams, memories of her younger days came back to her.

#

She was sitting in the passenger seat of the old green Morris Minor. Her mother was driving. They were going to see Granny Petrie, who was in an old folks' home and wasn't long for this world, her Mum said. Her grandmother often didn't even seem to know who they were. Stevie quickly got bored with these visits, and often got into trouble—like the time when he stuffed the ancient Mrs Blenkinsop's ear trumpet full of tobacco from Mr Wallis's tobacco pouch. And had been about to light it when their mother noticed and hastily grabbed it from him. So Mum hadn't really objected when Stevie—or Steve, as his dignity now preferred him to be called—had claimed a prior arrangement to stay overnight camping out in a tent in the garden with his friend Duncan.

A big car—a Daimler, Aurora recognized from a previous car trip with Stevie, who'd kept up a running commentary on all the vehicles they passed (there weren't that many in their part of Scotland in 1950)—was waiting in a side road for them to go by.

No! It *wasn't* waiting. It was turning directly into their path!

Aurora saw her mother's foot jab at the brake. Too late. They ploughed into the side of the Daimler, slewed across the road. A horsebox, coming in the opposite direction, caught them a glancing but violent blow. The noise was terrible. They lurched to an abrupt stop in a ditch.

Her mother's head had gone through the windscreen, and the steering wheel was embedded in her chest. There was blood everywhere.

Aurora realized that some of it was hers . . .

#

Aurora blinked tears from her eyes and shook her head. She must have suppressed that memory all these years—and no wonder. She had believed until today that she had come out of the accident without a mark, whereas she knew now that she'd had a broken arm, internal injuries and many cuts and abrasions. She had been in hospital for only two weeks, but while she'd been there the news had been broken to her, none too gently, that she no longer had a mother. Or a grandma, for Granny Petrie had passed away on the spot upon hearing of the death of her favourite daughter-in-law.

Of course! That had been the beginning of Aurora living in homes, and running away from them, and becoming generally wild. But she remembered that, before she'd left the hospital, the doctor had commented that she was lucky to be alive, and expressed amazement at the speed with which her injuries had healed.

That hadn't been the only occasion, either. Other incidents now came to mind—like the time she had plunged a hand into the synthesizer at that strange concert. She couldn't remember why she had done it, now, but she could still see the shower of sparks, smell the burning flesh, see the startled and horrified look on Lefty's face, eyes white and wide in his dark face. She should have died, with full mains voltage passing through her—but she hadn't.

She saw now that it had been only a matter of time before this ultimate test was reached. And, if she hadn't been on Mars, out of reach of Earth's modern medical techniques which could in all probability have re-attached her old arm, she might still not have discovered the truth—or passed the test.

Aurora mopped her brow with her left hand. The memories had left her drained and trembling. She needed a drink—but there wasn't any booze here. Perhaps something medicinal, though?

No. She banished the thought. She was surely old enough to know better!

#

Somehow the media back on Earth got to hear about Aurora's arm. The crew had agreed to keep the information quiet, at least for a while, until they were quite sure what was happening, but someone must have leaked it. Accusing glances were cast about the small base. Who among them had a secret but lucrative contract with the TV and videomedia companies? Bryan Beaumont was the most likely suspect, as he had worked as a journalist for *Nature* and other scientific journals and popular e-mags. But he denied it. More likely Mission Control had been the source of the leak.

It didn't really matter, Aurora pointed out. They couldn't have kept the news to themselves for long, anyway. As it turned out, the media's attention worked in their favour, since this human-interest story produced far higher viewing figures on the home planet than had the report of a short-lived steam vent or any of their other geological or meteorological discoveries—important though those were to the scientific community.

Even so, she wished the spotlight had not been drawn to her.

Or did she? Was there, deep down, a secret wish for her strange story to become known, so that she could stop masquerading—and perhaps some sort of explanation might come to light? It was in the lap of the gods now.

At last the dust settled and life at the base got back to normal. Although, actually, as far as Mars was concerned, the dust did not settle. As was common at this season, a planet-wide dust storm arose, and for a while operations outside the Hut and the Lander became difficult—sometimes impossible. As Spring had come to the southern hemisphere, the dust storm had started in the great 1800km basin of Hellas Planitia (what an asteroid impact *that* must have been!), right around the other side of the planet. Soon the whole of the little world was shrouded in an ochre haze. Only Hayashi Minako, the meteorologist, was daring to go outside. Wearing a special environment suit, she was setting up equipment to record the wind speeds, density of dust and other data. Since she was outside anyway, she also tended the electrolysis apparatus, set up nearby to extract oxygen and hydrogen from water ice—one of the reasons for choosing this site. The oxygen was used for life support, the hydrogen would be needed later, and both could be recombined in a compact fuel cell to provide power when the solar cells were inactive.

The rest of the team—including Aurora, whose arm was now almost normal, apart from its baby-pink colouring—twiddled their thumbs impatiently. They were awaiting the opportunity to send out an expedition, using both rovers, into the tributaries of the Noctis Labyrinthus—a vast network of canyons and crevasses which lay to their east, and which was connected eventually to the mighty Valles Marineris, the 4800km-long seismic rift in which America's Grand Canyon would have been utterly dwarfed and lost.

Noctis Labyrinthus, the Labyrinth of Night! Aurora shivered with anticipation. Both the artist and scientist in her yearned to go there. As they had passed over it in orbit, awaiting instructions to land, she had gazed at it through the telescope to see clouds of fog form in the steep valleys as the early-morning sunlight struck east-facing slopes and vaporized ice which had formed there during the night.

Bryan Beaumont had a penchant for rock music of the Sixties and Seventies, and among the private possessions he'd been permitted to take on board with him had brought, instead of the modern sound-cards, old-fashioned compact discs of what had once been LP records. To pass the time, even while he worked in his cubicle to catch up on collating lava and ash samples, he played music by some of what had once been known as "progressive" groups, such as Pink Floyd, King Crimson, Grateful Dead, UFO . . .

In keeping with his taste in music, Beaumont's appearance was boyish. His thick, reddish hair almost always looked uncombed, as he was forever pushing it back out of his eyes. His manner was exuberant, and he became almost excessively enthusiastic about anything which took his interest. Unfortunately those interests tended to stray into areas usually thought of as pseudoscientific, sometimes earning him the censure of his colleagues. There was no doubting his high intelligence, nonetheless— which was perhaps why they tolerated his excesses. As the mission progressed, Aurora realized that she found him quite attractive, but he never appeared more than orthodoxly friendly towards her, and her own inexperience in romantic matters meant that she never felt able to make a first move. In any case, she rationalized, that kind of thing was all much too difficult in the close confines of the base.

As Aurora passed him one day she stopped in her tracks. For a moment she stood frozen to the spot, goose-flesh rising on her back and neck as the memories came flooding back. He was playing the Gas Giants' album!

Beaumont looked round at her curiously.

"Anything wrong, Anne?"

Aurora pulled herself together. "No, I—I just realized I'd forgotten something. By the way, I've meant to ask you before: why do you always play that old music? You can't even have been born when that stuff was around."

"Oh, I was practically weaned on it. My old man had a great record collection, and I've always found it more interesting than the sterile mush that passes for music nowadays. Or neopunk—that seems to be an excuse for anyone who can play three discords on a synguitar! No, you take the disc that's playing now. Can you believe it, my parents met at that concert, in London, England! They said it was the most incredible gig they ever went to. Yet the group—the Gas Giants, they were called—was only a support act, and they just vanished soon afterward. Weird, isn't it? They . . . "

He was obviously all set to go into more detail, but Aurora made to move on. Before she could, Beaumont picked up the flat plastic case which had held the disc and peered closely at it. It held a smaller reproduction of the original album sleeve.

"Hey, d'you know something? That girl—Aurora, she called herself—looks just like *you*, Anne, except her hair is much longer. See?"

Aurora pretended to look at it. "Mmm, I suppose she does, a bit. Anyway—gotta go." She swung away abruptly, Bryan's gaze boring into her back like a laser beam.

Why was she always being reminded of that damned concert? Against her will, her head was again filled with those strange images. To take her mind off them, she decided to make a painting of Noctis Labyrinthus, based on the overhead video view, and see how accurate it turned out when she got there. She loaded the videodisc and found the image she wanted.

It would be the first time she had painted since the accident, and she took up the light-brush with some trepidation. But she need not have worried; very soon she was applying deft strokes. She had unhesitatingly chosen a spot among the complicated intersecting rifts, and the scene which took shape was so real that she might have been there in person, right now. She used the airbrush effect subtly, and fog swirled over the lip of the canyon and softened the outlines of the broken cliffs beyond.

The air in the Hut was stuffy, heavy with odours of cooking and bodies and the acrid smell of electrical apparatus, plus of course the ever-present Martian dust. One of the Apollo astronauts had said that moondust, inside the module, smelled like gunpowder. Mars dust, Aurora thought, was like a combination of damp dog and paprika. She yawned, closed her paintscreen, and decided to take a look at Mars in real time. She reached out to switch over to the orbiting cameras, then changed her mind and decided to use the big high-definition flatscreen on the far wall of the Hut. As she passed Beaumont he looked round almost guiltily and blanked his computer screen. *Secretive*, she thought.

As was normal, the big screen showed the outside view. It had not been considered worth the technical problems or expense of fitting actual windows to the converted fuel tank. She watched a large, rather dim star raise itself blearily from the western horizon. As it rose higher it revealed a misshapen disc. Phobos. She knew the inner moon would pass through more than half of its cycle of phases and set four and a half hours later in the east, to rise again eleven hours afterwards. Then a smaller but brighter star appeared and overtook Phobos. That, she knew, would be their Orbiter, waiting to take them home but meanwhile completing the best high-definition survey of the whole planet ever made, either working autonomously or, if they needed to choose a specific area—preparatory to a ground exploration, for instance—under human guidance.

Both the orbiting and landing craft had names, as was customary. There had been much argument over them. Gods such as Ares were always warlike, so had been ruled out. Finally, the orbiter was named *Schiaparelli* and the lander *Lowell*, after the two early astronomers who had been the most prolific and influential observers of the red planet. True, Lowell had also been responsible for many misconceptions, with his assertion that the canals he claimed to see were artificial watercourses, created by intelligent Martians . . . but at least he had brought Mars into the public's awareness, and its imagination. The crew generally ignored these names, however, and rarely called the two craft anything other than Orbiter and Lander.

The fact that the Orbiter was passing overhead would not prevent Aurora from seeing the other side of the planet in real time. Three small satellites had been placed in strategic orbital positions so that the whole of Mars (apart from small areas around the poles) could be viewed at any time. The satellites also served as communications relays. Unfortunately, one of them had failed to achieve its proper orbit, so there were occasional blind spots. This was not one of them but, even so, not only was the great asteroid-impact basin of Hellas almost certainly obscured by dust but it was currently night on that part of the planet.

It wasn't Hellas she wanted to look at anyway. She keyed in the appropriate coordinates and there was the huge, dark cone of Olympus Mons, rising above a sea of ochre suspended dust. From it long dark streaks extended northwards, just as they had in November 1971 when the unmanned Mariner 9 probe first arrived. Already the Big Three volcanoes—Arsia, Pavonis and Ascraeus—could be seen thrusting their peaks above the clouds. Perhaps the planet-wide dust storm was starting to subside, and their expedition could soon start?

Noctis Labyrinthus

Aurora stepped down from Rover 2, walked forward a few metres, and looked over the canyon edge. This felt like a school outing, and she could imagine laying out a picnic on the flat area of sand to her right. *Spam sandwiches, hard-boiled eggs, tomatoes to eat like an apple; but no one* ever *remembers the salt* ... Hayashi Minako sat on a boulder, assembling an anemometer. Nearby, Bryan Beaumont examined chunks of basalt. Claude Verdet was already a tiny figure in the distance, his long legs letting him bound over boulders and narrow crevices like a mountain goat. Rover 1 was still approaching over the plain of Syria Planum, completing its 700km journey.

At first the walls of the canyon dropped steeply, revealing varicoloured layers of lava flows, but then the slope became more gradual as banks of talus—debris flaked off over millennia—piled up, leading down to the floor. There were several spots where it would have been quite easy to descend to the sandy bottom. In places the bedrock seemed to be exposed, though it was possible, instead, that large boulders had fallen from above and, partially buried, were mimicking patches of bedrock showing through. That was something for the first traverse to discover. The signs of erosion, presumably by water, were quite clear.

The big question to be answered was: were there any signs of life down there? The sometime presence of water was beyond doubt. Could there be fossils, no matter how primitive? Or, better still, might there be living organisms? The results from probes like Britain's *Beagle 2* and later unmanned missions had been inconclusive to many scientists, sadly.

Meanwhile, the most important item was to unload and set up the Blimp.

Aurora set to with a will, unpacking the incredibly thin but strong material of the envelope while Vitali Orlov erected the struts for the cabin and motors.

"Why can't we use a proper aeroplane?" Aurora asked, more to make conversation than anything else.

The Russian engineer pulled a face. "Oh, when we decided early in mission planning that only way to explore large area of very difficult terrain is from air, we looked at various designs for aircraft, but no good." Orlov normally spoke perfect English, with an American accent—he had spent some years studying at MIT—but occasionally, especially when he felt he was "lecturing," his sense of humour led him to parody the stereotypical Russian.

"Plane would have to travel six times faster in Mars air than it would on Earth to give same amount of lift, yes? Would need two-and-half times as much power, too. Then there is power-plant. Air-breathing engine with propellers or jets—no good! Have to use rockets, electric power, or glider? Need be glider with bloody big wingspan. So, no plane. Many problems. No runway. Small range. Big wings hard to pack to bring here too. You see difficulties?"

Aurora nodded, then said "Yes. I see. Well, anyway, I can't wait for my turn in the balloon."

"Is *not* balloon! Is what we call hybrid—part lighter-than-air, part aerodynamic airship, yes? And needs only quarter of power—less, even—than on Earth. Is filled with hydrogen—quite safe: no oxygen in Martian atmosphere to make explosion. Electric power for propellers from solar cells. Easy!"

The envelope was almost laid out on the desert. "But it's enormous!"

The gasbag was in fact just over one hundred metres long. But only its size was intimidating. It was being filled with stored hydrogen from the electrolysis plant back at Base; this was extracted from water-ice—H_2O—which of course produced twice as much hydrogen as oxygen. The latter was used for their life-support packs. Once the bag had been inflated and the cabin attached, the Blimp floated above the ground, tugging gently at its tethers in the light wind. It was obvious the Blimp was going to be a joy to use, and simple to operate.

By the time the task was finished, the Sun was settling redly into a bank of haze, back in the direction from which they had come. The remains of the dust storm created a splendid display of colours, with separate layers of orange, crimson, magenta, violet and prussian blue swirling towards the zenith. Stars appeared, and Aurora wished she had time to fetch out her paintscreen.

Later, she told herself, shooting off a few frames with the tiny digital camera she always carried on her suit.

The crew spent the night in their rovers, which were relatively large and well equipped. Tomorrow they would erect another inflatable, this time full of oxygen, as a pressure dome. Officially, this should have been their first job, but they had all been eager to see the Blimp aloft, and one more night of slightly cramped discomfort would do them no harm.

#

Their camp was not in the best position for a test flight, as they were near the top of the Tharsis bulge—the volcanic upland area that dominates Mars's northern hemisphere. This meant that the atmosphere was even thinner here than elsewhere on the surface. But nearly all of their flights would take them westward, towards Valles Marineris, and where it was safe to do so they would actually be descending into the canyons, within which the air was actually measurably thicker than up on the surface.

Such was the excitement among the crew that straws (actually lengths of electrical cable) were drawn to see who should be first to go aloft. All of the members of the mission had, as an essential part of their training, several hours of flying experience back on Earth, but that would be of little help when it came to controlling this strange craft in an alien atmosphere. The Blimp could carry only one person plus about fifty kilograms of equipment. The two women tried to claim an advantage, on the grounds that they were lighter, but were promptly told that they would have to take their chances along with the men.

It was Claude Verdet who drew the lucky short straw, and his thin black moustache almost met his ears as he beamed with pleasure. He settled himself in the fragile-looking cabin—actually no more than a framework, open at the sides but with a transparent plastic shield curving from front to back. The propeller, angled downward for takeoff, began to rotate, the tethers were released, and the Blimp surged upward.

The silvered gasbag rose quite rapidly for a few metres, then hovered, a bright alien object against the dark sky, the rosy early-morning sunlight illuminating its underside.

Aurora was suddenly overcome by a wave of emotion and staggered, clutching at the side of the rover next to her for support. She had a powerful feeling of *déjà vu*; what could it be?

She saw the dirigible superimposed on an image of a broken brick wall, a crooked chimney stack, flames, blackened wooden rafters pointing to the sky at unlikely angles. There was a roaring noise in her ears. Other pictures crowded at the borders of her consciousness, demanding to be let in, but she swept them aside.

Some of her colleagues were looking at her strangely, or with concern, and Robert Lundquist, wearing his stern possibly-a-medical-emergency face, was advancing towards her.

Aurora waved him away, almost angrily.

"It's all right. I'm—OK. Just went weak for a moment. Didn't sleep much last night—must be all the excitement!"

She managed a weak smile.

"Are you sure?" asked Lundquist. "Is your arm bothering you?"

"No, really, Bob. It's nothing."

But her mind was whirling. It hadn't been one of her flashes, even though it had possessed something of the same quality. After all, the flashes had to be products of her imagination, didn't they? This had felt like an actual experience—a memory.

She brushed the frantic thoughts aside and concentrated on the Blimp's ascent.

Verdet had now angled the propeller so that he was slowly turning to face down the canyon. He gave them a wave as he moved off, and his voice, high with excitement, came over their helmet phones.

"*C'est magnifique!* The view is amazing from up here. The canyon keeps subdividing for as far as I can see. There's still some fog further off, though, hiding the floor, so I'll wait 'til it burns off before I try to go higher and take mapping photographs. Meanwhile, I'll put this ship through its paces, OK? Oh—over."

The Blimp dwindled in the distance, occasionally rising or falling, or turning to explore various tributaries. The rest of the crew watched it until it became a silver star, then they quietly dispersed to go about their various duties.

Orlov stayed at Rover 1. He was in charge of erecting the living quarters and also setting up the communications link, which would relay voice and pictures through its powerful transmitter to the big S-band dish at Base—which had been left unmanned, except for computers, digital recorders and robotic maintenance equipment—from where they would be beamed onward to Earth. As radio waves took nearly twenty minutes to reach the home planet, conversations were impossible, and unless there was an emergency transmissions from either direction were sent in daily bursts.

By mid-morning, having completed various chores around the camp, Aurora set off on her own to explore the canyon floor, taking samples as she went. She had already noted several spots where fan-shaped slopes of debris reached almost from rim to floor, making it quite easy to descend, though she still took great care. Her progress was made more difficult by having to take a trolley—a small cart which was normally pushed or towed, but which had a small electric motor for use when required. It carried a spare oxygen pack, water and food tubes that could be plugged into her suit, and her geological equipment and sample containers—areological rather than geological, strictly, but few bothered to make the distinction.

From time to time she reported her progress to Orlov, who seemed glad of her company, if only by voice. The colours here were more interesting, with clearly visible layers in the walls revealing ash and lava flows. Her feet sank, sometimes several centimetres, into soft sand (or "fines", as it was technically known) and dust, some of it no doubt blown from above, some eroded from the walls. Much of the time she walked in violet-tinted shadow, but the sunlight reflecting off the walls above gave her plenty of light. A glint of white on some ledges suggested ice or frost that had not vaporized.

She was reminded of other gorges that she had explored in her long life, particularly the Gorge of Samaria on Crete. But she didn't expect to find stepping stones across a river in this canyon! She smiled to herself. That trip to the Greek Islands had been an interesting one, with much to intrigue a vulcanologist. She mused about Knossos and Santorini—Thera, as it was sometimes known—and the legend of Atlantis. Although shunned by orthodox scientists, the idea of ancient civilizations, perhaps as advanced as humans were today, yet becoming extinct due to some natural or manmade catastrophe, had always held a fascination for her. Once, many years ago, the very world on which she was now walking had been the focus of humanity's hopes of finding another civilization, but they had been dashed with the advent of space probes. Still, one never knew . . .

"Hey, Vitali, I think I just saw a little green man dodge behind a rock!" she said into her mike. The only response was a crackle.

"Vitali? Come in, Rover 1!"

Nothing.

Looking back, she saw that she had made a number of twists and turns. The canyon was deep, overhanging in places, and her radio signals were undoubtedly being blocked by its walls. Her suit radio was much too weak to reach the Orbiter or any of the satellites, so could not be relayed by them. She cursed herself for not thinking of that earlier. Indeed, she realized, she would have to be careful not to get lost without the aid of radio to guide her. But then she reassured herself: the tracks left by her feet and the thick tyres of the trolley would help her retrace her steps.

She continued on her way, still picking up samples, for a while, then sat on a flat rock to attach a container of self-heating soup to the connector on the front of her suit. Moments later she was sucking the soup through a tube. It was not exactly delicious, but was welcome for all that. The yeasty smell of it filled her helmet until drawn away by the suit's circulation system. She looked down at the container. Green. Sometimes she yearned for a sight of green grass, or a tree. Or of blue sky.

She glanced at the oxygen readout. About half an hour left before she needed to change the tank. She moved on. Shortly she found herself traversing an area of what appeared to be bedrock, swept clean of dust by a wind that swirled through the canyon, funnelled by walls which at this point were close together. She could see the little eddies and dust devils which it raised as the gorge subdivided yet again into left and right forks.

Near the junction, was that a smooth rock or a beached whale? Yes, and just near it—surely those were three or four seals, sunbathing.

Aurora became aware that a red light was blinking inside her helmet. It was time to change her air, before she really started hallucinating. She sat down, her back against the trolley, reached over her shoulder and unclipped the oxygen module from her pliss pack (PLSS, portable life support system, known as "pliss" since Apollo times), sealing its tube. Placing the almost spent unit aside, she pressed her back against the new one until she could clip it on. Oxygen hissed briefly as she opened the tap, then its flow again became unobtrusive. The new air tasted metallic. She put the used tank back on the trolley for recharging. As she did so, she noticed a transparent plastic tube of bright green balls, left from her last golf game.

Gazing at the rock over which she was now travelling, it occurred to her for the first time that her footprints were no longer visible. Remembering, with a smile, children's stories in which the hero had paid out a ball of string in order to find his or her way back, she decided to place a golfball at strategic points on her way. Their microtransmitters would help guide her back along her route.

The sunlight was now striking only the top few metres of the walls, bouncing down as an amber glow. She must turn back soon, before sunset.

But there was an intriguing black shape up ahead, and she wanted to investigate that first . . .

The black shape turned out to be a cave entrance, angling down into the canyon wall and giving every impression of having been formed by water; there were even wavelike striations in the entrance. She ventured cautiously inside and turned on her suit lamp. It was reflected back in myriad points of light. Ice crystals, and—yes, icicles! Here where the sunlight never reached, melt-water filtering down from above through crevices had frozen and grown down, like stalactites, perhaps over thousands of years, maybe much longer even than that. She felt like a tomb robber or a vandal as she snapped off the tiniest sample for later analysis.

She continued to make her way along the passage. Even the ground beneath her feet was now ice-covered. *Careful: it's slippery here . . .*

Even as she had the thought her feet were swept from beneath her, and she hit the ground with a body-shaking thump which knocked the breath out of her. As she tried to rise she felt rather than heard a rumbling sound, and the daylight vanished as the roof fell in.

Aurora felt exasperated rather than afraid. This was the second accident she'd suffered that had been caused by the collapse of a roof—the previous one being the roof of a lava tube. She'd be getting a reputation for being accident-prone.

Well, I don't appear to be hurt, she thought, *apart from a bruise on my new arm.* She'd fallen rather heavily on that arm. *Nothing broken, anyway. Of course, if something were damaged it would probably heal or grow again . . . but not if I run out of air first! Going to have to dig myself out . . .*

It did not take long to realize that this was easier said than done. She was wedged awkwardly, giving her little room for movement. Plus the chunk of roof that now blocked her way out was huge—far bigger than she'd realized—and even in low gravity she wasn't going to be able to move it.

A Martian Mystery

Back at Camp One, the crew were getting worried. Vitali Orlov had called them together in the pressure dome, the Igloo. "The last contact I had with Anne was over four hours ago. Communications were getting a bit weak and intermittent, and when I couldn't get through any more I assumed it was just that the canyon walls were blocking the signal, and she'd realize this. But she must be well into her second can of air by now, and I'd have expected her to be back in range."

Bryan Beaumont asked: "What about Claude? Shouldn't he be back by now, too?"

"According to the original plan, yes, but he was doing such good work and having such a good time that I let him stay up longer than scheduled. It's OK—he's still in radio contact, and he's on his way back."

"Well in that case cannot we ask him to keep an eye out for Dr Pryor?" asked Minako. She never used first names when talking about people, though she sometimes did when talking to them.

"Yes, I already have," replied Orlov.

Even as he spoke, the Blimp hove into view, now reflecting the rays of evening sunlight which streamed across the plain and threw the canyons into purple shadow.

Orlov spoke into his microphone. "Come in, Claude. Any luck? Over."

"Sorry. I've been down as low as I dared, and used my floodlights, but there's no sign of her. Afraid I can't stay up much longer; the batteries are getting low, and the solar cells won't be charging much now. But I have enough power for one more sweep of those tributaries to the north, in case she strayed into them, if you wish? Over."

"Roger, Claude. Do that. But don't take any chances—and be down before sunset, right? Over and out."

As the airship manoeuvred so that its tail elevators faced them, then drew away, Orlov snapped, "Right, I think it's time to organize a search party. I've been cooped up in this place all day, so I'll lead it. Bryan, will you take over here? The rest of you, get suited up—those of you who aren't already—and we'll go down into the canyon. And bring extra lights." Then, grimly: "Oh—and, Robert, I don't need to remind you to bring your first aid kit..."

A few minutes later, as he lowered his helmet into place, Orlov grimaced and said to Beaumont, only half-joking: "Damn that woman! Why can't she obey the mission standing orders—never get out of radio contact? And why can't she stop getting herself into trouble?"

"She gets very wrapped up in what she's doing," said Beaumont in her defence. "But she knows her stuff. Anyway, personally I think she'll come walking in any minute with a faulty radio."

"I know, I know. And I just hope you're right."

The party picked their way severally down the talus slope to the floor of the canyon and slow-footed along it in a straggling line. They could travel much faster than Aurora had, since they were not stopping to examine and collect samples, but they didn't go so fast that they didn't take time to shine their flashlights into every likely crevice and offshoot.

"A person could get lost here and never be found," said Minako pessimistically.

"It must be being so cheerful that keeps you going!" came Beaumont's voice over their radios. He was monitoring their progress.

"Please! Keep the airwaves clear in case Anne is trying to contact us—unless anything important comes up," ordered Orlov.

After that the party moved along in silence apart from an occasional muffled oath as someone stumbled over a rock. The gorge was almost entirely in darkness now. Phobos appeared over the western rim for the second time that day, on its endless journey towards the east. The little moon's dim light did not help. Their figures flickered like pale wraiths as light beams glimmered from silvery suits and swept away again.

\#

Aurora was, to her own surprise, having some success. Recognizing that she could never hope to move the slab of rock that had blocked the original entrance, she was probing at the roof directly above her. This consisted of loose rocks and something like shale. Stones were raining down on her, bouncing off the visor of her helmet, but as long as none of them cracked it, she felt she might be able to break through to the surface.

She tried not to think about the fact that she only had two hours of oxygen left. This would barely have been enough to get her back to camp even if she'd already started walking. Once again she cursed herself for an idiot, and resolved to go by the book in future.

"If only I get out of this alive, that is," she muttered. She twisted to get a better grip on a rock, and winced as she realized that her leg also hurt. The rock shifted, came loose and fell—straight towards her helmet.

She ducked her head out of the way as much as she could in the limited space.

Then, with a crash and a shower of debris, the whole roof fell upon her.

Her heart thumped as for a moment she thought she'd been buried alive.

However, she calmed herself swiftly. She was on Mars, not Earth. On Earth her strength would have been unable to move the mass of rubble, but in the lesser gravity of Mars she found she could—with a colossal effort—wriggle free and clamber up the slope of fresh detritus to the surface.

Only a thin line of sunlight now illuminated the rim of the canyon. A fine spindrift of dust from the desert caught the rays and formed swirling trails which twisted against the russet sky like cirrus in an Earth sunset. She located her trolley and grasped its handle with her right hand, changing her mind rapidly as pain shot up her arm. She swapped hands and triggered the little motor; so long as she was on a relatively flat surface, the motor would give her greater speed.

I must look a sorry sight! she told herself wryly. Her suit was stained and dirty, though fortunately not torn; her helmet's faceplate was scarred. She was limping. Although the temperature around her was already over 60CE below zero, she was sweating with effort.

"Horses sweat. Men perspire. Ladies *glow!*" she told herself. It was something her mother had used to say. Thinking about her mother brought back the image she had seen when—was it only that morning?—the Blimp was taking off. She remembered that for many years her mother had been proud of some silk underwear she had made, she said, from a German parachute. The parachute from a—what was it? A landmine? The thing had landed on their house when Aurora was a tiny baby—too young to have any actual

75

memory of the event. But memories of what she had been told as a little girl were returning.

There was something about a barrage balloon—red-lit from below; a crackling roar—and a German parachutist who had helped them. And her brother Stephen, walking. Poor Steve. He had died of cancer only last year; she had not been able to go to his side, much as she had wanted to. How could she, when she looked like his daughter or even his granddaughter? She had been keeping in touch with him only by an occasional phone call and e-mail.

She shook a bead of sweat out of her eyes and wrinkled her nose. Ugh. The inside of her suit was becoming decidedly smelly. Where was she? Her mind was wandering, and she was nearly exhausted. Oh, yes, Steve. As a boy he'd been paralysed from birth, and then he'd got up and walked after being buried when the roof fell in on him, or something. (Well, it had been *her* turn to be under a collapsing roof this time!) The story had all sounded very unlikely; and yet, in the light of her own recovery from a severed arm, did it really seem so impossible now?

Could there be something *special* about her family? Or was it—? Yes, that must be it. Stephen must have had some of the same quality she had. But no, no, that couldn't be the truth. He had aged naturally, and he certainly hadn't beaten cancer—though he'd been 86 when he died. Perhaps you got only one chance. Perhaps the—the talent, or whatever it was, burned out after one apparent miracle? Would she start ageing now, and heal no better than anyone else? But then she seemed to have had several lucky escapes already, to say the least . . .

Her mind spun, in a turmoil. Her faceplate had misted up, the suit's circulation and cooling system unable to cope with her exertions, and her eyes smarted as salty sweat poured down her face. She couldn't go much further.

A bright glow swam blearily across her visor, growing and spreading. A wave of relief washed over her. "The Blimp!" she shouted, rushing towards the light. Of course! They'd have asked Claude to look for her when she was overdue.

She operated the built-in wiper inside her faceplate, and at the same time flicked on the radio. There was a crackling hiss of static (a diminishing roar; a blue-white flash against a dark sky). The light, now that she could see more clearly, seemed peculiar. It could only be described as white tinged with reddish blue. It was brilliant, and she could not make out the outline of the airship behind it. Yet the light itself seemed to be spherical, with—yes—with scintillating points moving inside it, like tiny glittering mirrors. And a mist swirled around its edges. What was going on?

She stopped, still several metres away from the light. It moved up and down, quite rapidly. She took a step towards it, still uncertain what to make of it. It moved away from her, undulating with a strange, switchback motion. She spoke into her microphone: "Come in, Claude. Is that you? This is Anne Pryor—stop messing about, will you? I'm about done in!"

The only answer was a rushing noise which grew louder and faded, it seemed, with the motions of the light. With startling abruptness, it blinked out, only to reappear fifty metres away. It pulsated, and now appeared more orange in colour. Suddenly it swooped upwards, hovering near the rim of the canyon, so that she could see every detail of the rocks. Then it either shrank in size or flew away from her so rapidly that she couldn't tell which.

It dwindled to a spark, and vanished.

Aurora sank to the ground and wept; with disappointment, with frustration, with sheer exhaustion. Yet even as she tumbled into the depths of despair part of her mind was nagging at her excitedly.

If this hadn't been the airship—and it obviously hadn't—then what *had* it been? Could it be some form of life, or maybe even a Martian machine?

But her brain was overloaded—with memories, with sensory input, with wild theories and, again, with exhaustion. It responded with the gift of unconsciousness.

#

The search party had reached a place where three canyons branched off from a wide amphitheatre.

"How on Earth—damn that expression!—how the hell are we going to find which branch she took?" asked Robert Lundquist.

Orlov, as he had done time and again, tried to contact Anne on his radio, with no more success than before. His flashlight beam swept into one of the branches, moved on, then swiftly swept back. He gasped.

"I think there's a—a—*plant* over there!" he exclaimed, moving towards the green object. For a second he thought it was some sort of phosphorescent fungoid growth. Then the virtual image of his imagination flipped his vision to reality and he recognized it for what it was. A golfball.

"I think I know which way she went," he said. "And, if one of us tunes in our RDF, we might be able to find her more quickly. You do it, will you,

Minako? I want to keep this frequency clear for speech."

Not too long afterwards they found Aurora lying slumped against a low hill of sand. At first they feared she was dead, but Lundquist quickly checked for vital signs and pronounced her alive, if not completely well. He connected a new oxygen tank. Orlov and Minako lifted her onto a collapsible stretcher, and the party made its way carefully back to the Igloo.

#

Aurora's fears that she might have lost her powers of recuperation proved groundless. After only a day in bed she became restless and wanted to be up and about again. Lundquist allowed her to take on the task of keeping an eye, or ear, on the intercom, in case of urgent messages—a very light task.

There was something she had been wanting to do. She got out her paintscreen and gazed at it for a moment, wondering when she would have an opportunity to go outside again and use it. Then she brought it to life. On the screen was the painting she had done based on the view from orbit.

Yes, she had been right, no doubt about it. The scene she had created mainly from her imagination was almost identical with the area of the canyon where she had had the encounter with the strange glow, apart of course from the lighting conditions. She shook her head and switched off the screen.

Bryan Beaumont had brought with him, for relaxation, a minisynth—a tiny keyboard capable of producing the most incredible range of sounds. Last night he had been entertaining the rest of the crew with it in the Refectory—the tiny communal eating area of the Igloo. He was not a very good player, to be honest, but personal talents were encouraged and appreciated when most other entertainment was of necessity canned. He had left the instrument there, and since everyone else was outside Aurora switched it on and ran her hands over the keys.

It was almost the first time she had played any instrument since 1972, and a half-smile of nostalgia quirked her lips as she ran through a version of "The Seagull." She wondered what Synth or Herbie would think of the technology of this instrument compared with the old—what was it? Ah, yes: the old Moog. Were they still alive? They could well be, though they must by now be in their late seventies or even eighties. Did they still listen to rock music? She laughed aloud at the thought of Herbie, perhaps in an old folks' home, nodding his head and annoying his neighbours as Hawkwind's "Silver Machine" blasted from his speakers.

For a moment images crowded the edge of her subconscious. She had pushed them away when the Blimp first lifted, and she pushed them away again now. They made her uneasy. But somehow she knew that one day she would have to let them in once more.

She was quite oblivious to the fact that Beaumont came in through the outer airlock while she was playing. And he did not betray his presence, but stood behind the thin plastic curtain-wall of the Refectory, listening to her playing, his lips twitching in a smile.

The negative side of her quick recovery was that next day, once Orlov saw she was fit, he gave her a severe lecture on the dangers of making extended sorties unaccompanied, of getting out of radio contact, and of generally not obeying rules. She accepted this harangue meekly, and finally, seeing that she appeared contrite, he took pity on her by praising her resourcefulness in placing the golfballs.

"If it hadn't been for those we might not have found you before your oxygen ran out," he said. "Now, what's all this nonsense about dancing lights?"

Aurora had tried to tell her story once she recovered consciousness, but Lundquist, assuming she was delirious, had tranquillized her. Not before Bryan Beaumont had heard enough, though; and with his mystical streak he had immediately started plaguing the others with theories about UFOs, energy lifeforms and other not very scientific suggestions. When they poured scorn on him he claimed that he had only been joking, but it was obvious to all that he had been more than half-serious.

Lundquist had summed it up when Beaumont had left the room for a moment. "Wishful thinking!" he'd said with a grin.

"I promise you," she told Orlov now, forcefully, "I wasn't seeing stars due to a blow on the head, I wasn't delirious, and it wasn't imagination. At first I just thought it was the Blimp, come to find me. But it was like a glowing sphere, white with a reddy–blue tinge . . . "

"You mean violet?"

"No, I don't. There was red and blue light in it, but not mixed. Sorry—I can't explain it any better. And I'm supposed to be an artist! Anyway, every time I moved towards it, it moved away. And it sort of weaved about, and bobbed up and down, like this—" She waved her hand, gracefully. "And then it just—shrank—and vanished."

"You didn't manage to photograph it, I suppose?"

"Come on—I was hardly in any state to think about my camera."

"No. Sorry. Well, I suppose I'll have to mention it in my next report to Earth. But I really can't give it much emphasis without more evidence. You do see that, don't you?"

Aurora nodded. "Sure. Can I go outside now?"

"Ha! I don't know if I should let you! Yes, OK—but just stay in contact from now on, you hear?"

Aurora was on her way to the suiting-up chamber of the Igloo when she was waylaid by Bryan Beaumont. His face bore an expression which puzzled her. Serious, yet with a hint of—what? Triumph? Whatever, it was obvious that he could hardly control his impatience.

"Can you spare a moment, Anne?" he asked.

"I was just going outside."

"Oh. Well. I did rather want a word." He pushed back his unruly sandy hair.

Aurora sighed. "Is it about those lights?"

"Eh? Oh, no—although I would like to talk to you about those some time too. No. You see . . . " He appeared almost embarrassed for a moment, and looked about him as if checking that they were not overheard. Then he said in a rush: "During the last couple of days I've been—sort of making a few enquiries. I looked up your records in the database. Yes, you almost caught me once with your info up on the screen. And then I got a friend back on Earth to check a few things. And, well, it rather seems, doesn't it, that Anne Pryor didn't exist before around the year 2000?"

Aurora flushed. "How *dare* you pry into my records."

"Look, I was just kind of interested at first. After all, you must admit, you're a bit unusual, what with your arm growing back and all! No, let me finish!"—as it seemed Aurora was about to interrupt again. "Yesterday I heard you playing my minisynth. How come you never told me you could play! You're good, aren't you—as good as your lookalike! Yes, I also spent some time watching my videodisc which includes stuff I'd collected about the Gas Giants—partly from an old tape my father had of an archive recording off some old rock channel on TV. And—come on! I don't see how you could *be* Aurora, but you must at least be related. Are you her daughter, or what? I mean, apart from the fact that you look a bit older, you're the spitting image. Those violet eyes . . . "

Aurora was silent for a long minute. "You must realize that whatever you're suggesting could be disproved in a moment," she said. "For instance, it just happened that my records were destroyed in a fire in 1999. But—if you can wait until tonight, I just might have something else to say . . . " Then, as she saw his face light up: "I only said *might*. Tonight?"

"OK. It's a date.

"Dream on, boy!"

#

But that night there was more excitement. Minako had taken out the Blimp during the afternoon. She had less flying experience than the others, and had intended to make only a short trip to accustom herself to the controls. But, as everyone else had found, the experience of seeing the network of canyons unfolding beneath her had been so fascinating that she'd not wanted to come down. There was no particular reason for Orlov to insist she did, so, as long as she kept in radio contact, he let her carry on.

However, as the shrunken Sun was almost touching the horizon he was about to radio her to tell her to get back within the next few minutes when her voice, unusually high and excited, came over the speaker.

"I saw a light down below! I went quite low over the spot where we found Dr Pryor—it's quite wide there—and was about to switch on my lights—for a second I thought I had—when I saw this ball of light moving about right below me, down in the dark canyon. I went even lower, and it sort of skipped out of the way and disappeared. But—I think I got a shot of it before it did!"

While they were eating their evening meal, Claude Verdet brought up the digital image he had made on the computer screen. It was not very impressive, but it showed an overhead view of the aptly named labyrinth of intersecting canyons. The desert was redly sunlit, with boulders casting long shadows, but the gorge was in darkness.

Except in one place, where a spherical light-source cast enough illumination to make the walls visible. Had the watchers not known that none of them had been down there it could have been an astronaut aiming a lamp upward. Indeed, one could almost imagine a pale figure behind the light.

"You know what they're going to think, back on Earth, don't you?" said Beaumont, examining the screen closely. "'It's a fake'—that's what they'll say. They'll say we've done it to keep interest alive in the Mars project and ensure funding for the next phase."

"We'll all swear an affidavit if it comes to that," protested Aurora. "Surely they'd have to believe us then?"

"With any luck, maybe we'll get better evidence, anyway," said Orlov soothingly. "But it means we're going to have to set up a night-watch—with instruments, at least." Apart from the airglow experiment, they'd been switching off pretty well all the instrumentation at night up to now.

Minako added, casually: "If you send them my pulse and blood pressure graph for the moment when I saw that light, they'll know it was something unusual!" For Minako, it was almost a joke.

It was time for Orlov to make his daily transmission to Earth, and he left, taking Verdet's video card with him. The rest of the evening was spent in heated argument, theories about the light or lights being put forward by one and torn apart, or occasionally supported, by the rest. Although Aurora several times felt Beaumont's eyes on her, there was no opportunity for them to have a personal conversation. She found she felt quite disappointed about that.

After an hour or so, Orlov returned. "The folks back at Mission Control seem quite interested in the lights," he informed them with conscious understatement, "though not exactly over the Moon." This was greeted with hoots of derision, as were all such corny remarks. "Anyway, tomorrow we're to set up a video camera on the surface, rigged in such a way that it can cover the valley floor with a wide-angle lens. I think I can arrange a mechanism that will alert us if it picks up anything brighter than someone lighting a cigarette."

"Somehow I don't think you're taking this seriously!" commented Aurora.

"What's a cigarette?" asked Verdet gloomily. He had been a heavy smoker back on Earth. There had been a strict no-smoking policy since they'd left. Smoking would have been impossible outside anyway, in the thin, oxygen-poor Martian atmosphere, and anywhere else there was too *much* oxygen in their canned air for a naked flame not to be dangerous. Even without these considerations, it'd have been highly anti-social to fill their communal living and working spaces with cigarette smoke.

After a moment Verdet joined in with the laughter of the others.

#

The next night they at first clustered around the viewscreen to watch the image from the video camera. But, even though its sensors could be adjusted to show wavelengths from infrared to ultraviolet, nothing out of the ordinary appeared. Eventually they lost interest, and left it up to the alarm system to tell them if there was anything worth watching.

Beaumont caught Aurora's arm as she was about leave for her tiny cubicle. "Yesterday you said you might have something to tell me," he reminded her, his voice hoarse.

She stood for a while, her eyes on his face, then led him to her cubicle. "I like you, Bryan," she said once they'd got there, "though I don't much like the way you've been digging into my past life. I suppose you've discovered that I'm British too? Scottish, actually."

"Well, actually, no—though I did have a strong suspicion, from your accent." He emphasized the "actually" with an upper-crust accent. "So where were you around 1972? I could go on digging, you know. Even your initials are the same—A.P.—though in your recording days you were known as just 'Aurora'. Of course, only a rock-music freak like me would see any connection—I guess you just got unlucky . . . "

Aurora hesitated, playing with a lock of blonde hair. Then a mixture of expressions crossed her face: stubbornness, quickly replaced by resignation, submission; relief?

"I was in London. I'd been dossing around, getting into drugs, all sorts of shit like that. Then I met this guy who was in a group—yes that's right, the Gas Giants—found I could play, and the rest is herstory!"

"Hers . . ? Oh, yeah, I get it. But how *old* were you?"

"As a matter of fact I was thirty-two—but I looked about sixteen or seventeen, as you know. I've always looked younger than my age."

"Well, sure, but that means you'd have to be . . . " He did a quick calculation. "Seventy-eight? Jeez! This is crazy! I mean, I sort of knew it—well, I thought it—but . . . it's got to be impossible!"

"So's growing a new arm. Do you think I don't find it all impossible, too?"

"You mean even you don't know why? You're sure you're not the result of some secret Nazi genetic experiment, or something?"

Aurora smiled faintly. "Not that I know of. I age slowly, I heal quickly, I don't get ill or catch diseases, and, as we've now discovered, I seem to be able to regenerate new limbs. My theory is that I'm some sort of genetic mutation. In which case there must be others like me, somewhere."

Bryan sagged back in his plastic chair, gazing at her as she sat cross-legged on her cot. "I can't take it in," he said weakly. "Tell me some more about yourself. Will you, please?"

She plunged right in and told him her life story. The whole saga tumbled out. Her childhood, the rock scene, her late education and jobs. He let her go on until he knew just about everything there was to know about her. When she had finished it was after two in the morning, and they were both whispering, as everyone else was asleep. Snores in different pitches came from the direction of Orlov's and Verdet's cubicles.

"Incredible!" Bryan breathed at last.

Aurora grinned at him. Bryan's cheeks were flushed, and he was running his fingers rapidly through his hair. She realized once again how fond of him she'd grown over the previous months. Now, after the last few hours, they were closer than they'd ever been before.

"I'm sorry. I shouldn't have made you tell me. But . . . "

Aurora leaned forward and gave him a sisterly kiss. "It's all right. To be honest, it's a relief to tell somebody at last. D'you know how long I've been keeping this to myself?" The atmosphere between them was charged now. Bryan kissed her back. Then they kissed again, and it lasted longer than either of them had expected.

When at last they broke apart he looked embarrassed. "Tell you the truth, I've always fancied the pants off that girl on the record sleeve." He stood up. "I'd better go . . . "

"Yes, I think perhaps you had," she said, smiling at his departing back.

#

She awoke, somehow surprised and even disappointed to find herself alone, inside her sleeping bag. Had last night been a dream? No—it all came back to her. It was such a relief finally to have confided in someone. But her relationship with Bryan Beaumont could never be the same again . . .

She relaxed languidly for a while, then got up and took what passed for a shower—a sponge-down in a litre of water from a metered instant heater. Oh, for a real, tingling needle-shower, she thought. She supposed she should be grateful that it was her turn, since even this facility was rationed to one shower per three days per person. Long ago there had been much more water on the surface of Mars. Some day, when humankind decided it was time, there would again be more. For now, it was locked up underground.

It seemed almost strange that work at the camp continued as normal. Life took on a new dimension for Aurora. She rarely had an opportunity to be alone with Beaumont, and when they did go into a huddle in the Refectory she felt that everyone's eyes were on them, and that there must be gossip.

The days passed, until their researches around Noctis Labyrinthus were almost completed and only a little aerial mapping remained. In two days they should return to Base Camp.

And all this time the light in the canyon had not reappeared.

Discovery

Next day Aurora went to Vitali and announced: "I want to go down the canyon again, to where you found me." Seeing that he was about to interrupt, she continued quickly, "Look, that light was real, and we can't just leave here until we've found out some more about it. I know it may sound crazy, but I have a feeling that it might be triggered when someone passes close by. That's why the video camera up at the rim has never seen anything. Well . . . look, I know it's a long shot, but this whole thing is pretty weird, isn't it? It's got to be worth a try?"

Orlov grinned, his teeth white in his black beard, and held his palms towards her in surrender. "What took you so long? OK, OK! I was going to suggest that we took another look at that spot, anyway, since that's where Minako saw the light too. But no solo trips this time, right? A party of us will go see."

Aurora smiled. "Thanks!"

That night, an hour before sunset, four figures descended into the gloom of the canyon and set out at a brisk pace along its floor. They slowed as they reached the wider area, with its hummock of sand, in which Aurora had been found. No light appeared.

"Let's go on a bit," she suggested. "I found a cave with icicles in it down here. As you know, that particular cave collapsed on me, ahem, but there might be others there. I didn't have much of a chance to look."

They traversed the floor, passing over bedrock, then sand, then more rock. No further caves were found.

Finally, Orlov said, "We'd better get back."

As they neared a corner where the gorge turned in a forty-five degree bend, Claude Verdet, who was leading, stopped and pointed. His voice came softly in their helmets. "Look. See—ahead there?"

The jutting rock was limned by a soft glow.

They moved towards it, treading softly as though their footsteps might scare something away. The glow brightened, silhouetting the features of the cliff.

They rounded the corner.

And there hovered the ball of light, just as Aurora had described it. It was about two metres from the ground, but as they advanced it rose to twice that height and bounced softly up and down.

Belatedly they remembered their cameras and other equipment, and began making recordings and taking measurements. The sphere sank slowly lower and, as they stood still, approached them.

"It's like an animal, wanting to come close, but wary," Minako whispered.

Bryan's going to be so sick he missed this, thought Aurora. But he and Lundquist had had to stay behind, Beaumont to send their daily message to Earth, the doctor to make his medical report.

The sphere elongated slightly, its interior sparkling. Its colour pulsated, first a reddish tinge predominating, then blue. Suddenly it became pear-shaped and split into two, like a dividing amoeba; then the two halves merged again into one. The ball faded to a dull red, rose higher—and winked out.

There was a collective sigh.

Verdet was the first to speak. *"Fantastique!"* he breathed.

"Beautiful!" agreed Orlov, while Minako merely nodded, unable to speak.

Aurora, too, said nothing. She felt only a great sadness that the light had gone.

Orlov spoke, more briskly. "Come on, let's get back. I'm going to send this stuff to Mission Control tonight, and ask them to agree to a longer stay at this camp."

Mission Control agreed.

#

Now that the evidence was incontrovertible, the news of the lights broke on Earth. The newspapers, the newscasts and the internet were filled with excitement. Hard copies of some of them were printed out in the Igloo and passed around to much merriment and some annoyance.

LIFE FOUND ON MARS?
MARTIAN UFO DISCOVERED.
GREAT BALLS OF FIRE!
ASTRONAUTS HAVE SPOTS BEFORE THE EYES!

Not surprisingly, theories were hatched in abundance. After a while most of the crew ignored the popular press, which seemed to be fixated on alien lifeforms, tiny spacecraft and Martian ghosts, and concentrated on the reports of scientists who, like themselves, were studying all the data: the wavelengths of emitted light, spectroanalysis, electrical potentials, radioactivity, and anything else they could discover. Beaumont did still browse through the mass media, partly for amusement but also just in case anyone did come up with an interesting idea, he said. Most of the others (including Aurora, privately) thought he protested a little too much.

However, among the expedition members it was Beaumont who came up with the best hypothesis, backed up quite quickly by scientists on Earth.

When he first advanced it he appeared almost sheepish. "As I think most of you know," he said, "I've taken a sort of interest in UFO phenomena for some time. Not that I believe in little green men or anything like that, of course!" he added hastily. "But you must admit there are some interesting cases, and they need explaining. Well, the best explanation I've found is earthlights.

"It has been known for, oh, thirty or forty years that lights and glows in the sky have been associated with various areas around the world. In England, for example, there's Glastonbury Tor, Silbury Hill and the whole Warminster region. In Utah there's the Uintah Basin—the locals call them spooklights there. And so on. In some cases, records go back hundreds of years concerning balls of light—some say "like a rising Harvest Moon," that sort of thing—which bob around certain hills or mountains. Sometimes they're round, sometimes cigar- or rocket-shaped; which is why lots of people thought—still think—they're spacecraft. Going further back, they were called Will 'o the Wisp, or thought to be ghosts, spirit lights, or whatever.

"But genuine researchers suggested they might be due to ball lightning, or some sort of plasma effect—or to "earthquake lights," associated with tectonic activity. That doesn't mean there had to be an earthquake in the area; quite the opposite, in fact, because a 'quake releases energy quickly. It seems the lights and glows can be caused by low-magnitude seismic activity—any kind of gradual release of pressure that has been building up in underground rocks, modifying local electrical conditions."

"That's right enough," confirmed Aurora, interrupting his long, eager sermon.

"It could be a piezoelectric effect—you know, when you put pressure on some types of crystal, electrical charges are formed on their surfaces. You could easily get ten thousand or even a hundred thousand volts per square metre in rocks below ground. It might be due to friction, or to the fracture of rocks. But there's research going on all the time, and whole new areas of geophysics are appearing." He looked embarrassed. "Well, you all know that, don't you! But whether it's friction, heat or pressure—there's an effect called rock-crush, too—I'm sure you see the point. If it can happen on Earth, why not on Mars? After all, we had evidence of seismic activity when Anne found that steam-vent at Arsia."

Claude Verdet spoke up. "I've come across some of this research, too. But I understood that it's more likely to be an atmospheric effect. Isn't it true that, when some fracture lights were spectroanalysed, they found no trace of elements from the rocks, only from the air?"

"Apparently," replied Bryan. "They tried experiments in the laboratory in various gases and in a vacuum. The spectra showed distinct lines from the gases. But there's no reason why the Martian atmosphere shouldn't produce the same sort of effects as Earth's, is there?"

"None that I can see right now—except that it's so thin," said Verdet with a frown. "But we obviously need to set up some new experiments, don't we?"

Everyone agreed with this, though Orlov seemed highly sceptical of the earthlights hypothesis. However, he couldn't suggest any better idea, and they certainly needed to find out as much as possible.

That afternoon they set out again, armed with new apparatus, some of it jury-rigged by Verdet and Beaumont with Aurora's help. For a while it had looked as though she would have to remain at the Igloo, but Minako took pity on her and swapped duties. So she was with the four men as they approached the famous spot.

As before, nothing happened as they approached. The sky above the canyon glowed a dusky crimson, which rapidly became purple, then almost black, with a scattering of bright stars, while the ragged strip of light on the uppermost parts of the wall shrank to a broken line and vanished. For a while they explored various small tributaries using their halogen lamps; then Orlov gave them the order to return.

Suddenly there was confusion. Orlov stumbled over a boulder in the darkness. As his huge bulk crashed down, the ground beneath him gave way and he disappeared into a crevasse barely wide enough to take his body. They all heard his cry of pain. Then he lay still.

At almost the same moment a glow appeared almost directly above him. This time it was not a solid-looking ball but indistinct—an amorphous mass inside which seemed to be a swirling motion.

Lundquist took charge. "Claude, help me pull him out. Carefully now! You two"—to Beaumont and Aurora—"there's nothing you can do for him at the moment, so carry on with your experiments. Vitali wouldn't want you to waste time!"

Aurora whispered, "Well I'm glad it wasn't me again . . . " but no one seemed to hear her. For one thing there was a rushing noise, like the wind through trees, in their headphones.

The light was solidifying now, its pinkish glow taking on a roughly spherical shape. Then it elongated, as before, and seemed about to split. But instead it hung like a vertical dumb-bell, its outline pulsating. A windblown eddy of fins wriggled its way, snakelike, along the floor. The light moved in the opposite direction.

With a shock, Aurora realized that it was taking on a human shape. Wasn't that an arm, beckoning? "Look! It's a figure!" she cried aloud.

There was a moment's silence. Then Beaumont said doubtfully: "Well, yes, I suppose it *does* look a bit like one. But don't get carried away!"

Verdet and Lundquist had laid Orlov on the low sand-hill. He moaned loudly enough to be heard above the roaring noise which rose and fell in their helmets. Lundquist waved Verdet away as he examined his patient—as well as he could, with both of them encased in suits. His first priority was obviously to ensure that Orlov's suit had not been punctured in the fall—the big Russian had fitted into the crevasse like a cork into a bottle. But the suit was intact.

Verdet had heard Aurora's comment and Beaumont's response. "Sorry, Anne, I have to agree with Bryan. It *is* a curious shape, but a figure—?"

Aurora was certain that for a few moments she had seen a gowned figure, its hidden feet not quite touching the ground, gesturing her to approach. But she was wise enough to keep her silence; she didn't want her crew-mates to start questioning her sanity.

"Come on over here!" called Lundquist. "I need your help now. Can you leave your instruments recording? I should have thought to bring a stretcher, but I didn't. Damn. If we all place a hand under him, though, he won't be difficult to carry in this gravity. I've splinted his left leg as best I can, but the main thing is to keep him as level as possible."

As they retreated, looking back over their shoulders, the light resumed its spherical shape, rose, dimmed and flickered out.

#

Orlov lay on his cot, his face white. His leg was broken, but would heal in time. Far more significant was that he had no feeling in either leg. It seemed that the lower part of his spinal column had been damaged, and he could not walk. This was not just a personal disaster for him but a major crisis for the expedition as a whole. The rest carried on with their duties; it was all they could do.

There was desultory talk, in private, that it would be interesting to see if the strange "Martian force" that had healed Anne's arm would work for him too, but as the days passed and they were due finally to return to Camp One, there was no sign of improvement.

Aurora visited Orlov alone one evening while the rest were in the Refectory debating the light. He appeared to be asleep, long black lashes lying on his rather swarthy cheek. For a moment she saw superimposed on his face her brother's. They were as dissimilar as one could imagine, except that both had dark hair. Steve's face had been long, ascetic, bespectacled. Orlov had regained some of his colour, and had not lost his appetite, so his face was still round, yet with high cheekbones, and bushy eyebrows and a full beard.

She suddenly remembered once more the story of how Steve had been paralysed as a small boy until being cured when that strange "German" had touched him. Suppose—? Like many people, Aurora had during her long life had little contact with serious illness or injury other than her own. As an adult she had never witnessed a serious automobile accident or a plane wreck; had never even visited a hospital.

Tentatively, she reached out her right hand, and ran it over her crewmate's legs and round to his pelvis—he was lying half-turned on his side—and then on into the small of his back. Was it imagination, or did she seem to feel a heat that was more intense than his body temperature?

"Why, Anne, I didn't know you cared! And we all thought you and Bryan were an item!" His eyes opened, and a smile played briefly over his lips. Then he frowned. "But, if I may ask, what *are* you doing, exactly?"

Her hand jerked away as though scalded. *So they do know about Bryan and me!*

"I—I'm sorry. I thought—maybe—I could help. Stupid of me, but . . . "

A sharp voice came from behind her. "Help? How, Anne?" It was Lundquist. "I just came to check on my patient, but I must say that I—" He stopped.

"Do that again!" he ordered.

Aurora was confused, not knowing whether the order was addressed to her or not.

"Vitali! Your right foot! Wriggle your toes again!"

Orlov did as he was told, incredulously, then rotated his whole foot. He swung himself off his bed and placed the foot on the ground. The other stuck out in front, being encased in a light but rigid plastic cast.

"Help me up," he said, his voice tight. They took hold of his arms and got him to his feet, while Lundquist reached for Orlov's aluminium crutch and held it out to him. The Russian knocked it aside and took an awkward, stiff step forward. Then another. Lundquist and Aurora walked alongside him; then she loosened her grip. Orlov almost fell, then lurched forward, right into the Refectory a few paces away.

He grinned at the open-eyed, open-mouthed faces that were turned towards him. "Good evening, my friends! Yes, you see before you a miracle! It appears that Dr Pryor can heal not only herself but others."

"Oh, now, look!" protested Aurora. "We don't know it was anything I did. I mean, it's just as likely you were going to get better by now anyway. Isn't it?"

Orlov's face was serious now. "I *felt* it," he said quietly. "I wasn't asleep, you know. When your hand passed over me, I could feel a—a sort of tingling warmth in my bones. And then it was like an electrical iron!"

He reached down and unsnapped the cast from his left leg. Flexing the limb, he said: "Hmmm. It doesn't feel quite right yet, but—" He walked in a circle around the tiny room, limping only slightly.

Lundquist spoke wearily. "Before you start doing the cancan, Vitali, sit down, will you? I want to examine that leg."

Aurora was trying to avoid Beaumont's eyes, but could feel them upon her.

"I think you ought to tell them, Anne," he said softly.

She looked around at their puzzled, expectant faces, and sighed. "Damn!

Oh, all right. I suppose there's no point in postponing the inevitable."

And once more she poured out the whole story, or as much of it as she thought they needed to know.

When she had finished, there was a stunned silence. Then Claude Verdet exploded: "This is a total fairy tale. I don't believe a word of it! Is it supposed to be some sort of joke?"

"Any of you can check Anne's records. I did," said Beaumont. "They go back as far as 2000, which is what you'd expect by looking at her. But the ones for more than a few years ago—well, they're plausible, all right, but anyone with even a remotely suspicious mind can tell there's something wrong with them. And then there are a lot of correlations with an Alison Petrie who seemed just to sort of . . . fade out around the time that Anne Pryor started becoming prominent. You can trace the whole 'ancestry' back if you know what you're doing. Anyway, Claude, you've seen with your own eyes how her arm regenerated—and now there's Vitali. You can't argue with facts! Can you offer a better explanation? Anne's something special."

"But if all this is true it means that you're a phoney, Anne! Your degrees—your doctorate—you haven't earned any of them . . . "

This was Minako, almost glowering. Aurora had noticed a slight, veiled hostility from the meteorologist before, but had put it down to the fact that, as the only other woman on the expedition, she might resent Aurora's blonde good looks; Minako herself was short and thickset, with a rather coarse complexion, and looked a full decade older. Perhaps, though, her jealousy was not personal but professional?

"Oh, don't worry, I'm fully qualified," said Aurora airily. "I claim nothing that I haven't worked hard for and earned. The only things that are phoney about me are the *dates* on my forged documents and computer records. Haven't I proved I can do my job as well as any of you?"

There were nods, and nobody else seemed prepared to argue.

It was already well into the early hours of the morning, and everyone now appeared inclined to go to their beds and think over this strange development in private. Before they parted, though, Orlov said: "I think we should keep this among ourselves—at least until we've discussed it again. We don't want Mission Control to think we've all gone off our—what is it you say, Bryan? Oh, yes—off our trolleys! *Niet?*"

Nobody disagreed.

Artefact

It was 07.30, Mars time; the fact that the Martian day was so similar in length to Earth's—Mars rotates in twenty-four hours and thirty-seven minutes—made life easy from the point of view of sleep periods and the like. The crew were packing the rovers for their return to Base the following day. Already the Blimp had been deflated, despite complaints from Aurora that she had never been allowed to fly it—Orlov had half-promised her she could do so back at Base Camp. For the moment, at least, the rest of the party seemed to have accepted her extraordinary story; there was little they could have done otherwise.

"Only one more night here," said Beaumont. "It feels like going home from a holiday. Er, Vitali?"

Orlov looked up from strapping together some tripods. "I've a feeling you're going to ask of me a favour."

As he often did when broaching "fringe" subjects, Beaumont looked at the floor as if embarrassed. "It's just that there's something I've been wanting to try, and this is my last chance," he said.

"Go on. I'm listening."

Beaumont hesitated, then said: "Dowsing." He hurried on, as if expecting to be laughed at. The other crew-members, who could overhear the conversation clearly on their phones, stopped what they were doing and gazed at him with a variety of expressions. "I've tried it back home, and it does work. Nobody seems to know quite how, and sometimes it doesn't—especially when you try to subject it to scientific conditions—but trying it here couldn't do any harm, now could it?" He was almost pleading.

"I mean, if there's something in that canyon, some . . . *focus*, I might be able to find it."

Orlov shook his head, and for a moment Beaumont thought he was refusing. But he saw the resigned amusement on the man's face.

"Yes, all right," said the Russian. "Anything for a quiet life. But do you have the equipment for this?"

"All I need are two lengths of metal wire or rod. One to one-point-five mil in diameter and, oh, thirty centimetres long."

Finding such items proved more difficult than Beaumont had expected, but finally he was allowed to cannibalize a spare telescopic aerial. All watched with interest as he cut two pieces to the same length and bent them, less than halfway along, to a right-angle.

"I've never tried this with gloves on," he said as he walked across the nearby ground in a straight line, elbows bent, holding the rods like some old-time cowboy with a pair of six-guns.

"Are you expecting to find water down there?" asked Minako sceptically.

"Oh, no, of course not—not *here*! But that's the interesting thing about dowsing. It's not just about water. You can find whatever you want—or try to. You just, well, sort of ask questions. But I'll have to go to the canyon to do it, because that's the point of interest. What I'm hoping is that I'll find some evidence that our seismometers were perhaps not sensitive enough to register—of underground stresses, or electrical currents. Something like that.

"It's a strange thing, you know, that stone circles and other megalithic sites often seem to be a focus not just for earthlight phenomena but for the energies that dowsers detect. I've felt it myself at the Rollright Stones."

Seeing the scepticism on their faces, he turned away sulkily.

"Well, I *have*. You'll see."

Claude Verdet muttered: "Are you sure you're not a doctor of parapsychology?"

If Beaumont heard the remark, he ignored it.

#

Later in the day—there was no need to wait for darkness, Beaumont pointed out—he, Aurora and Orlov walked once again along the canyon. This time the sunlight shone down brightly, bouncing off the sepia and ochre rockfaces. When they reached the spot, Beaumont marked out a rough grid by dragging his foot in the sand, and began to walk in straight lines holding his two bent rods quite loosely in his hands, the longer arms parallel and pointing straight ahead. He had stripped the ink containers out of two ballpoint pens to use as plastic handles into which the rods fitted, free to rotate.

For the first three traverses, nothing happened. Then, as he walked close to the spot where Orlov had fallen, the horizontal rods moved smoothly inwards until they crossed.

"Ahhh," he breathed.

"Is that the equivalent of a hazel twig pointing downward?" asked Aurora.

"That's right. Will you put a marker here, please?"

She obediently placed a green golfball on the spot, and he continued walking.

There was no further sign of activity; the rods continued to point straight ahead.

After three more traverses Beaumont stopped. "Right. Let's see what we've got here."

From a pocket in his suit he produced a crystal pendant which Aurora could remember seeing around his neck. Walking back to the marker, he held the pendant like a pendulum in one hand over the spot. It began to oscillate.

"Is it water?" he murmured, apparently to himself.

The pendulum continued to swing.

"Metal?"

The pendulum began to rotate clockwise. Inside his helmet, Beaumont nodded,

"Now, how deep is it? Is it more than ten metres down?"

No response.

"More than five metres? More than two metres? More than *one* metre?"

He looked surprised.

"If this thing's telling me the truth, whatever it's found is only a few tens of centimetres at most below the surface. In which case . . . "

He began to dig in the soft fines. Soon he had excavated a sizeable hole, and his arm could hardly reach the bottom. Orlov and Aurora stood at the edge, looking down.

"Damn. Ah!" His gloved hand rubbed the sand off something solid. At first it seemed to be a smooth boulder, but as he wiped the fins off it became obvious that it was metallic. It looked shiny, new.

"Help me scrape the regolith from around this, will you, guys?"

The other two knelt around the hole and scooped out sand and dust.

Slowly, a spherical object was revealed.

"I don't believe I'm seeing this!" said Orlov. "Hang on a moment! I must take some pics before we go any further."

Aurora thought of asking Beaumont if he'd buried the object there himself, but bit back the joke.

Orlov said: "Wait here. I'm going to call the others."

He scrambled up a scree slope which he hoped might be high enough that his radio signal wouldn't be blocked by the solid rock walls all around. Seen by the two below, his suited figure sparkled in the sunlight as he climbed higher and finally stopped, one arm hooked around a rocky crag.

Although conversation was faint and scratchy, he succeeded in making contact.

"They're on their way," he told Beaumont and Aurora as he clambered back down.

Soon afterwards the others arrived. Verdet used his video camera to record the moment when the object was lifted clear of the hole. It stood a little over a metre high and consisted of two joined spheres, one about seventy centimetres in diameter and the other not much more than half that, and partly embedded inside the larger one. Both were of a shiny but greyish metal and almost featureless. The smaller sphere had a black band running round it and a small circle, full of dust, inscribed in its top. From the bottom of the larger sphere, and apparently moulded seamlessly into it, extended three elegant, narrow fins or legs, presumably to serve as a stand.

Suddenly the little party became aware of a familiar rushing sound, as of a distant waterfall, in their helmets. Looking up, they saw that, even though it was full daylight, the lightform was faintly visible against the shadowed wall of the canyon; it was transparent enough that they could see the rocks through it, and gave the impression that it was fizzing. Aurora was reminded of a firework set off in daytime.

The light floated lower and hovered, and again the globe elongated into a shape which could almost be human, though even Aurora could not have sworn to this now.

There was surprisingly little conversation. Everyone seemed too stunned for words.

Then Orlov said: "Well, I think I can speak with some authority when I say that we shan't be moving from this camp for some time after all. We have to stay where the action is, don't we? So we'd better get back and start unpacking again."

"There go the comforts of home!" muttered Beaumont. "Do you think we should take this—whatever it is—back with us?"

"I don't see why not," said Verdet. "We've taken measurements all around, and got plenty of still and video records of where it was found. We can test it better back at camp."

This time Lundquist had remembered to bring the collapsible stretcher in case of emergencies. They appropriated it to carry the artefact.

"Is it OK to lie it on its side, though?" asked Aurora. They all assumed that its intended orientation was as found when buried, with the engraved circle on the small sphere at the top.

Orlov shrugged. "Maybe it will tell us if it doesn't like it," he said.

As they placed the structure on the stretcher the lightform hovered close by, as though monitoring their activities. It followed them as they marched away, then seemed simply to fade.

"I feel sad," said Minako.

"You think this thing and the light are connected in some way?" asked Beaumont.

"Well, don't you? It seems logical, doesn't it?"

"Yeah. Maybe the—the object . . . What are we going to call it, by the way? Maybe it's done its job."

Aurora said, "I think it's some kind of beacon."

"Could be," said Beaumont. "Beacon. That'll do as well for a name as anything, for now." Then, to Orlov: "Look, it doesn't need all of us to carry it back, does it? I'd like to carry on dowsing over a wider area. After all, where there's one object there could be more."

"OK. But you're not staying here alone. I want to go back and examine this thing. Anne and Claude, will you stay here? I want one of you up on that scree slope. You can contact the camp from there; and be sure to make a report at least every five minutes. We don't know what we've got here, so whatever you do keep in touch. Is that understood?"

#

Beaumont continued striding across his grid for nearly an hour, with no further reaction from the rods. Heaving an exasperated sigh, he sank down onto a boulder.

"I'm going to take a drink, then I'll move along the canyon, over that hump." He indicated the low, sandy hill which rose towards one side, where a talus slope began to rise, narrowing in an inverted V towards the rim.

They all took a rest, then Verdet reported to Base what Beaumont was about to do.

Almost as soon as Beaumont stepped onto the incline, his rods jerked violently together.

"Wow! What's this?" he exclaimed, obviously surprised by the strength of the reaction.

He continued criss-crossing the low hill, but his rods refused to part. "Whatever's down there, it's *big*!" he said squeakily. Verdet repeated this into his helmet mike for the benefit of those back in the Igloo.

By noting where the rods allowed themselves to be separated and where they stayed insistently together, Beaumont and Aurora marked out a rough circle nearly ten metres across. Then, to the surprise of the others, Beaumont snorted with laughter.

"Sorry!" he said. "But this suddenly reminded me of an old black-and-white movie I saw on TV once. Must have been made in the Fifties. *The Thing*—that was it! A bunch of scientists were at the North Pole or somewhere icy, and they marked out this circle—a shape they could see under the ice. It was a flying saucer—of course! Hey! I hope we don't find a creature like they did. It was a sort of human carrot, and if I remember rightly it was after their blood. That was before Spielberg started making movies where the aliens were goody-goodies . . . "

Aurora smiled patronizingly. "Yes, well, we don't want to let our imaginations to run away with us, do we? Don't you think we ought to call the others here, to see what it is we've found?"

Verdet called Orlov to ask what progress was being made back at camp. He reported to Beaumont and Aurora that, the Igloo having now been repressurized, Orlov and Minako had shed their environment suits. They were avoiding touching the Beacon, limiting themselves to various instrumental tests. There was radioactivity somewhere within, it appeared, but not at any dangerous level, and there was a strong magnetic field. Nothing else, so far.

"You may not have noticed," added Orlov, "but the Sun's getting low. You'll be in shadow very soon down there, and by the time we got to you it would be virtually dark. So I suggest that, as long as the area's well marked, you come back here to the Igloo now and we'll all go out again early tomorrow."

Verdet agreed on behalf of the other two.

Before they returned, Beaumont walked over the area holding his pendulum. It told him that whatever lay below him was metallic, and deeper than the Beacon had been. The depth was no more than two or three metres, though, according to the pendulum.

"I can't be sure, but there might be an even bigger mass buried below. There's something peculiar about it. Maybe this is just the tip of the iceberg." As it often did when he launched himself upon a theme, his face lit up with enthusiasm. "Hey, perhaps we've discovered a whole Martian city, buried down there!"

"Careful! We're getting into the realms of fantasy again," warned Aurora.

"Well, don't you think all this *is* pretty fantastic?" he retorted.

#

Early next day the party, short only of Verdet—left to man the communications desk and with instructions not to touch the Beacon while alone— straggled along the canyon. By the time they reached the circular area Aurora and Beaumont had marked out the previous day, a widening band of amber sunlight was creeping down the wall to greet them. They had brought trolleys packed with tools, extra oxygen and food packs, with the expectation of a long day ahead.

The hillock was made of fairly loose sand and dust, together with some rocks, and soon a haze filled the air as they scooped and dug away at it. The crevice into which Orlov had fallen, only a few metres away, was in bedrock, and it soon became apparent that it was the narrow end of a crack that rapidly became wider, ending in a dust-filled crater.

And in the crater was . . .

How were they going to tell Earth? It was fortunate they could transmit images. Otherwise no one would believe them when they reported that they'd found a flying saucer . . .

Well, not quite a saucer, but near enough. The object was certainly circular, but it was shaped more like a doughnut or an old-fashioned home-baked pie. On its upper surface, where the central hole curved down into the interior of the vehicle (if that's what it was), grey metal merged imperceptibly into transparent perspex or something similar. This rose, in the centre, to a low dome. The perspex-like material was slightly yellowed and a little scarred, making it milky and translucent in a few places. Peering through it, they could dimly see an instrument panel inside what could surely only be a cockpit or control cabin some three metres across.

As they began to excavate the underside, it soon became evident to them that this was more complicated than the top surface, being scalloped or terraced in a number of concentric rings. As they continued digging they came across obvious signs of damage. The vehicle was not horizontal, but tilted at an angle; at its deepest point, where it was almost embedded in rock, the metal of the underside was badly crumpled around a hole which seemed to have been some kind of storage area, perhaps for a rover or similar very large vehicle.

#

Back in the Igloo that evening, the whole crew gathered in the Refectory. Orlov had ordained that they all take showers, in view of their physical exertions, and they had changed and eaten. Now they were slouching in their chairs. He had made his report to Earth, and sent as much data as he could. The response had been predictably stunned. He had left the scientists and media "experts" to mull over the news.

Now it was time for their own inquest.

Since it was thanks to him that the discoveries had been made, everyone tacitly agreed to let Beaumont have his say first.

"I think it's pretty clear, isn't it? What we have here is an alien spacecraft that has made a crash landing. Its crew managed to throw out, or plant, a distress beacon to attract the attention of a rescue party. Which, for some reason, never came."

"Mmm, yes, that does seem a plausible explanation," agreed Orlov. "But it begs a lot of questions. Why doesn't the Beacon, if it really is a beacon, put out radio waves? Why didn't another expedition come after the first? Why did they come to Mars—a dead world? Why didn't they make contact on Earth? They'd obviously have been capable of doing that if they'd wanted to."

"Perhaps they did," said Bryan. "Let's face it, there have been enough reports over the years of—well, you know, UFOs and all that . . . "

"For God's sake, let's not get into all that crap! But there's another point," said Verdet. "The craft is so small. Surely much too small for a starship. I can't believe that it could have contained enough fuel, no matter what they might have used. It's not as if it were a ramscoop, or something exotic like that, using interstellar hydrogen for fuel; they'd have needed to bring their own fuel with them wherever they went. And it's not big enough to contain enough air, whatever they breathe, however efficient their recycling, for them to reach the Solar System from another star. Don't forget, they would have had to travel at least five light years and more likely twice that—there are nine or ten stars within ten light years or so of here. Probably they'd have had to come a lot further than that."

"Perhaps it's only a sort of landing shuttle," suggested Beaumont, apparently not put off by Verdet's earlier comment. "Maybe there's a mother ship still in orbit out there somewhere."

"Oh, come off it," said Lundquist. "There's no way we wouldn't have detected an object that big, anywhere in this part of space, with all our probes and deep-space scanners."

"You're forgetting one thing," argued Beaumont. "Mars does have two quite peculiar satellites, and we haven't got round to taking a good look at them yet. Maybe one of them's an asteroid ark. If we were to send a proper expedition to Phobos, which is in a really odd, low orbit for a *natural* satellite, we might find that, deep below its dark, carbonaceous exterior, there lie tunnels—living quarters—motors or some sort of drive mechanism . . . "

"Steady, boy," murmured Aurora.

"Anne . . . Aurora, you haven't had much to say so far," remarked Orlov.

"No. To be honest, I'm feeling—well, a bit overcome by it all. I can't see anything wrong with any of the arguments we've heard, really, yet I don't think any of you have hit on the answer. But I'm afraid I can't suggest anything better. I'll . . . I'll need time to think about it."

"Anyway, if Phobos were some kind of generation-starship or ark, surely we'd see some sign on its surface," said Minako.

"You mean like 'PLEASE ENTER TWO BY TWO'?" said Beaumont with a grin.

Minako ignored his interruption. "We've got plenty of high-definition images from unmanned probes, after all. And, even assuming you're right and this is a shuttle that crash-landed, why haven't we picked up anything from the mother ship itself?"

"I know you all think I've got too much imagination," said Beaumont carefully, "but sometimes that's what you need at moments like this. Don't you see? All this could have happened centuries ago, before we even had radio. Or thousands of years—millions—back in the days of the dinosaurs, even! I know that UFOs and flying saucers are dirty words nowadays, but you can't deny that ship *is* sort of disc-shaped, just like the ones that people have seen for centuries."

"Which have never contacted anyone except some hicks out in the sticks," drawled Lundquist. "And which, if I might remind you, you've already explained away very nicely as being due to earthlights."

"Just because some—or even most—examples of a phenomenon can be shown to be due to one cause doesn't mean that it's the *only* answer," snorted Beaumont. "There could be many explanations for similar-sounding reports." He became aware of the scornful looks around him and added: "I'm just acting as Devil's Advocate really, you understand?"

"Anyway," Aurora interposed, "it doesn't really look as if our Marslight was due to rocks fracturing or rubbing together or whatever, now, does it? Not now we've found the Beacon."

The discussion continued for another hour, but everyone felt tired and eventually they decided, one by one, to call it a day.

It was as well that they'd turned in early, for they were woken before dawn by an unscheduled message alarm from the comm desk. The news of their discovery was filling the media back on Earth. There was widespread public hysteria.

After centuries of waiting, Earth knew that it was not alone.

Open Sesame!

. . . People are reacting in different ways. There's a huge rise in the sales of books and data-wafers on astronomy, exobiology and SETI—the search for extraterrestrial intelligence. Radio astronomers have been "listening" for signals from other stars since the 1970s, with no success, even after they set up a radio telescope on the far side of the Moon. And a huge increase in the membership of UFO societies and what are sometimes spoken of as "nut cults."

The presenter smiled disarmingly so as not to offend any member of her audience.

At the same time, many people are turning to the churches. Some just want to know the answer to the question: "Did God make the creatures who came in that spacecraft, as He made us—and do they therefore have immortal souls?" This is a question which theologians were trying to answer long before we had this concrete proof of the existence of life beyond Earth, so it will be interesting to see if they come up with anything new.

New religions are springing up, too, mostly based on the "Was Christ an astronaut?" hypothesis. They believe that the brilliant Star of Bethlehem which the Three Wise Men followed—meaning that it moved—was a "mother ship" in low Earth orbit and that Jesus came down from it by some method, presumably as a baby . . .

#

Orlov grimaced disgustedly and turned down the volume. "What the hell have we started?" he asked no one in particular. He selected more random sections from the recording that had been transmitted from Earth, commenting: "Lots of UFO reports . . . Texas farmer's wife abducted by alien in a gown . . . Spherical lights over Stonehenge . . . what rubbish! Come on. We've got work to do.

"Claude, you'll want to look over their life-support system, and Bob, we might need your biological expertise—well, who knows? There may be bodies in there. I have to go, too, because we'll probably need an engineer if we're going to get inside the ship. Bryan: your . . . special skills have proved pretty useful so far. That leaves Minako and Anne—is it OK if we keep calling you Anne?—to deal with the comm desk and see if there's anything new to be found out about the Beacon. Is that OK with everyone?"

Minako and Aurora eyed each other a little warily, but everyone nodded. The field team departed, laden with tools and instruments. They were planning, en route to the spaceship, to put a relay on the canyon rim so from now on there would be direct radio contact between the two groups.

Minako busied herself with the communications desk. Aurora, feeling rather depressed at being left out of the main action (but it was for the first time, she consoled herself), went over to the table where the Beacon sat.

Wearing surgical gloves left out for her by Lundquist, she tried to lift it and found that, even allowing for the low Martian gravity, it was remarkably light. By swinging it gently, she found that most of its mass seemed to be centred somewhere near the base of the large sphere. A power source, perhaps. From the depths of her memory came an image of a doll she had once owned, for some reason called a Kelly; you could knock it, hit it, kick it, but it always swung upright. Probably you could have done the same with this if it hadn't been for the tripod of thin legs on which it stood.

She took one of these in her hand and gently pushed, then gave it a screwing motion. Still with no sign of a seam, it silently vanished into the sphere. Almost simultaneously the other two did the same. She snatched her hand away, the other still supporting the artefact. But there was no real need, she found, for the Beacon did indeed remain upright, balanced on its low centre of gravity. It rotated at the slightest touch.

Suddenly she felt a compulsion to touch the Beacon with her bare flesh. She knew it was against her instructions—but what harm could it do? If the thing was going to pick up any micro-organisms, it would have done so by now; they had no isolation procedure for anything this large. It seemed unlikely that it would itself hold any contamination not already present in the rocks and dust of Mars.

She peeled the thin, transparent glove off her right hand. For some reason she thought of Bryan. Nowadays he touched her hand whenever he could—but spacesuits were so impersonal! She imagined Mars with a breathable atmosphere, and the two of them walking hand in hand down the canyon, without a care in the world, a light wind ruffling their hair. For months they had breathed nothing but canned air. And it was becoming a bit stuffy in here, to say the least. Minako, she had noticed, had a strange odour; or perhaps she used an unusual perfume?

She sighed, then glanced round guiltily. Minako was still at the desk, screened from her. She could hear Orlov's voice from the speaker, describing the ship, with its transparent dome on top. Somewhere a relay clicked and a motor hummed. It was never quiet on this expedition, she mused. Even alone, out on the surface in a spacesuit, there were noises from the circulation system, or the radio. Or her own amplified breathing.

To reassure herself that she would not be observed as she conducted her illicit experiment, she popped her head round the door into the radio section and asked: "Any news from the dig?"

Minako looked up. Did she look guilty, too? If so, why? She said: "Not really. They've nearly uncovered the rest of the ship, and they're making tests. Vitali's looking for some sort of door or handle—some way to get inside it. How are you getting on?" She did not really sound interested. Aurora told her about the retracting legs. Minako nodded, and Aurora withdrew.

Back alone with the Beacon, she reached out her naked right hand (Her *new* hand: was that relevant? Probably not.) and touched the artefact. If she had expected something spectacular to happen, she was disappointed. It did not spring open, there were no sparks, no electrical shock.

The surface was warmer than she'd expected, and it seemed to become faintly warmer still—and wasn't that a faint humming, felt rather than heard? Then she realized that the black band around the upper sphere was no longer black. The change was not great, but it now glowed an intensely deep ruby red. An image popped into her head: a bubble, or dome?

Aurora became aware of a faint crackling sound behind her, and wheeled around. The lightform was hovering there. As before, but much more quickly, its spherical shape elongated, became pear-shaped, and took on a distinctly human form. This time there was no doubt about it. It was a white-gowned figure, with pale hair visible under a hood, pale eyes gazing straight at her. It was semi-transparent, like a hologram. And it was beckoning.

Aurora spoke, softly. "What do you want?" She moved forward a step, and the figure shied away, like a frightened animal. Yet still she felt that it wanted her to approach.

She took another step, very slowly—*If it goes away much further it'll pass right through the outer wall*, she thought—and reached out her right hand.

A tingling shock ran through her, and her brain seemed to turn cold, then freeze solid. The room vanished and she saw what seemed to be a close-up of the surface of a soap bubble, its sheen a play of shifting yellows.

Then she slumped to the floor.

#

At the excavation site, Orlov had found a very slight depression in the skin of the craft, and had been pushing his palm against it, hoping that it was some sort of lock. All to no avail. He had just sat down to take a sip of fruit juice with glucose when the transparent dome disappeared.

He thought it might have retracted into the metal skin, but if so it had been too quick for his eye to follow. He noted the time on his watch and tongued his recorder. Then he shot off some pictures, both flat and holo.

What had caused the sudden change? Nobody had been closer than a couple of metres at the time. He imagined an ancient mechanism, perhaps triggered by something he had done minutes ago, coming out of its long sleep and becoming activated. Perhaps the electrical systems of the craft were solar-powered, and were only now recharging in the weak morning sunlight after having been buried for millennia?

The other three had noticed the change at last and, with startled exclamations, were gathering around.

Suddenly Minako's voice came through their helmet phones, sounding worried.

"Base Camp to field party. Dr Pryor has just collapsed, near the first artefact. I don't know what happened—I just found her. Come in, please. Over."

Lundquist instantly took charge. "Roger, Minako. This is Robert. Is she still unconscious? Over."

"Yes—no. I think she's coming round. A moment, please." Obviously off-mike: "Are you all right, Dr Pryor? What did you do?"

There was a pause, and some sounds off.

Aurora's voice, rather shaky, came next. "Sorry to scare you, folks. I was examining the Beacon, and that light appeared behind me. I—I touched it." She omitted to mention that it was with her bare hand. "I got some sort of shock, and passed out. I know it was silly of me, but it seemed a good idea at the time. The light's gone now. Oh, yeah, that black band around the little sphere? It was glowing a dull red just before the light appeared. But it's black again now. Er, over."

Orlov's heavy brows drew together.

"I rather think you may have done more than you thought," he mused thoughtfully. "What time was it when you touched that thing, do you know? Over."

"About eleven-ten, as near as I can say. Why? Oh, over."

"Well, at exactly eleven-eleven and fifteen seconds, the central cockpit of the spacecraft opened. Don't you think that's rather a coincidence? Over!"

A babble of conversation broke out then, until Orlov bellowed "Hold it!" loud enough to burst their eardrums.

"Anne, if you're quite sure you're OK, let's clear the airwaves now and get on with our jobs. I suggest you take a rest—and don't touch that thing again. Roger? Over."

"Roger"—rather reluctantly. "Over and out."

Shrugging away the conundrum, the big Russian engineer got back to work. He crawled gingerly over the curved torus shape, and peered down into the cockpit—for by now it was obvious that this was indeed a cockpit. There were two reclining seats made of some black plastic material which still looked supple, and an instrument panel which contained surprisingly few controls. The panel was likewise black, but set into it were pale grey keypads and some clear crystals which he could imagine as glowing lights. They sparkled in the yellow sunlight which blazed down from the sky above.

There were two rectangular panels that might have been digital readouts, but they were blank, and what was obviously a large blue-grey viewscreen, nearly two metres across and half that in height, which followed the curve of the wall. It too was blank. Below and to the left of the instrument panel was an oddly shaped recess: two hollow hemispheres making a figure-of-eight, the upper being smaller than the lower. The same shape appeared as a symbol emblazoned above the screen. It had some characters inside it.

Orlov looked back at the other three questioningly, and seemed uncharacteristically unsure of himself. "Anyone object if I'm the first to go inside?" he asked.

"No, of course not—you go right ahead. You're the boss!" said Lundquist, and the rest grunted agreement.

Orlov gingerly lowered himself down into one of the seats, wondering how he would get out if the dome suddenly reappeared above him. It didn't.

The seat could have been designed for a human. It was just the right height and at the right distance away from the control panel for his arms to reach the keypads. The viewscreen was just below his eye-level, but he could have seen the outside view through the canopy, had it been in place. As a pilot, he approved. He felt that he could fly this thing right away—if only he knew how, and if it still worked.

He gazed around. There was a short section of curved wall uncovered by instruments; surely an access door for the rest of the ship. He stood up and examined it for handles or other signs of an opening. But, as with the exterior, there was nothing but a slight depression, and, though he placed his hand on this and pressed, nothing happened. He sighed. It looked as though they were going to need Anne—Aurora— again. But why? She had proved to be a total enigma, yet she seemed to hold the key to all this, somehow. Indeed, but for the presence of her and Bryan, the team would now be back at Base Camp, taking rock and ice samples.

Base Camp—?

"Damn!" he suddenly exclaimed.

"Anything wrong, Vitali?" asked Lundquist.

"Nothing in here. Funny what you think of at the oddest moments. Here I am in the middle of the greatest discovery of the generation—of *any* generation, most like—and I've just remembered I made a mental note to do something about our supplies. With everything that's been going on I'd forgotten all about it until now. Unforgivable of me."

The others immediately knew what he was talking about. There was a logistics problem with their current situation. They were supposed to have gone back to Base Camp days ago. Naturally, they'd brought more supplies than they'd expected to have to use, but, with the protraction of their stay out here, now even the reserves were running low. They were going to need more food, oxygen and water very soon.

Verdet said: "So someone's going to have to take a rover and collect some stuff. No problem, is it?"

"I can't let one person go alone. It means we're going to lose two people for a while. Oh well, it can't be helped. We'll discuss it back at the Igloo."

Orlov climbed out of the control cabin, slid down the curving metal until his feet hit the ground, and walked a few metres, taking in the whole scene. The craft was now fully exposed except for a buried section near the damaged portion, which lay on bedrock. He went over to Verdet.

"What are your feelings about this?" he asked. "It seems to me that it couldn't have hit from much of a height, or the damage would be greater. I'm not even sure that it made the crater it's lying in—I think that might be a previous meteor impact. Either that, or the lower part of that ship is a *lot* denser than it looks."

"*Oui.* I agree. It seems it must have come in at quite a shallow angle. Maybe it was trying to land in the desert, but couldn't make it, and had to fly along the canyon a little way. But something else is bothering me. I've been running some tests on the skin. It's an alloy, but nothing too unusual: nickel, steel, titanium, carbon, a few other traces. But I've also been looking at the erosion patterns, and at signs of oxidation by all the peroxides in the Martian soil— it's pretty corrosive stuff. Well, I've got a positive result on both, but . . . "

He looked at each of them in turn. They looked back expectantly.

"How long would you say this ship has been here?" he asked.

Beaumont replied, "As I said the other night, it could be millennia. Granted, it wasn't buried very deeply, but with the winds on this planet blowing the dust around, that doesn't prove much, does it?"

"It's that very dust which creates the problem—or, at least, the erosion the dust causes. That and oxidation. You see, both tests agree that this craft can't have been here for more than about a century. That's with a margin of error of, oh, plus or minus fifteen years at this stage. But I'd opt for less than a hundred years."

There was silence at this. The four men stared mutely at each other. This wasn't a result they'd expected.

Then Orlov said, "Well, anything's possible, of course, though that's pretty recent. As we said before, you'd have thought that Earth would have seen or heard something from them. But there's always an explanation. Those flying saucers of Bryan's, for one. Wasn't that term coined in the nineteen-forties?"

"Hey!" yelped Beaumont, "Don't lump me in with the ufologists! Mind you, you've got to admit they have a point when they say the reason nobody in authority's been contacted might be because the aliens have a non-intervention policy."

"I was about to say, couldn't you have misinterpreted your test results in some way?" continued Orlov, looking at Verdet. "I mean, if that alloy is more resistant than you're assuming it is, that would change everything, wouldn't it?"

"True." The Frenchman nodded. "But I don't think it's the answer. Wherever this thing comes from, metals are metals. It doesn't contain any 'strange unknown element,' like you read about in sci-fi stories."

"Used to," muttered Bryan, wincing. "And it's *SF*, Claude, not 'skiffy'."

"*Pardon?*"

"Nothing. Forget it."

"Anyway, Claude," said Orlov, "I'd like to go through those results with you when we get back."

"Sure." But Verdet did not look happy about it.

Another Discovery

Deciding which two crew members were to return to Base to fetch supplies was difficult, but it was finally agreed that Verdet and Minako should go. Aurora and Beaumont seemed essential around the alien craft; Orlov's engineering knowledge might yet prove important; and Lundquist, as physician, needed to be with them—in addition, his knowledge of life-support systems was almost as great as Verdet's, and it was always possible that his knowledge of biology and allied subjects would be required.

Rover 2 set off soon after dawn, the early morning sunlight sparkling off its bubble canopy. A miniature dust storm obscured its progress as it drove almost directly into its own long shadow.

Hardly had it disappeared from sight than a message warning flashed on the comm desk. It was William Emmart—himself a US astronaut, and an old friend of Orlov's—at Mission Control.

Vitali, United Press and TV have asked us to confirm the contents of a press report they have received, from an unrevealed source. And I'm not surprised. Isn't it enough that you've discovered an alien ship, and Martian ghosts, without all this stuff about Dr Pryor healing you of a broken leg and paralysis? And her being nearly eighty years old into the bargain, with forged records! Come on guys! What are you trying to do to us? This is all a joke, isn't it? Please tell me it is! Over.

Vitali leaned close to the microphone. "Sit on it, Bill, please. We'll get back to you later. Over and out."

He looked round at the other three. Aurora and Beaumont were about to suit up ready for the day's examination of the alien craft. Lundquist was to remain by the comm desk today, and also intended to examine the Beacon microscopically.

"OK, who's the joker?" asked Orlov. He was obviously angry. He continued, caustically: "You all heard that. Correct me if I'm wrong, but we did agree to say nothing about that little incident, did we not? So who's got themselves a little contract on the side, writing for the popular press?"

He looked pointedly at Beaumont.

Beaumont reddened and looked away, but firmly said, "Not guilty." He turned to Aurora. "You know I wouldn't do that . . . ?"

Aurora nodded.

"Don't look at me," said Lundquist. "I'm still trying to come up with some sort of rational explanation, and I'm the last person here to want this sort of story to get around. Christ! This whole expedition's become some sort of pantomime! I'm sorry, Anne," he added quickly, "It's not your fault, and I'm only too aware that you did more for Vitali—not to mention yourself—than I ever could have. Come to think of it, I could well be redundant." He softened this with a grin. "But we came here as a scientific expedition, expecting to do some research, prepare the way for a later permanent base, see how much water lies below-ground as permafrost, stuff like that. And look what we've got ourselves into. I sometimes wonder if I'm dreaming. Perhaps we all are . . . "

As Lundquist ran out of steam, Orlov said: "In that case it must be one of those two on the rover."

"I can't see Claude sending that message."

Aurora thought of Minako's veiled hostility to her, and remembered the woman's guilty look when Aurora had walked in on her at the comm desk, but she remained silent.

Lundquist, however, said: "Minako has always seemed rather keen to volunteer to remain here on comm duty."

"Whichever of them it was, I think we'd better say nothing until they get back. Then, perhaps, we'll hold an inquest. Let's get out in the fresh air. Well, you know what I mean."

#

Beaumont had been widening the area of his dowsing, in case any more artefacts or other evidence might be scattered around. Having failed to find anything in the local tributaries to the canyon, today, after dropping the rest off by the spaceship, he drove Rover 1 to the desert just above the site of interest. The others would, at the end of the day, climb the scree slope for the drive home.

Aurora was not sure what she could do that might be constructive, so she stayed close to Orlov as he climbed once more into the cockpit, which had remained open.

"Curses!" he said. "I meant to bring the Beacon back here with us today. There's not much more we can find out about it back at camp, and I still think it may have acted as some kind of key to open the canopy of the spaceship."

"You do realize," said Aurora, "that we've never found a trace of radio waves emitted by that thing? Anyway, if it was something I did back at camp that caused the canopy to open, the message would have had to have passed through a hell of a lot of rock. Our radios couldn't do it."

He shrugged. "Maybe they didn't use radio. Nothing about them would surprise me any more."

She climbed down into the cabin with him. Having examined the control panel and its various instruments, she placed her hand on the slight indentation in the wall that he'd said he felt sure must somehow control the door's opening mechanism. Like the Beacon, it felt warm to her touch—and did she feel the same sort of faint vibration?

She pointed at the big figure-of-eight-shaped recess under the instrument panel, noticing it for the first time. "Vitali," she said eagerly, "I think we've just discovered . . ."

"Yeah," said the Russian. "I was just coming to that very same conclusion myself. Looks like that's where the Beacon belongs. *Double* curses on me that I didn't bring it today! We'll have to—"

At that moment Beaumont's voice came over their helmet phones, loud and excited. "Can you two drop whatever you're doing? I think I've found something interesting here!"

Vitali and Aurora looked at each other, and wordlessly clambered out of the cabin. She gazed up at the canyon rim. The ascent would have been a stiff one under Earth gravity, but did not look too difficult here, especially as the scree slope served as a ramp. They started climbing.

Small flakes of rock shifted under their feet, and little avalanches of sand cascaded back into the canyon. They had to hold onto larger rocks, testing them for solidity, as they pulled themselves up to the serrated edge. For the final part of the ascent they had to go up over a series of platforms or terraces of rock very much like sedimentary layers, dusted with fines, where the level surface of the plain had apparently slipped and sunk several times, creating a set of giants' stairs with treads perhaps a metre deep. A curved bite had been taken out of the rim at the top.

As their heads peered over the edge, they could see Beaumont as a tiny figure nearly a kilometre away.

"He might have driven over to fetch us!" said Aurora crossly as they tramped towards him, their feet sinking a centimetre or two into the soft regolith, the duricrust crunching like dried mud.

Beaumont was kneeling by something, looking at it intently, and making gentle scooping motions with his hands.

When they reached him they found that he had excavated quite a deep hole, itself inside a wide linear depression which stretched away from the canyon rather like a dried-out stream bed, though quite straight.

"I think this was a small crevasse, originally, but it's filled up with sand," he said by way of greeting, not looking up. "I started by dowsing along it, just out of interest—I thought I might be able to detect how deep it went. About five metres, as a matter of fact. But two metres down . . . "

He pointed to the bottom of the hole he had dug.

A metallic-gloved hand protruded from the dust.

For a moment Aurora felt as if her eyes were whirling in their sockets. Giddiness washed through her. It wasn't possible! She re-focused. The glove was still there, and it looked so much as if it had come from one of their own spacesuits that for a moment she visualized a crazy scenario in which Verdet had murdered Minako and buried her . . . or vice versa.

She shook her head to clear away the fantasy.

Orlov took holos of the gloved hand from various angles and then they started to dig deeper.

The rest of the arm appeared, then a helmet. It was a transparent bubble, though, like the canopy of the spacecraft, it was yellowed and slightly opaque.

Soon they could see the top of a head. The brow was mottled ochre and brown, but the cranium was covered quite thickly by grey or white hair. They unearthed another arm, then the shoulders.

"It reminds me of when I fell into that crevice down there," said Orlov. "I wish we had Robert with us—not that I'd expect him to be able to do anything for this poor fellow, but . . . "

More digging, and more of the torso came into view, then a leg, which seemed to be twisted at an awkward angle.

"I just don't believe this!" said Beaumont. "He's got to be *human*! Surely?"

There was no doubt that the figure was of human proportions, with head, jointed arms and legs—even five fingers. The head, when they were able to see the face through the yellowed plastic, was discoloured and wrinkled, and reminded Aurora of a mummified ape she'd once seen in a museum. But then how would a human astronaut look after being buried on Mars for unknown centuries? Or was it less than a century? No one really seemed able to accept Verdet's findings on that.

The suit was made of a silvered material, very much like their own, and, far from being hardened and cracked, it seemed even more supple than theirs. It bore no insignia or other markings, although there was a small black box on the chest. The backpack was slim and curved, unlike their angular pliss equipment, but it was dented as if by some sort of blow.

It took a lot more careful work before the figure was completely free and could be removed. They kept Lundquist informed on progress, and he in turn passed on the information to Earth, together with Orlov's acid addendum that this was a piece of news that had been "officially" approved for general release.

Lundquist was almost beside himself with impatience to examine the astronaut's body, so they strapped it carefully to the carrier on the back of the rover ("But don't bring it inside the cabin, in case of contamination—in either direction," he had instructed them) and headed back to the Igloo.

Soon they saw its white dome, half-shadowed, rising above the horizon like a third, but Moon-sized, Martian satellite.

#

Inside the Igloo, Lundquist had rigged up an isolation chamber using transparent plastic sheeting and an electric fan to produce an invisible curtain of air. Any bacteria or other micro-organisms from the alien body would be filtered out and could later be examined with his tiny electron microscope. Inside, he wore an environment suit which would be decontaminated after use.

The others stood around, like family visitors at a hospital, powerless to help but impatient to know the result of the operation. Through the tantalizing reflections on the gently undulating plastic they watched as the physician, after completing his examination of the exterior of the spacesuit, unclipped the black box on its front and laid it aside.

Then he removed the helmet. They crowded closer for a better view.

Two cloudy greyish eyes stared back from deep sockets. The face was wrinkled, the skin waxen and yellowish. A few flakes of dried flesh dropped away from it abruptly, making Aurora jump.

Stupid! she said to herself.

The spacesuit opened easily, with no obvious zip or velcro fastening; it simply peeled apart. The figure had worn some sort of undersuit, but this seemed brittle and tore almost at a touch. Lundquist placed samples of the material into sealed containers.

After what seemed an eternity, most of the body had been uncovered.

"I don't believe any of this!" said Lundquist into his helmet mike. "It just has to be some kind of hoax." He peered out at Orlov. "Are you sure the Soviets didn't send a man to Mars some time in the Seventies, and keep quiet about the mission because it ended in disaster? Your people used to do that kind of thing, you know!"

Before Orlov could reply, Lundquist continued: "Actually, I should have said 'send a *woman* to Mars.' This cosmonaut, or whatever it is, is a human female, about thirty years old when she died, I'd say. Oh, there's no doubt about it"—he spoke above the hubbub of conversation from outside his "tent"—"and don't start talking about parallel evolution, please, Bryan! I'll need to do a scan of the skull, but from what I've seen already I know that the pattern of the teeth is fully human. Look: on each side, two incisors, one canine, one, two premolars. OK, no wisdom teeth, but that's not unusual. There's no doubt she's human. And look at the ribs . . . There's no chance that an alien species could develop in exactly this way. This lady was born on Earth.

"Mind you, there are a few trivial differences, but even those could be confined to this individual. The toes—see?"

He had pulled the spacesuit right off one leg. No one paid any attention to Aurora's sudden hiss of indrawn breath.

"They're hardly there," Lundquist continued. "Very short and stubby, and practically joined up into one. But I've seen similar variations before—in the children of radiation victims, for instance. There are a few other minor oddities, too, but nothing that suggests she's not human.

"Vitali, if you're eager to make a report to Earth, you might like to take down a few notes—save me getting out of this suit? There are some more tests I want to make before I do that . . . "

Orlov grabbed a notebook and pen and tried hard to keep up with the medic's rapid-fire commentary.

"I want to make sure the medical specialists at Mission Control know this report is absolutely official and authentic," the burly Russian remarked to the rest during a rare pause. "Otherwise there's no way they're going to believe it. Let's face it, they won't anyway!"

He carried on writing, moving his lips as he did so, echoing Lundquist's words in an undertone. "Remarkably good condition . . . no bacterial decay in tissues . . . probably frozen very quickly . . . some breakdown of cells due to ice crystals . . . probably protected by the fact that it was buried . . . kept at fairly constant low temperature . . . "

This went on for several more minutes until Orlov exclaimed, "Stop, stop! Surely that's enough?"

The normally quiet and reserved Lundquist seemed to realize for the first time how long he had been talking, and grinned. "Yes, of course. Sorry! Got carried away. Go ahead and transmit that."

Orlov did so, along with other details of the discovery. He played down the dowsing aspect, Aurora noticed. She glanced at Beaumont and saw that he'd noticed this as well.

They waited with some trepidation the forty minutes or so before they could expect a response from Earth, still on the far side of the Sun in its orbit, though now getting daily closer.

When it arrived, the message from Earth was all that they had expected:

> . . . please transmit video and visual scans at earliest opportunity. On no account allow contamination of or by crew. Ask Dr Lundquist to make personal contact with us as soon as he is able—our Chief MO, Dr Sodhi, wants to ask some questions.

There was more of the same. Then came a message from Bill Emmart which they had *not* anticipated:

> . . . story of Dr Pryor's healing of Commander Orlov, and of her apparent age—and other unusual attributes—has somehow leaked to the media. We are attempting to trace the source, but no luck so far. I'm afraid she'll have to face a full inquiry on her return, though in view of her achievements on this mission it may not be too great a worry! However, the TV and media are having a field day, as you can imagine.

I don't know how this new discovery of yours will affect things, except perhaps to take the heat off Anne. At the moment, the rock-music world has gone mad, and the Gas Giants' album is being re-released along with some video footage someone's found. Anne's—I mean Aurora's—face is everywhere!

There's a movement to send invalids to Mars; they seem to think that Mars is some sort of Lourdes ... Meanwhile, you probably won't be too surprised to learn that the second Mars mission is being brought forward, and enlarged, using a Venus swing-by to reach Mars more quickly. You'll be gone before they arrive, of course; though there has been a proposal that a couple of your crew-members might be able to stay on the surface until the second expedition gets there. That would allow you to bring back the, er, body. But it's only a suggestion so far.

Mission Control, out.

The team-members stared at each other.

"Damnation!" said Aurora.

Orlov looked furious.

Lundquist, still inside his tent, seemed disgruntled—had they really believed his report?

Beaumont, after a momentary look of panic, seemed almost gleeful. "Now the shit's really hit the fan! Don't you see? This is going to make all those hide-bound-fogey scientists, living in their ivory towers, open their minds at last! Every aspect of science is going to be affected!"

"Have you quite finished trotting out the clichés?" enquired Orlov. "Because, if you have, we've still got work to do. For a start, would you like to report the latest developments to those two in the rover—and find out how they're getting on? They should be halfway to Base by now."

Bryan switched wavelengths and made contact with the rover. Minako and Verdet reported tersely that their journey was proving uneventful, and they were preparing to stop to rest for the night.

"D'you think Minako's safe with that Frenchman?" asked Beaumont when he had switched off.

"Is *he* safe with *her*?" countered Aurora. But her attitude to him did not seem as warm as usual.

A little later the four of them retired, exhausted by the day's events. But none of them slept much. Their dreams were haunted by strange images.

Especially Aurora's dreams.

Inside the Spaceship

Next morning at dawn, fog rolled down the canyon, undulating like a soft, pink quilt over a restless sleeper. The same three as yesterday waited for the Sun to burn it off before they departed for the spaceship, taking the Beacon with them. They left Lundquist behind to continue his tests on the dead female astronaut and make his full report to Earth.

Once they'd reached the spaceship, Orlov climbed into the cockpit first. Beaumont lowered the Beacon carefully to him before he and Aurora got in as well; there was plenty of room for all three. Orlov gingerly slid the Beacon into its hole. It fitted so precisely that it looked as if it had been moulded there.

With no sound or warning, the transparent dome appeared above them.

"Hey!" cried Beaumont, leaping up and pushing at it with his hands.

"Don't worry," said Aurora, speaking with a calm that surprised her. "If it opened once it will open again."

"I just hope you're right," said Orlov. "But what made it open and close? We've been taking for granted that it needs your hand on the Beacon to get this thing functioning, Anne, but it looks as if we were wrong. So *what*'s controlling it? And suppose it runs out of power—what do we do then?"

Aurora pointed at the Beacon. "If you were right about this thing opening the canopy the first time," she said, reaching towards it, "it must act as some sort of remote control. It should work here, too."

She touched the smaller sphere confidently with her gloved hand.

Nothing happened.

She touched the larger sphere.

Still no result.

They tried to remove the Beacon from its recess, but now it appeared to be welded into place, seamlessly.

"Great! We're stuck. Let's try the instrument panel," said Beaumont, a note of desperation not far beneath the surface of his voice, no matter how flippant he tried to sound.

Every control was dead, unresponsive.

I'm surprised we're all being so relaxed about this, thought Aurora. *Bryan's obviously scared shitless, but none of us are remotely near panic. It's almost as if the ship itself were telling us we'll be OK . . .*

Orlov changed his suit comm channel to that of the Igloo. "Hello, Robert? Come in please, over."

The only sound in their phones was a wash of static overlaying a tinny squawking noise.

"Damn, damn! We shouldn't *all* have got inside!" said the engineer angrily. "One of us should have remained outside at all times—we *knew* that."

He turned back to the Beacon and tapped it as sharply as he could with his gloved knuckle. It made a dull echoing noise. He tried to grasp it with both hands.

"Hold on!" said Aurora. "Do that again."

"Do what?"

"Knock on the Beacon."

He did so, and it made the same sound. "That's just the sort of noise it made back at camp. Oh, you mean it shouldn't, now that it's so firmly in place?"

"No, Vitali, you idiot! Just *think*—we shouldn't be hearing it at *all*. Unless . . . "

"Unless there's air in here. And plenty of it," said Beaumont. He paused. "So who's going to take their helmet off?"

"Nobody. Their air could be poisonous to us," said Orlov firmly.

"Robert says that astronaut is human," said Aurora. "If she is, surely she must have breathed the same air as us."

"But it could have gone bad, or changed, or something, in the length of time this thing's been lying here," said the engineer firmly. "Even if it *is* less than a century it's been sealed up here."

"So we all die of suffocation in our suits," said Beaumont. "Nice one. You're not thinking straight, old chap."

He put his hands to his helmet.

Orlov moved as if to stop him, but Aurora put a restraining hand on his arm. "If he takes it off just for a moment—just enough for a sniff—it shouldn't do him any harm. Don't forget, Robert hasn't found any harmful micro-organisms on either the Beacon or the body—and it's hardly likely there's cyanide or something in the air."

"All right," said Orlov grudgingly. "But I take no responsibility."

Once again, in the face of an unknown quantity, he had become indecisive and nervous, Aurora noted. Quite unlike his usual bluff, confident self. At such times his Russian accent thickened, yet he spoke English even more correctly, if anything.

Beaumont lifted his helmet.

His nose wrinkled. Then he opened his mouth and took a deliberate breath.

"Best air I ever tasted!" he said. He winked at Aurora. "That's from an old movie, too. Remind me to tell you about it some time."

"Are you sure?" asked Orlov worriedly.

"Oh yes. It was *When Worlds Collide.*" He raised his palms towards the glowering engineer. "Sorry, sorry! Come on, try it for yourself. There's a sort of—sort of *ozony* tang to it. And it's cold. But it's as good as anything I've breathed on this trip so far. Better, in fact. It's beginning to stink a bit in the Igloo, don't you think?"

The others removed their helmets, Orlov very slowly, as if ready to replace it at the slightest hint of anything untoward. The accentuated rise and fall of his chest betrayed his anxiety further. Aurora felt her own heart racing.

"Phew. Well, that will help a lot," Orlov said at last, the taut muscles of his face relaxing. "And isn't it getting quite warm in here, too? It should be freezing, surely?"

"Never mind that. We still have to get that canopy open—and find out what's in the outer part of this ship."

Orlov looked round at Aurora, surprise on his face. She was removing the upper, torso section of her suit.

"I know we're celebrating a bit," said Beaumont, "but there's no need for a striptease, is there? Not that I'm complaining, you understand."

Ignoring him, Aurora reached out her bare hand and touched the Beacon. Almost at once, the black band glowed dull red, pulsing a little.

After a few moments its glow became steady and then the canopy vanished.

They dived for their helmets, but they'd hardly had time to move when the canopy reappeared again.

"What did you do?" asked Beaumont.

"I haven't told you before, but when I touched this the other day, back at camp, I'd taken my glove off." Aurora glanced guiltily at Orlov. "OK, OK, I know I shouldn't have, Vitali, but it seemed—necessary."

"It's all right," said Orlov with a wry smile. "You needn't apologize. Or explain. I've gotten the message by now that you're a law unto yourself, here on Mars."

"Hmm. Well, anyway, it seems that it needs to be touched by bare flesh—or perhaps it's just that its power is low, so it needs that extra human contact. I'm just guessing . . . " She looked from one to the other, hesitating.

"I hate to say this, but as to how I did it, well, I just *thought*. Honestly! I literally thought *open* and then *close*, visualizing the canopy—and it *did*. And it comes back to me now: just before I passed out, back at the Igloo, a picture of the canopy had come into my head. Even though I hadn't seen it by then. I thought I was just imagining it after hearing your descriptions, and then I fainted so I forgot all about it."

Orlov said, "Can you open the canopy again, Anne? We'll have to put on our suits and helmets for a while, until you close it once more. I must try to contact Robert. It will be interesting, afterwards, to see how quickly the air refills this chamber again—assuming it does."

It took the three of them a few minutes to work out how Aurora could safely touch the Beacon with her bare hand yet keep her suit on for when the air rushed out and the Martian cold rushed in. In the end it was Aurora herself who pointed out the obvious. It was cold on Mars, but not *that* cold: she wasn't frightened about exposing her hand on its own to the environment for a few seconds. She picked up her suit and removed the padded outer mitt from the end of one of its flaccid arms. Underneath there was an airtight inner glove, silk-thin but made of material that offered adequate insulation against the chill for up to a few minutes—the system had been designed to allow astronauts to perform any emergency fine manipulations with their hands in the depths of space. The inner mitt was course integral to the arm of the suit; she borrowed Beaumont's belt-pick to cut it loose. So long as she always kept the outer glove on, the inner was redundant.

The three of them donned their suits. None of them could stop looking at Aurora's exposed hand. It was alive and yet outside the confines of any man-made structure. Whatever their brains told them, their instincts were yelling that this was an anomaly—a supremely vulnerable anomaly.

"The Beacon itself is going to be cold," said Beaumont abruptly. "As cold as the air. It's going to freeze the moisture on your skin. Your hand's likely to stick to it . . . "

She shook her head at him. "It's got its own warmth," she said. "That's another thing I found out."

He quietened.

Fixing her gaze earnestly on Orlov's, Aurora reached out to the Beacon. *Open,* she thought.

It did.

"See?" she said, rapidly pulling on the thick outer mitt. "Nothing to it."

Her ragged breathing, loud in their helmets, belied her words.

Orlov grinned at her, then popped his head above the level of the cabin and spoke to Lundquist, explaining what had happened. The physician was relieved to hear from them—he'd been trying to raise them without success.

"I think we could just about hear you," said Orlov. "You sounded like Donald Duck. There seems a lot of static in here, though. Can you hear it? Over."

"Yes, it's still there, but 'way in the distance. You're coming through loud and clear now. Over."

"We're going to try to close the canopy again, so don't worry if we go off the air for a while," explained Orlov. "With any luck, we'll have more news about the interior when I speak to you again. Over and out."

"Over and out," concurred Lundquist.

"OK, Anne, do your stuff," said Orlov, nodding.

The band was still glowing ruby red. More relaxedly this time, Aurora removed her glove and put her fingertips on the Beacon, thinking: *Close.*

A moment later the dome once more covered the bright sky with its pattern of scars and milky markings.

Beaumont started to tap the Beacon in a regular rhythm. Slowly the "thunk" became louder. As soon as he was satisfied the cabin was once more fully pressurized, he took off his helmet, clutched his throat and made a strangled sound, his tongue protruding, eyes wide.

"*Doctor* Beaumont, behave yourself! This is a serious scientific expedition!" said Aurora, turning away to hide her smile.

Orlov chuckled briefly, but then sobered. "Anne's right. A bit of fun's OK for lightening the tension, but there's such a thing as crying 'Wolf!' too often."

"Right-oh, message received." Beaumont did his best to look apologetic.

Ignoring their byplay, Aurora placed her ungloved hand in the small depression on the blank wall and frowned in concentration.

Nothing happened.

Acting on a hunch, she went over to the Beacon and put her hand on it instead, still focusing her thoughts on the wall.

There was an audible *click!* and a section of wall opened—but only a little way. It stopped leaving a gap of some fifteen centimetres.

Beaumont and Orlov grasped either side of the opening, pulling hard, trying to widen the gap.

The sides of the opening wouldn't budge.

The band on the Beacon had turned black again.

"I think it gets exhausted," said Aurora. "It must recharge itself somehow—perhaps just from solar power. Though it wouldn't have got that when it was under the sand." She looked exhausted herself, her face drained of colour.

"Doing that takes it out of you, doesn't it?" said Beaumont solicitously, putting an arm around her shoulder.

"Yes. It was the same when I played with the Gas Giants. I used to feel physically washed out after every rehearsal, every gig. Mental powers, whatever they are, seem to require a lot of energy." Fitting actions to words, she took a long swig of glucose drink from her suit pack.

Orlov unhooked his suit flashlight and shone it through the gap now opened in the cabin wall. Peering, he let out a long, low whistle.

Beaumont and Aurora stepped to his side. The bright halogen beam reflected from three curved rows of seemingly semitransparent ovoids, placed one above another, but staggered. There must have been at least three dozen.

"Eggs! It's like in *Alien!*" said Beaumont. "That's another classic old movie, you know," he added for Orlov's benefit.

"Can't you be serious for a moment?" said Aurora vexedly.

Beaumont looked contrite, but only briefly. It was obvious he was in his element. "I wish we could get inside."

Aurora, the colour returning to her cheeks, touched the Beacon again. As if in sympathy, the red colour glowed once more along the black band, but fluctuating. Her brow creased. Then, with a faint rumbling sound, the panel opened completely to form a doorway over a metre wide. As with the canopy, none of them saw it actually move.

"Abracadabra! Your wish is my command, oh master. I mean, mistress," muttered Beaumont.

"In your dreams," drawled Aurora automatically.

The three stood around the entrance as if afraid to go inside. In the end Beaumont was the first to put a foot over the threshold. As he did so, light came on in the shadowy chamber. It had no apparent source, and it faded in gradually—like dawn on a stage set. Within a minute the entire area was bathed in a soft yellowish light, not unlike early-morning sunlight.

The "eggs" gleamed dully.

Softly, as though they might wake someone, they moved over to the semi-circle of ovoids. Each was nearly a metre and a half long and, while they looked as if they should be translucent, it was impossible to see anything of their contents—assuming there was anything to see, that they weren't just solid.

Beaumont wiped his hand over one of them as though clearing a misted or dusty car windscreen, but whatever was making the "egg" opaque was either inside or a quality of the material, for his efforts had no effect. There was no dust inside the ship except what they'd brought in with them.

Orlov, noting there was a faint line running around the midpoint of each ovoid, tried to pry one open. His efforts, too, were wasted.

He looked questioningly at Aurora.

Sighing, she placed her bare hand on the nearest egg. Soundlessly and smoothly, the upper half swung upward. They all stared, speechless.

Inside was a baby.

A tiny human baby, no more than a few months old, its eyes closed, its tiny hands clenched.

"*Close it!*" ordered Orlov sharply.

Aurora simply pushed the lid down, and it remained that way.

"We don't do any more until we have Robert with us," said Orlov.

"Hibernation!" cried Beaumont. "It *has* to be. That would explain how the craft could be so small! It had no crew except that woman—the pilot—who was perhaps trying to get help after they crash-landed. But it carried lots of babies in hibernation so that when they reached a suitable planet . . . "

"Let's leave the theorizing until later," said Orlov. "But you might like to consider how *human beings* came to be visiting Mars from another star. And there's still the question of what fuel this ship used. Look how much space is taken up by these . . . these incubators. Or deep-freezes. Whatever."

"Well, that's obvious—" started Beaumont.

"Enough!"

The Russian put on his helmet, and it was obvious from his expression that he expected the others to do the same. As they left the chamber the light inside faded away behind them.

When all were fully suited up, he nodded to Aurora.

The band on the Beacon was an intense red-black that made Aurora think of infrared. The light hurt her eyes, as if it were shining far more brightly than she could see. She concentrated on thinking of the canopy open.

It did start opening, but then, like the door panel, it stopped. Even half-open, however, it gave them plenty of room to climb out.

Orlov looked back down into the cabin before he slid off the side of the vessel to the ground. "I was just thinking," he said to no one in particular, "that this cockpit was open for quite a while before we came back and closed it—before Anne closed it. You'd have thought at least some dust and sand would have blown in and piled up on the floor.

"Interesting."

#

Lundquist, via the relay on the rim of the canyon, reported that Minako and Verdet had made good progress and were almost back at Base Camp. He had the impression that they had fallen out over something. Verdet was obviously curbing his comments.

Told about the discovery of the baby, Lundquist wanted to come straight out. But by the time they had returned with the one rover, grabbed new supplies and pliss packs, then turned around and came back to the ship, it would be sunset. Lundquist wanted to do it anyway, pointing out that the alien ship had its own lights; but Orlov vetoed the idea.

"Better to make a fresh start tomorrow," he said. They all sat down to take some food and liquid before the trek back to the Igloo. Purple shadows crawled up the canyon wall.

#

That evening, most of their time was spent listening to and sending messages to Earth. The public at large might not yet have heard about the discovery of the babies but it was making the most of what it did know.

The established churches were divided on Aurora's healing powers, some sects wanting to canonize her, others wanting to have her exorcised as an instrument of the Devil. The Church of Jesus Christ Astronaut wanted her to agree to be its new Leader, and was aggrieved when Aurora refused. They were said to be considering adopting the dead female astronaut in her place. Perhaps the spaceship had been Mars's own Star of Bethlehem—only it had crashed?

Many Christians saw no problem with the human appearance of the woman. Had not God created Man (and presumably Woman) in His own image? they asked. So wouldn't the people He placed on other planets also be in His image?

"Poor old Darwin must be turning in his grave," commented Beaumont. "And what will the Christ the Astronaut lot say when they hear about our babies? A whole cargo-load of Baby Jesuses!"

To everyone's surprise, Orlov turned on Beaumont angrily and grabbed his shoulders.

"I've had about enough of your snide remarks!" he shouted, his cheeks red. "All scientists aren't atheists, you know. Me, for example. I'm not ashamed of my religious beliefs, even if I do usually keep them to myself. Do you really think our wonderful Cosmos came into being by accident?"

He subsided as rapidly as he'd erupted, his arms dropping to his side.

Aurora drew Beaumont away to sit beside her. "You know, you *have* been rather a pain in the arse today, Bryan," she said. "Why don't you cool it now?"

His only answer was a glare.

Aurora knew something of Orlov's background; of how his father had been an elder of the Russian Orthodox Church, serving directly under the Patriarch of Moscow. The old man had kept his faith despite his life being made a misery during the attempted suppression of religion by the Communists, but lived just long enough to see the revolution that had taken place in the early 1990s, with the collapse of the Soviet Union setting millions of his fellow-countrymen once again free to observe their religious practices. The events of the past few days must have been very difficult for Orlov—especially having Beaumont's perhaps unintentionally tasteless remarks to cope with on top of everything else.

"Sorry," said Beaumont barely audibly in Orlov's direction, having apparently thought all this through for himself.

They went to their bunks that night in a subdued mood. They squabbled among themselves often enough, usually half in jest, but serious flare-ups were rare. The Igloo seemed much smaller than usual, the walls encroaching, the air heavy.

"We Have a Problem . . ."

Next morning Verdet called in to say that all was well back at Base Camp. He and Minako had collected everything on their list, and were about to return. Orlov started to fill them in on what had been happening, but Verdet, oddly, interrupted to point out that they had seen and heard most of the exchanges with Earth on the main comm desk. He did not seem to want to elaborate, and he did not put Minako on the air to them.

Meanwhile Mission Control was still relaying the news and views from their home planet:

> *Anthropologists have so far been quite unable to come up with a tenable hypothesis for the presence of an apparently human female astronaut on Mars. The great public out there are not so restrained, though! One of the favourite theories is based on Erich von Däniken's ideas, first put forward in the nineteen-sixties. He claimed that the ancient "gods" were alien astronauts—responsible for everything from the Pyramids to the lines on the ddesert at Nazca, which were (of course) runways for spacecraft. Some people have modified this to claim that these aliens took away cavemen from Earth fifty thousand years ago. The descendants of those human deportees have now returned, having grown up among and been educated by the aliens. Get it?!*
>
> *Another favourite is Atlantis. According to fans of the lost continent, refugees from the ancient super-civilization escaped in spacecraft just before their volcanic island blew its top and vanished without trace below the waves, leaving only the scattered isles of Thera. They found a habitable planet of another star, colonized it, and their descendants are now coming back to explore the*

Earth. Their first attempt, eighty years or so ago, may have failed—but they'll try again!

Quite why they went to another star instead of just moving to another continent on Earth doesn't seem clear.

None of these theories is being taken seriously by the scientific establishment, of course, but you have to admit there could be some seed of an explanation buried in some of them—and, as I said, no tenable "serious" ideas have come up yet. But you guys can rest assured that we're working on it. I guess you are too, huh?

Mission Control, over and out.

"I can think of another theory," said Beaumont. He had regained his good humour, though relations between Aurora and himself were definitely strained. "It's not new, of course, but what if humankind—all life, even—was originally brought to Earth from another star system? It didn't have to come on a spaceship, it might have somehow "seeded" itself—spores drifting through space—that Martian meteorite even!—that kind of thing, anyway. There'd be no need for parallel evolution then. We'd all have evolved from the same stock."

"I can't buy that," snorted Lundquist. "Life in the near-vacuum of outer space, drifting between the stars?"

But Beaumont was warming to his theme. "Yes, why not? Suppose an Earthlike planet blew apart for some reason—a nuclear war or something. We know that life *can* exist in a vacuum, and at extremes of temperature—look at those still-viable spores that were found on *Surveyor* by the astronauts on Apollo—Apollo 12, I think it was. Yes, the second Moon landing. And how some desert plants and even animals, like that frog, can encapsulate themselves and remain dormant for years and years, until the rains come.

"Well, look, there has to be some explanation for what we've found, doesn't there? It's no use throwing out every suggestion just because it sounds a bit way-out!"

The others nodded tolerantly.

#

This time all four returned to the alien craft, leaving the comm desk on automatic. Orlov, Lundquist and Aurora climbed in through the half-open canopy, leaving Beaumont outside as a safety precaution—though whether there was anything useful he could do if they got trapped inside seemed doubtful. He seemed happy to dowse a few areas he had so far missed. It was obvious to Orlov that Aurora was equally happy that Beaumont should be some distance away from her. The big engineer thought *Lovers' spat* to himself and made no comment.

The door panel was still open, just as they'd left it.

"See? There's still no trace of dust anywhere—not even what we must have brought in with us yesterday," he said. "I think there has to be an automatic vacuum cleaner somewhere."

"Now why doesn't that surprise me?" murmured Lundquist.

Aurora stripped off her glove and used the Beacon to close the canopy over them. After allowing time for the cabin to pressurize, they doffed their suits.

As they entered the chamber, the lights again brightened.

Orlov tried to see where the air had come from, but there was no sign of a ventilator or duct. He turned his attention instead to the floor, and started carefully pacing from the dully gleaming ovoids to the centre of the cockpit.

"I thought so," he said. "The cabin and chamber don't take up all of the space inside this ship. There's an outer ring. That would explain where the propellant goes. Or went. Or maybe it houses some sort of drive mechanism. There's room there for *something*, anyway."

Lundquist made for one of the "eggs" and tried, like Orlov had yesterday, to pry the top open.

"I'm afraid Anne's the only one with the magic touch," said the Russian with a smile.

Aurora put her hand on the first ovoid, and it opened as before. Lundquist at once peered closely at the infant inside, and applied various instruments.

"The baby's about three months old," he said almost immediately. "But it's not hibernating, alas—it's quite dead. Perfectly preserved, though, as you can see. And the limbs are still flexible, the flesh soft."

He peeled off the baby's one-piece garment, which was of a very soft grey-white material with a pearly sheen. "It's a he," he said. Freeing the tiny foot, he pointed. "See? The toes—they're like the woman's. Stubby, and virtually joined together. And with hardly any nails. Strange."

He frowned, then said: "Anne—could you open another egg, please?"

She did so. This time the dead body was that of a girl, of about the same age and in exactly the same condition as the boy.

She opened another five before they stopped. Of those opened, four contained boys, three girls. Their apparent ages varied between two and six months.

This puzzled Lundquist. "If this is some kind of starship, carrying a crew in hibernation, I'd have thought they'd be bred specially, and all be the same age. But then what do I know?"

"A crew of babies?" asked Orlov.

"Well, the usual thinking is that they'd grow during the voyage, even though "asleep," so that after, say, fifteen or twenty years at a speed somewhere near that of light, they'd be old enough to start colonizing a new planet. The ship itself would be almost entirely automated, of course."

He moved one of the pathetically small corpses. Aurora fought back the urge to vomit as the tiny limbs splayed like those of a raw chicken on its way to the oven, but Lundquist seemed unperturbed as he leaned forward again to examine the interior of the empty capsule. He was about to speak once more when Beaumont's voice sounded tinnily from his helmet, lying nearby.

"I forgot all about him!" Lundquist whispered embarrassedly, picking it up.

"I said, 'That wouldn't work'," Beaumont drawled. "I was thinking about it yesterday. Those—coffins—they aren't big enough to allow for growth. Unless we assume the containers are organic in some way and are supposed themselves to grow, or something really alien," he added. "No. There isn't room in the chamber for that."

"I was about to say the same," muttered Lundquist, looking slightly aggrieved. "And also, apart from a sort of absorbent area below the babies, which seems to have acted as a sort of super-diaper, there's no sign of any waste-management system such as you'd need on a really long voyage."

"I'll tell you something else," came Beaumont's voice again. "If those babies were supposed to grow up . . . and, now that I think of it, why *didn't* they? Their age means the system must have gone wrong soon after they left home, yet that woman arrived alive and able to go out on the surface. Where was I? Oh yes, if they were supposed to grow older and be able to colonize some presumably uninhabited world when they arrived, shouldn't there be some sort of learning system along with them? I mean, I can accept sleep-learning, but I didn't see any sign of a gadget to do the educating. Can you?"

"Would we be able to recognize it if there was?" asked Lundquist.

Even so, he and the other two re-inspected the two babies and their opened capsules. Sure enough, there was no sign of speakers, electrodes, screens or anything that might have represented a sleep-learning system. Lundquist told Beaumont as much—adding irritably, as he hefted his helmet yet again, that they would have to install a better communication method between the inside and the outside of the craft.

"They may be human-*looking*, but it's all so alien," sighed Orlov while this exchange was going on. He'd been prowling around the chamber, prodding at the walls away from the row of cocoons.

"I've found another of those depressions," he said suddenly, placing his palm in it. "Anne? Could you oblige?"

Aurora placed her hand in the little recess, and tried to visualize a door ajar. The problem was, she didn't know exactly where the door might open, or what it would lead to. She glanced through the open entrance to the cabin, where she could just see the Beacon, its band still glowing—though more faintly, perhaps? While the image of the open door was still in her mind, the panel under her hand vanished. In its place there was suddenly a large open rectangle.

She had a momentary view of brown rock and what appeared to be a sand dune—but at the same moment there was a thin howling sound as air started to rush out of the chamber. A freezing sensation numbed her limbs.

For a moment she panicked, and started to dart towards her spacesuit. The others, their eyes wide, began to pick up their helmets. Then, realizing what she must do, she created a vivid mental picture of the door panel closed.

And it was.

Within moments the air was back up at full pressure again. The temperature, thankfully, also rose. They had all started to shiver.

"Whew! That was close," breathed Lundquist.

From the helmet he was again holding came Beaumont's voice, loud and anxious.

"Hey! Can you hear me? What's going on in there? Dust and sand suddenly started erupting from underneath the ship! Did you start up the motors or something? Are you all right?"

Orlov laughed, a little shakily. "Yes, thank you, Bryan. Sorry about that, but we just opened another door—and it led into the damaged section and nearly let all our air out!"

"Oh, is *that* all? Well, I guess that's a relief. I wonder what used to be in that space? We haven't found anything that would fit."

"Hmmm. Good point. Keep looking!"

Turning to the others, Orlov said, "There doesn't seem to be a lot more we can do in here, apart from taking lots of video and stills to send back to Earth. Won't they just love this!" He gestured towards the control cabin. "But maybe we can get something working in there. Or perhaps Anne can. After all, there seems to be power somewhere. The lights and air still work."

Beaumont's tinny voice said, plaintively, "Can I come in there with you? Honestly, I just can't concentrate on doing anything else out here. And it doesn't look as if I can be of any use outside, does it? The controls of that thing seem to be in Aurora's hands." It was the first time he had called her by that name publicly, but nobody seemed to notice.

"We'd have to open the canopy and repressurize," said Orlov. But the others agreed to take pity on Beaumont; if the controls could be made to work it would be a great pity for him to miss the fun. So the two men donned their helmets and Aurora put on her suit, her right hand still free.

She imagined the canopy open. The red band brightened momentarily, and the dome started to open, jerkily, seeming to dematerialize a few centimetres at a time. Air began to whistle through the gap.

Which got no wider than about eighteen centimetres, then stopped.

She tried again. The space doubled, but staunchly refused her efforts to make it any larger than that.

Orlov tried to push his way out.

The band went dull black.

"Damn! This is useless!" said the engineer, still trying to squeeze his chest through the gap.

Lundquist pushed the glove onto Aurora's hand.

Orlov cursed again, this time in Russian. "I can't get out through here!" he growled angrily at Aurora.

"It's not my fault," she snapped. "It's all down to that thing." She pointed at the now lifeless Beacon.

The Russian calmed down. "Yes. I apologize. Let's see if someone smaller can get out. You first, Anne."

She pushed her helmet and shoulders through the gap. "No way," she gasped.

Lundquist came to the rescue. "It's our plisses that are the problem. We can unclip them. There'll be quite enough air in our suits and helmets to get out—as long as we clip the plisses right on again outside. Bryan, it'd be good if you could help. We'll pass them out to you."

Aurora and Lundquist were soon outside, plisses back in place. Then it was Orlov's turn.

As he had feared, his bear-like figure would not pass through the crescent-shaped space, no matter how he wriggled and pushed.

He tried one final heave and—

"I'm stuck!"

The combined efforts of the three others could not pull him through. At last they were able, however, to push him back in.

He sank into one of the control chairs, panting with exertion, and re-attaching his backpack with difficulty. "Now what?" he growled, sweat streaming down his face and dripping from his beard, his faceplate misted.

"Perhaps we could cut the canopy, or break it?" suggested Beaumont.

"Not a chance," said Aurora dismissively.

"There's nothing for it, then, I'm afraid," said Beaumont to Orlov. "You'll just have to stay in there until power returns to the Beacon—transmitter, whatever the thing is. It always has before, so there's no reason to suppose it won't do it again. We can keep you supplied with oxygen, food, whatever you need. Don't worry—you'll be fine!"

Vitali grinned weakly. "Yes. Fine. Easy enough for *you* to say. Sure."

He didn't sound at all sure.

Another World

Aurora and Lundquist stayed with Orlov. They had with them a trolley containing food and drink packs and spare oxygen. Beaumont drove back to camp to report to Earth and to prepare to bring further supplies, should they be needed. Rover 2 was almost back from Base. Minako and Verdet were close enough to have picked up much of what had happened via the relay station perched on the lip of the canyon.

It was very lonely by yourself in the pressure dome, Beaumont discovered. He found he could not bear to allow his thoughts to dwell on what he was doing on this strange world; on the immensity of space around him; on the vast distance to Earth; on the unimaginably vaster distances between the stars. So he stayed at the comm desk in case he was needed.

He tried talking to the pair on Rover 2, but they seemed singularly uncommunicative.

He prepared a message and video to transmit to Earth.

At 22.07, Mars time, he saw a light appear on the western horizon. It grew brighter and separated into two. Hillocks and dunes became outlined in yellow–white. At last the red glow of the Rover 2 cabin's night-driving lamp became visible, revealing the dark silhouettes of two figures.

Finally, dust swirling in the glow of its headlights, the vehicle came to a halt. There was a delay while the occupants checked their suits, helmets and backpacks, then the hatches swung upward like a gull's wings and the two scientists stepped out.

It was obvious as soon as Minako and Verdet entered the dome that there was something wrong between them.

Beaumont allowed them to de-suit and to relax with some refreshments before he broached the subject. "All right, what's up with you two? You can cut the atmosphere in here with a knife since you came in!"

Minako's eyes blazed, and Beaumont, remembering a remark once made by Aurora about the Japanese woman's strange odour, for a moment wondered if he had accidentally hit the target. She had bags under her eyes, he noticed; they didn't make her any more attractive.

Verdet passed a hand over his short, crinkly black hair and said nothing.

"If you don't tell me I'll start using my notorious imagination!" threatened Beaumont, smiling to try to lighten the mood. "Let's see: two of you, alone at Base Camp. I know, Claude made a pass at you, Minako, and you slapped his face!"

"Oh, shut up and don't be ridiculous," snapped Minako. "We're not all like you and Dr Pryor, you know."

For a moment she looked as though she instantly regretted that remark. She continued rapidly: "If you must know, he accused me of being responsible for the leaks to the media about Dr Pryor and her amazing powers. I've told him time and again that it wasn't me, but he just keeps repeating that I had more opportunity than anyone else, because I often volunteered to stay at the communications desk."

Beaumont's face fell. "Oh. Ah. So that's it." He turned to face Verdet. "She's right, Claude. I can't tell you how I know, but it definitely wasn't Minako. Now, kiss and make up?"

Verdet looked for a moment as though he would refuse. Then he summoned a grin, leaned over and planted a peck on the embarrassed-looking woman's cheek. "Sorry, Minako. But you must admit . . . "

"That's enough!" said Beaumont. "Let's leave it at that. And I don't know about you, but I'm about ready to turn in. Think of poor Vitali, Bob and Anne . . . "

#

Next morning, after a brief report to Mission Control, the three from the dome took both rovers out to the spaceship. Today they brought extra supplies, so that in the event of anyone being trapped inside the craft again they'd be able to survive a day or two in relative comfort until the Beacon recharged itself. Assuming it *did* recharge itself.

Orlov had spent an uncomfortable night, but was pleased to see that

Minako and Verdet had returned safely. The shrunken Sun peeped over the rim of the canyon, and soon the alien craft gleamed in its rays. The partly open canopy glittered.

Finally Aurora said, "Well, I guess this is the moment of truth."

As though they had rehearsed it, Lundquist unclipped her pliss. She climbed the smooth skin of the craft, flattened herself to squeeze under the canopy, and dropped inside. Lundquist passed her backpack through to Orlov, who attached it again. The whole operation took only seconds.

She grasped the fingers of the glove, whipped it off, and placed her hand on the Beacon.

Nothing happened, and despite the gadget's inner warmth she felt her hand growing rapidly cold and numb. She prepared to pull the glove back on.

And then the familiar ruby glow appeared, spreading around the band on the smaller sphere. Aurora breathed a sigh of relief—and she wasn't the only one. She put the glove back on, at the same time "thinking" the canopy fully open.

"Do you think everyone *should* come inside?" she asked Orlov as the others crowded the opening. "And what about you? Are you all right? Do you want to go back to camp?"

"They may as well come in. I think I would have a mutiny on my hands if you found something vital when you tried the controls and they missed it. As for me—I've got only one problem, that I didn't want to take care of in here unless I had to." He smiled uneasily. "But if I can just go outside for a moment . . . "

She knew what he meant, because she likewise always tried to arrange matters so that she didn't have to use her suit's toilet facilities unless absolutely necessary. Unlike the arrangement of various tubes and diapers—nappies, she still called them—used in earlier suits, theirs did have a sort of double-airlock system that allowed them to relieve themselves and bury the results, sealed in a non-degradable and detoxifying plastic pack, when out on the surface. There had been a strong faction in favour of bringing home all waste matter, so as not to contaminate the Martian or space environment, but the prospect of saving weight had won the day—every gram of waste material left behind on Mars represented an extra gram of valuable samples to be brought home in its place.

Arrangements could doubtless have been made with those outside to pass out baggies, but she could sympathize with Orlov's sensitivity. *He must be very uncomfortable by now,* she thought as he left hastily.

When he returned, the whole team was clustered around the instrument panel, Minako and Verdet having examined one of the ovoids and its tiny contents. She closed the canopy, not without some trepidation.

On the way to join the others Aurora touched the Beacon. "For luck!" she said.

She sat down at the control panel for a moment, then placed a finger on the largest and lightest-coloured of the grey keypads.

Almost at once the blue-grey screen flickered with coloured patterns, which dissolved into swirling dots.

Then a face appeared, wavering for a few moments as if in a distorting mirror before reappearing with crystal clarity. It was the face of a man, apparently aged about forty. He was dressed in a close-fitting grey suit not unlike those worn by the babies, though darker in colour. A skullcap hid his hair. His eyes were violet.

The screen now seemed like an open window, and the man was so lifelike and three-dimensional that, involuntarily, she put out a hand to touch him. She felt only a cold, curved surface.

Aurora tapped the light grey keypad a couple of times, and a voice became audible, getting louder. "It just seemed logical," she said, anticipating an un-asked question. Like the picture, the voice was so clear and had such presence that they all found it hard to believe the man was not right there in the cabin with them.

"I thought our holos were getting pretty real, but this is something else!" said Beaumont.

"Ssshhh! What is he saying?" asked Orlov.

But the man's speech was unintelligible. Yet it seemed tantalizingly familiar.

"Hey, didn't he just say 'temperature'?" asked Beaumont.

"I thought I heard some French words—and German," observed Verdet.

"And Japanese," added Minako.

In fact, elements of every language they knew seemed to be there. All felt they could almost sense the meaning of what the man was saying. He seemed worried, and there was a sense of urgency, as though he were trying to warn of some peril. But of course they had no way of knowing for whom the message was intended.

The image broke up into shimmering points again, and the sound became a static-like roar. When the picture steadied the man had disappeared, replaced by a view of a city taken either aerially or from a high hill. It was no city on Earth, of that there was no doubt. And, assuming the structures had similar proportions to those in an Earth city, it must be vast; yet the buildings were mixed among large areas of greenery and park-like areas.

"It reminds me of an artist's impression I saw of Atlantis," chirped Beaumont.

"Oh, per-*lease!*" said Aurora wearily. "UFOs were bad enough . . . "

"No, I'm *not* supporting that silly theory," Beaumont countered hastily. "Honest! But those concentric watercourses, and the low white buildings and pyramids—and especially that great volcano in the centre. You must admit, they do have that look about them."

Aurora somewhat grudgingly agreed that she had seen similar reconstructions of the capital of the legendary lost continent. Meanwhile, the view enlarged and began to move along some of the waterways and roads. Vegetation clung to the slopes of the volcano for more than half of its height. So the image *was* from some aerial craft. Behind the volcano, softened by distance, hung the outline of an even bigger conical mountain.

Orlov had set his video camera on a tripod so that it could make a continuous recording of what was on the screen.

There was a lot of plant life, which from this height could have been any kind of trees and shrubs, probably tropical. Some had bright flowers or fruit. There were ships or boats on the water; slim, gondola-like craft, some with masts and strange, square or triangular sails which did not billow or change shape but glittered silver-blue. On the roads were a few bubble-like vehicles, and a disc-shaped craft floated smoothly across the deep blue sky. White-gowned people moved on the footways and in the squares.

Aurora shivered suddenly.

Several times the scene blurred and wavered; once or twice it broke up completely. As long as it was clear, the voice continued, occasionally pausing as the view lingered, apparently to make some point. Aurora began to feel even more strongly that she should be able to understand what was being said, but maddeningly the meaning eluded her.

The viewpoint zoomed in on the peak of the volcano. The circular floor of the main crater was flat. In the middle of it they could see a smaller crater, covered by a transparent bubble; through the bubble they could make out rows of seats grouped around a dais. The focus tarried on a group of twelve people seated round a central circular table which looked to be made of marble. Seated onlookers leaned forward intently.

The narrator's voice stopped, and instead the voices of the twelve, both male and female, could be heard, discussing something in urgent tones. These looked older than the other people seen so far, and their gowns were of pastel colours rather than white; but all had fair hair and pale eyes, in which violet or green seemed to predominate. Their skin, though, was very tanned-looking—almost coffee-coloured.

Aurora felt her colleagues' eyes on her, though no one said a word. They were all strongly aware that these people bore a very strong generic resemblance to her, Aurora. It could hardly be a coincidence, surely— there must be some reason for it. But what?

The group of debating people dissolved, and the city reappeared, this time seen from almost directly overhead. The scene slowly rotated and the viewpoint became higher, so that the watchers could see more and more of the landscape. The outermost of the watercourses could now be seen not to close in a complete circle, but to widen again behind the volcano, creating a figure-of-eight, the closer portion being the smaller. Aurora was reminded irresistibly of the shape of the Beacon, although the similarity most probably was just happenstance, she thought. The inner watercourses were on different levels, being terraced on the lower, gentle slopes of the central volcano.

There was a fairly flat plain, much of it cultivated; but its fields were not laid out in neat rows or rectangles, instead being arranged in aesthetically pleasing shapes, with complementary colours meeting at their perimeters, an occasional contrasting hue making a startling counterpoint. The straight lines of the watercourses which radiated from the central, volcanic "islands" became gentle curves that meandered among the pastures. Around the city, the water formed three concentric rings. Other low buildings, perhaps farms, were scattered here and there.

It looked idyllic.

The view continued to rise, and several other, isolated flat-topped mountains came into view over a horizon which was beginning to curve, almost lost in a violet haze. The soft purple shadows were long, suggesting late afternoon. The depiction began to rotate again, until the Sun came into view.

No, not the Sun.

Two suns.

"A binary!" breathed Beaumont.

"That clinches it. This planet we're seeing certainly isn't in our Solar System, and can never have been," said Orlov.

Both suns looked reddish, but this could have been an atmospheric effect, since it was obviously near sunset. But they must obviously have a similar colour to each other. One was far larger in the sky than the other—though smaller than the Sun in the sky of Earth. The minor or more distant component of the binary was very small, but piercingly bright. The two stars appeared to be very close, though this could have been merely an effect of perspective. Several large sunspots pocked the face of the bigger or nearer star.

Beaumont peered closer. "Is it just a trick of my eyes, or do I see a bridge of matter between them?" he said thoughtfully.

Before anyone could answer, the view closed on the two stars and became either a computer-style animation or possibly a sequence of time-lapse photographs. A symbol like a tiny paintbrush appeared in the bottom right-hand corner of the screen.

The two stars seemed as real as before, and Beaumont's linking stream of gas could now clearly be seen flowing between them. The stars began to re-volve ever more rapidly around their common centre of gravity. As they grew larger in the screen, the surface of the more massive star could be seen to be churning like a pan of boiling liquid. Great evil-looking black whirlpools welled up, burst and shrank, to be replaced by others. Around the star's limb, huge scarlet flames came into being like fantastic ferns, changing shape as though blown by an invisible wind and reaching for the other star before shredding and fluttering into nothingness.

The view disintegrated and, for a whole minute, the screen was dark. When the picture returned, a night scene was visible. The watchers were back on the planet, standing on a hill. The city sparkled with lights, though there was none of the wasteful commercial glare of a modern Earth city, no neon colours or waving, laser-writing beams. The sky was full of stars.

Out of the corner of her eye, Aurora saw Beaumont nudge Orlov.

"Orion's Belt!" he whispered. "There's Andromeda. Cassiopeia. All the constellations we see from Earth. And the stars! There's Antares. Sirius. Betelgeuse. This star system can't be too many light years away from the Solar System."

"Sssshhh! Later."

It seemed that dawn was approaching, for the sky lightened to pink in what might have been the east. It brightened so rapidly that again they knew they must be watching a simulation of some kind. As if to confirm this, the paintbrush appeared once more in the corner of the scene.

The two suns rose. They were now so close that the eye could hardly separate them, and they seemed wreathed in swirling vapour. Then, as they rose perhaps five degrees above the horizon—

All four of the watchers reeled back, involuntarily bringing their arms up in front of their eyes. A globe of searing, violet-white light burst outwards from the double sun. Within seconds, steam burst from all the city's waterways, leaving cracked trenches. Trees burst into flames and were gone. The city as a whole vanished in smoke, shrouds of which streamed away from the blazing glow that hung above the horizon.

Gouts of orange flame burst from the central volcano. Then it split apart and the view was obscured by steam and smoke. Other balls of fire rose from various points. In moments, everything had gone, virtually vaporized.

It was almost exactly like the effects of a hydrogen bomb, but multiplied many times. Yet evidently the planet still remained, a blackened husk, the surface they could see sterile and barren, smoking. The sky was now almost black, the atmosphere having been driven off.

Dominating the inky night now was an object which was awesomely beautiful, despite the destruction it had wrought. A tiny, bright star, surrounded by expanding shells and streamers of gas which fluoresced in a spectrum of colours—red, green, blue, violet—in what must be a flood of ultraviolet radiation.

The view pulled back swiftly, and the horizon became clearly the curve of a rocky ball, a crescent of ghastly, shifting light. No moon was visible as the planet shrank until it was like a tiny marble in the centre of the screen.

The surrounding stars shone coldly, unchanged, uncaring, the Milky Way a pearly band.

The scene faded, and once again a blank blue-grey screen faced them.

#

There was silence in the cabin. Everyone was stunned. Nobody wanted to be the first to break the spell. All felt that they had just witnessed a disaster of colossal and overwhelming proportions. Minako's eyes were brimming with tears, and the men too looked close to weeping.

Aurora was affected most strongly. She sat as if paralysed, her eyes wide open and an expression of horror on her face. It was as though she had experienced a personal tragedy.

Finally Verdet said softly: "*Sic transit gloria mundi.*"

"Yeah—but *what* world?" muttered Lundquist.

Beaumont spoke slowly. "It was only a simulation, wasn't it? Perhaps a warning of something that could—or was about to—happen but hadn't happened yet? Otherwise, how could they have recorded it?"

Aurora abruptly came to life and shook her head impatiently. "That's irrelevant. By now it *has* happened—you could tell it was inevitable."

"We're all familiar with the scenario," said Verdet. "It's been in stories and movies often enough. An inhabited planet's star goes nova, and the indigenes—the aliens—are forced to emigrate. Perhaps they didn't have time to build a lot of ships. Or they sent them out in lots of different directions, in the hope that at least some would arrive at a suitable planet. This one we're in failed, or went astray. And of course, if nothing else, they'd try to save their babies . . . "

He looked at Aurora, the light of revelation in his eyes. "Of course! At least one ship *did* reach Earth. And you—*you* were one of those babies! That explains all your—differences. We could see the people looked like you . . . "

She nodded. All of this had of course already passed through her own head. And it made some sort of sense. Yet . . .

"There are still lots of problems to solve," said Orlov. "How those people can appear so human. Why this ship seems too small to have come from another star. Why . . . "

"Once we get the people back on Earth onto the problem, we'll find the answers," said Beaumont confidently.

Explanations

The team resumed their work in the alien ship in an atmosphere of unreality. The world they had seen blasted to destruction on the screen seemed to stay with them, somehow more real than the one they were on. A feeling of imminent disaster hung over them, even though they knew it was illusory. The catastrophe they had just seen must have happened long ago—hundreds or perhaps even thousands of years in the past.

As they worked they all removed at least the upper portion of their suits, as it had become warm inside the ship.

Aurora made two discoveries, one merely interesting, the other of more immediate importance to them.

"The ship must somehow be tuned to people of the race who built it; that's why I'm the only one who can operate it, and why the Beacon, or remote control, only works for me," she had said early on. Trying other keypads on the control desk she found that one key caused what were clearly numbers—many were even familiar—to appear on the two black rectangles, confirming the impression that they were digital readouts. But the numbers made no sense, and flickered through apparently random sequences.

Another key, though, caused the red glow of the band around the upper sphere of the Beacon to brighten or diminish.

"It's drawing power from somewhere to recharge itself," suggested Beaumont. "If the power's lasted this long, there must be a good chance that it's virtually inexhaustible."

"Hmm. Maybe," said Orlov. "All the same, let's keep an eye on that black band and make sure it stays red. If we're now draining power at a higher rate, it could be it'll fail suddenly, and then we'd all be trapped in here."

"Optimistic sod!" said Beaumont cheerfully.

Orlov returned to the wall of the outer compartment, which seemed to intrigue him. "There's a lot going on beyond here," he said. "This room occupies only a fraction of the entire ship—even allowing for that damaged storage compartment. Ah!"

On the flat bulkhead just beyond the capsules and their tiny pathetic contents he had found another slight depression.

"Aurora!" He realized that he had used her real name. It seemed obligatory to do so now, somehow. "Could you drag yourself away and work your magic over here, please?"

She left the control desk and looked at the recess. "Are you sure it's safe?" she asked. "You remember what happened last time. Or suppose there's some sort of dangerous fuel in there, or something?"

"I don't think there's any need to worry. Whatever fuel there is—if there's any left—it's bound to be safely contained; these people weren't stupid. If you're worried about radiation, don't be. Robert has checked for that already, and found only slightly more than the background count."

"OK." Aurora placed her hand in the depression, and as before a rectangular opening appeared. At first it was dark within, but when she stepped over the threshold a reddish light suffused the area.

Inside was machinery. It looked highly efficient, the construction seemingly simple—almost certainly deceptively so. A gleaming cylindrical tube, almost two metres in diameter, ran in a curve which followed that of the ship's exterior; it reminded Aurora of a proton accelerator she had once seen, though on a much reduced scale. Its surface, though smooth and coppery, reflected green and bluish whorls which swirled in continuous motion like oil on water. There were other metallic humps, plus some plumbing and cables, all tidily aligned across the floor and running up the walls.

Orlov was right behind her, avidly recording everything with his video camera, and almost immediately Verdet appeared with his holo recorder.

Then there was a cry from the cabin behind them.

"This one's empty!" Lundquist had been examining the egg-shaped capsules, mainly in an attempt to see what sort of life-support system had been attached to them. Previously they had opened only at Aurora's touch, but now an extra one lay ajar.

"I just put my hand on this one at the far end of the top row, and its lid felt loose," Lundquist explained. "So I put a fingernail in the groove and lifted—and it just swung up. There's no baby inside. You can tell that there used to be one—see the depression where it lay? Incredible that it's still visible."

The others came to look, but there was little comment. Just one more mystery to be solved, seemed to be the general feeling. Aurora was filled with a certainty that she knew only too well who the occupant of that cocoon had been, and from the glances the others directed towards her it was pretty obvious that they'd come to the same conclusion, but no one felt ready to put it into words.

"I want to take a look outside this ship, now that I know where the power plant is," announced Orlov, clearly desperate to say something—anything at all—to break the silence. "There are still sections that are partly buried."

Lundquist looked at his wrist, then shook his head in annoyance and picked up his suit. "It's getting quite late," he said. "That ... picture show took quite a while. Let's finish up now, shall we? You could take a look at the outside tomorrow when you're fresh?"

"Good thinking," said Orlov. "Home, everyone!"

#

Earth was equally excited by the new wonders revealed during that day. Mission Control agreed that it provided some answers, but also posed more questions. Their first priority was to have the data and the "movie" analysed by their top experts, using the most powerful computers, in the hope of discovering something about the star and planet from which the alien ship and its human-seeming occupants must have come.

Among the public, hysteria had reached epidemic proportions. Not that this was causing any real problems for the authorities—yet. Bill Emmart, who seemed to be on constant duty of late, reported:

> *Crank organizations and nut cults are crawling out of the woodwork everywhere you look. The ufologists are having a field day, saying "I told you so!" to anyone who will listen. And a lot of the great unwashed are listening, now.*
>
> *"You know, sometimes I wish you guys had just found some nice deposits of ice or maybe useful minerals we could mine. Even a fossil or two, some microbes perhaps. But no. You have to go and find a flying saucer full of babies, and scenes of the Apocalypse with special effects that make Spielberg look like Méliès. All you need to find now to make the public really happy is a fluffy animal or a cute*

robot with a squeaky voice! You do that and I'm resigning.
Mission Control, out.

There were many smiles at this, but Orlov did not join in. Although his words would not arrive for many minutes, he spoke into the microphone as though holding a face-to-face conversation. "If you'd been here you wouldn't treat it as a joke," he said sternly. "Simulation or not, by now a world and all its people have been destroyed. Why does God allow . . . "

He choked off any further words, but it was obvious to all that his faith had been deeply shaken.

Beaumont put a hand on his shoulder. "Not *every* inhabitant of that planet has died, it seems," he said softly, with a nod towards Aurora, who was sitting on a chair removing one of her indoor slip-on shoes. "There may be many more, scattered throughout the Milky Way. There may even be more of them on Earth."

In an obvious attempt to lighten the mood, he turned to Aurora. "What's up? Feet hurting, love? Want me to rub them for you?"

"I've never shown anyone this before," she said. "I've always been a bit ashamed of what I thought was a deformity, but . . . "

She raised her leg to show her bare foot. The toes were stubby and boneless looking, just like the astronaut's and the babies'. "I thought you all ought to know. There's not much doubt that I'm one of them, is there?

"But the point is: no matter how human I—*we*—appear, we're *not* human, *can't* be. Do humans regenerate new limbs? Do humans usually look like me when they're nearly eighty years old? Can they heal people with a touch? Yes, OK"—as she saw Bryan open his mouth to speak—"I know some people do claim to be healers, laying on of hands and all that. But they've hardly replaced doctors and modern medicine, have they? Isn't that right, Bob?"

Lundquist nodded. "There do seem to be substantiated cases, but, like all the so-called psi powers—including telepathy, clairvoyance and Bryan's dowsing—they seem to be fugitive, and recalcitrant when it comes to testing under scientific conditions. Which reminds me: I hope you're prepared to be a guinea pig for quite a while when we get back to Earth, Anne—er, Aurora."

"Huh. We'll see," was her only answer.

Beaumont got a card game underway—something which Aurora normally avoided whenever possible, seeing little point in such pursuits. However, there was a mood pervading the Refectory and anything which would help to dispel it should be encouraged, so she was the first to join in with him.

They played for a while, with Beaumont winning easily. After a while Minako, discouraged by a run of hopeless hands, dropped out and sat aside, obviously brooding on something.

Orlov tried casually to cheer her up, but she turned away his remarks. Then she said: "We have some unfinished business, I think, Dr Beaumont."

Beaumont's face whitened. "Oh. That."

"Yes—*that*. I think you owe me some explanation for what you said?"

Seeing that the others were looking from one to the other in puzzlement—except for Verdet, who clearly had at least some idea of what was going on—Beaumont explained, haltingly, about the misunderstanding between Verdet and Minako during their journey alone.

When he'd done there was a long silence. All eyes were on him.

Averting his eyes from Aurora, he said, haltingly: "OK. Yes, there's more to it than that. I'm sorry. You have to know."

He drew a deep breath and looked up at the Igloo's ceiling, as if a merciful Fate might—might *just*—do him a favour by sending a meteorite crashing through it to obliterate him.

"It was me all the time."

No one else spoke. No one took pity on him.

"I—I leaked the news to the media—or at least to a contact of mine in the media—on Earth."

There was another long pause and then Aurora's violet eyes blazed, a fearsome sight.

"Bryan, you *bastard*! How *could* you? After all we've been through together! I thought you were my . . . You *swore* to me it wasn't you!"

"Well, I couldn't find a way of just letting you all know, could I? Drop it nonchalantly into the conversation over the cornflakes in between asking you to pass the milk, sort of thing?"

His flippancy wasn't working, and he realized it quickly.

"I mean, it didn't really matter, after all—not until someone else was accused."

He shrugged, the sort of shrug an arrested criminal gives when he recognizes that the cops know everything, that the game's up.

"Oh, it's the old story. I got into bad financial difficulties. Those credit cards—they make it so easy, don't they? And I happen to like really expensive hi-fi equipment, and flashy cars, and top-of-the–range computers . . . It's amazing where it goes, isn't it? Well, they were threatening to sue me, and that could have ended my career in space if it was found out. Especially if I went to prison! I was lucky to keep it from them as long as I did."

He looked as if he were about to burst into tears.

"Yeah, I know it's a mug's game, but then I met this guy from a media company, and he said they'd pay off all my debts, with a bit on top—OK, quite a lot on top—if I'd report back any snippets of information that were, you know, exclusive. And all confidential, of course. They had no idea how lucky they were going to be!

"Anyway, I was offered big money if I came up with any 'scoops', and my contact had authority to act as my agent. They could have ruined my career if it got out, too.

"I suppose it all sounds a pretty poor excuse . . .

"Sorry, Minako," he said intensely, suddenly turning to her.

Then he looked directly at Aurora.

"I'm even more sorry it had to affect you. But you *were* the big news, weren't you? You can see, can't you? I had to do it." As though they were now totally alone, he added quietly. "It doesn't make any difference to—you know—us? I do love you, you know."

After a long moment the lines of Aurora's face relaxed, and she leant over and hugged him. "You great big softie!" she said, her Scottish brogue coming through. "It isn't really that important. They were bound to get hold of the news sooner or later, weren't they? But you *should* have told me about your problem. You should have been honest with me—with us all."

Beaumont now looked embarrassed. So did the others, though for different reasons.

Orlov, trying hard to look stern, said: "I can't say what action may be taken back on Earth—it's out of my hands, you understand. And now"—obviously keen to get out of the Refectory as quickly as he decently could—"I think I'll turn in."

"Yes, I'm feeling a bit of a raspberry, too!" said Verdet with something half-way between a grin and a leer.

"That's "gooseberry"," said Lundquist.

"*Comment?*" asked Verdet earnestly. There was a twinkle in his eye as he left.

Now alone in the Refectory, Beaumont and Aurora hugged each other. Soon the hugs developed into passionate embraces. After half an hour it was Aurora who said: "Do you think we could risk going to, you know, just *one* of our rooms tonight?"

#

Much later, Beaumont startled Aurora by suddenly sitting up straight in her bunk, nearly dislodging her onto the floor, and saying: "Of course, you realize we'll have to get married now?"

Aurora groaned, turning her eyes heavenward.

"No, I'm serious. I know it's considered, well, a bit old-fashioned these days," he said. "But why don't we, you know, make it all legal? That's if you'll have me."

"If only it were that simple," Aurora sighed. "Have you really thought it through? I've lived with my knowledge for a long time, and it's one reason why I've avoided . . . emotional entanglements up to now. By the time you're an old man I may look like your daughter. Could you live with that?"

"I could if you could. After all, it wouldn't be the first time a dirty old man had a beautiful young wife, would it?" He grinned, looking very young himself. "I do love you, and that's all that matters."

"Well, then . . . " She paused for a long time, staring at the ceiling. "Well, I guess the answer's 'Yes'. But let's tie the knot right away. Why wait? At least it'll give the media something different to talk about!"

"I wish we'd told them about us before," said Beaumont, stroking her hair.

Aurora said nothing. She was too busy nibbling his ear.

#

Next morning the report from Earth was fairly brief. Mission Control asked them to find out as much about the propulsion system of the alien craft as possible. ("Hah! Did they think I wasn't going to anyway?" huffed Orlov.) Experts were working to analyse the "movie," but it was too soon for them to have come up with any results. There was news from all around Earth of disc-shaped craft in the skies, some of them landing or crashing. A farmer in Berkshire, England, claimed to have unearthed a buried one while ploughing. Also in England there was a resurgence of crop circles, which had been debunked as a hoax 'way back in the 1990s. Needless to say, none of these claims had been substantiated, but the populace now seemed prepared to believe just about anything. As a corollary, every crank belief or theory was being disinterred and held up as having been true all along but suppressed by the authorities in a monstrous conspiracy.

White-gowned Druids were holding a ceremony at Stonehenge; they now claimed to be the true descendants of the star people. The stones could be made to prove it . . .

#

In the Igloo a very different ceremony was being held. Orlov had obviously been tickled to be asked to perform a wedding ceremony, as "Captain" of their expedition. He appeared wearing an impressive cosmonaut's dress uniform that no one had ever seen before—he must have brought it as part of his personal allowance.

Having got them all seated except Beaumont and Aurora, he performed the ceremony. He seemed like a strange blend of Russian Orthodox priest and American Justice of the Peace. His efforts were oddly moving.

To Aurora's surprise, Minako had come to her, rather shyly, on hearing the news of their intended marriage, and had offered her a golden ring. "It was my grandmother's," was her only explanation. Now, Beaumont placed the ring on the third finger of Aurora's left hand. It was a remarkably good fit. For a moment she stared at it incredulously. Marriage had never been on her agenda.

"I now pronounce you husband and wife!" Orlov announced proudly. Bride and groom exchanged a long, lingering kiss, to the accompaniment of applause and whoops.

During the party which followed, Beaumont asked Orlov how he came to have a knowledge of the US civil wedding ceremony.

"Oh, was married once, to American girl," replied the Russian, reverting to peasant mode. "Lasted three months. Three months too long. She tramp!"

Beaumont had brought his minisynth into the Refectory and, at Minako's request, tuned it to sound like something between a harmonium and an old church pipe organ. It was an unusual but evocative combination, and Minako displayed a hitherto undisclosed talent by playing a selection of Japanese folk tunes. There was much laughter at their attempts to dance in the confined space.

As the newlyweds left for a few brief hours together, Minako again entered into the spirit of the occasion, catching a bunch of paper flowers which Aurora had flung in her direction. Everyone clapped this, and there were more toasts in orange juice and cola.

"We should have had some good Russian vodka!" said Orlov.

"Hah! Saki is better," claimed Minako cheerfully.

"*Skol!*" said Lundquist, raising his orange juice.

Mission Control allowed the ceremony to be transmitted on TV and immediately thereafter released on videodisc and wafer, and around the world the public lapped it up.

Then it was back to work.

#

Out at the alien ship, all efforts were centred on clearing sand and rock from the rest of its perimeter and as much of the underside as possible. They set to with a will.

Verdet had half of his body underneath, clearing away soil from what looked like a piece of steering mechanism, when a shout came from Beaumont. "Claude—watch out!"

The heavy craft, no longer stable, suddenly shifted and tilted. It gave out a metallic groaning noise like a leviathan in pain, audible even through the thin air, and began to fall on him.

Orlov caught hold of his arm and yanked, and Verdet scrambled out with a fraction of a second to spare as the ship smacked down violently, causing a minor earthquake and showers of sand.

After that they were more careful. Not having for a moment expected an operation of this type to be necessary, they had not come equipped with any-thing resembling struts or props. But some of them began collecting suitably sized rocks which could be used to shore up the ship where it was exposed. The low gravity helped them to move quite large, flat boulders between them. It was of course quite impossible to move the ship, but they could at least try to prevent it from shifting again.

At last the greater part of the exterior was visible and the ship stood almost level. Minako walked around it taking video while Orlov and Verdet began their examination. Beaumont and Aurora climbed inside, as she wanted to see if any of the other controls would produce results, or even if there might be a further "movie" or other message. But for them to be able to work there comfortably for any length of time would mean sealing the interior so that they could remove at least the top parts of their suits. This would make it difficult for the others to come and go from the engineering section.

Orlov came up with the answer to that. "You go inside, and seal the canopy. Then open the hatch that leads to the damaged area, dash back into the cockpit and seal the central door behind you. After that you two can do whatever you like in there"—there were some sniggers over the suit radios at that, but he ignored them—"and we can enter from the outside through the damaged part, wearing suits—the hole is plenty big enough."

The red band on the Beacon now glowed steadily, so Aurora was able to follow his instructions without difficulty. As she tried to close the cabin door, though, it jammed partly open, just as it had when she'd first opened it. A fifteen-centimetre gap was left, through which air was whistling out. Already light-headed, Aurora tried again, and a third time.

At last the door closed.

"We'll have to watch that," said Beaumont as the pressure built again. "If it was an ordinary door we could oil it. But I haven't yet figured out how these doors work."

"Yes. And I wonder where the air keeps coming from?"

This was something everyone dearly wanted to know. With Lundquist helping them, they examined all the mechanisms now exposed, using radiation counters, magnetometers, even an ultrasound scanner and Lundquist's portable X-ray machine.

Attempting to cut open any of the machinery was of course not to be countenanced. If it ever became necessary, or allowed, it would probably be done by a later expedition, bringing experts in fields not previously anticipated to be useful on Mars.

They hoped it would never be necessary.

Where in the Universe——?

Vitali Orlov was making his report to Earth.

" . . . we found, by accident really, that when Aurora operated one of the controls a strong magnetic field was generated in a sort of dome or hump in what we call the engine room. *Really* strong—I wouldn't want to stay around it for long, though it seems to be shielded almost completely from the cabin by the walls and bulkheads of the inner section. Nothing else appeared to happen, though.

"There's no radiation to speak of, though what there is varies from place to place. We managed to get images of the interiors of some apparatus, and I'll be transmitting those when I've finished talking. Some of them opened remarkably easily—perhaps for ease of maintenance. That was a big help.

"Here's a summary of what we think we've found—though no doubt your experts will want to have their say.

"First, the ship seems to have an ion-drive for forward movement in space, vastly more advanced than anything we're working on. It doesn't seem to be the only method of propulsion, though. Some of the machinery is, frankly, inexplicable; we can't imagine *what* it does. But there is a big electromagnetic torus which extends right round the perimeter of the ship, except where it breaks at the ion-drive. Like an almost-closed horseshoe.

"There just isn't enough room for reaction mass for an interstellar mission, so this lends support to the theory that it must have come from some huge mother ship, or ark, which perhaps passed right through the Solar System and out again.

"If that's the case, though, surely you'd expect at least one scout ship—or whatever—to have reached Earth safely, so there should be more people like Aurora walking around. She managed to keep the fact quiet, so I suppose they could be doing the same—but perhaps now they could be persuaded to come out of hiding? Maybe you could broadcast an appeal, or something?

"Sorry. I'm supposed to be making a factual report, but we can't help ideas running through our heads, can we?

"There doesn't seem to be space inside for enough life-support—food, water and so on for the woman and the babies for more than a matter of weeks. A lot longer if they were in suspended animation, of course, but we can't find any evidence that they were. There's no cryogenic apparatus—nothing we can find that would place them in hibernation.

"There's always the possibility that they had invented some kind of drug, of course, of which only a tiny quantity would be needed. So Dr Lundquist has run blood and tissue tests on the woman and one of the babies. There are one or two unusual characteristics, but no unknown drugs—at least that he could detect.

"Now, air. They brought *some* oxygen with them; but they have a machine—which we're going to find very useful ourselves on future missions, if we can duplicate it. I'm sure we can crack it . . . Where was I? A machine, using some sort of catalytic process which converts carbon dioxide directly, continuously and apparently easily into oxygen.

"During its flight it would have converted the CO_2 breathed out by the occupants. Dr Lundquist thinks it is possible that the carbon left over was combined with other elements and transmuted into food. That would help solve the life-support problem, of course—but it's mainly theory at the moment. It wouldn't contribute much, in any case.

"It does explain how it keeps filling the ship with air. With carbon dioxide making up ninety-five per cent of the atmosphere of Mars, it just keeps extracting the oxygen. Easy!

"We ran a test with Aurora, and she thinks that mental—psionic, if you like—power may be used, at least partly, to control the ship, and even to regulate the motors. That would explain the lack of normal-looking electronic controls. But what she has done so far has scared her, and I agreed that we should take it no further. We certainly aren't ready to fly the ship! Though actually I'm pretty sure that would be impossible anyway—the engine section is too badly damaged. Pity.

"There's a huge mass of some kind at the centre of the ship, near the bottom. And I mean *huge*; makes us wonder if there's a tiny amount of superdense matter in there, perhaps forming some part of the propulsion system. Personally, I'm wondering if they were controlling gravity in some way. Maybe they invented some form of antigravity—it's not impossible, is it?

"We still don't know what to make of that quite large empty area which was the most badly damaged in the crash. It's a bit of a mystery.

"That's about all for now. Orlov, over and out."

#

He had hardly finished when he started to receive an incoming message that had been winging its way through the ether as he talked. As now seemed inevitable, their earlier transmission, which had included the scenes of destruction on the alien planet, had raised more questions than it had answered.

. . . our linguistics people are having some success. They say there's no way it could be a truly alien language. The syntax, phonetics, morphemes are typically human in origin. More on that when some sort of translation's available, but the message definitely seems like a warning.

Meanwhile, the stellar astronomers have been analysing the star-patterns that could be seen in the night-shot, and in the view from space at the end. As you must have noticed yourselves, they look very familiar, meaning that the star-system can't be too far from our own.

So our best computers were put to work plotting the constellations as they would appear from the closest likely stars. They change surprisingly little, actually, until you travel a long, long way, but the computers would be able to find very slight angular changes. You have to bear in mind that we've been looking for a binary or double star, which limits the field a bit.

We had a problem there. We couldn't find any star that fits within ten, even twenty light years. We extended the field, but no star would fit. We even got the computers to take into account the time a ship might have been travelling, compared with the time light takes us to reach us from various stars. No good. In the end we had to give up.

But one of our men, Shiro Takeda, pointed out what should have been obvious: if we were looking at constellations in the sky of a planet of another star, there should be an extra star somewhere—the Sun. For instance, if we were looking from a planet of Alpha Centauri, the closest possibility, the Sun would be in the constellation of Cassiopeia. But it just isn't there.

Takeda decided to try another approach. I won't go into the technical details now, but he was sure that those constellations, as they appear, could only have been seen from one solar system that fits the facts: our own, though presumably a long time ago. He took the computer-simulated sky back, even to millions of years. But he couldn't get it to fit that way, either . . .

There must be some other explanation—perhaps distortion due to some other effect. It's even been suggested that the process of your videoing the screen and transmitting it to Earth could be responsible for some distortion. and the computer's working on that. But personally I think this is clutching at straws.

If it was Earth, then obviously we still can't explain the double star, or the nova explosion. Frankly, we're baffled. Perhaps what we've been watching is nothing but an in-flight movie—someone's imaginary idea of an alternate reality? We don't know. But you'd better believe we're working on it . . .

Mission Control, out.

"Phew! What in the name of blazes have we uncovered here?" said Vitali.

Despite the excitement of their discoveries, and the strange results of the analysis, there was a sense of anticlimax and frustration around the camp, where the team was taking a much-needed rest day and performing neglected housekeeping chores. There was in any case very little more that they could do at the alien craft with the instruments they had with them, which had never been designed for this sort of discovery.

It seemed that the scene of action had moved to Earth. Yet scientists there, in many fields, must be itching for the opportunity to get to Mars themselves and do hands-on research on the ship—not to mention its humanlike "crew."

Aurora seemed particularly distracted. She would sit for hours, a puzzled, faraway expression on her face, and would sometimes not respond when spoken to until the second or third attempt.

Finally Beaumont sat beside her and put an arm around her waist. "What's the problem, love?" he asked gently.

She blinked and looked at him, her eyes slowly focusing. "Yes. You're the only one who could really understand, aren't you? You know all about those . . . visions I used to get. That most of the audience saw at that rock concert."

He nodded. "Go on."

"I've been getting them here on Mars, too. They won't leave me alone. Especially since we saw that film, or whatever it was. Sometimes I see them superimposed on reality. They fill my dreams. I think I'm going mad—it's like a sort of schizophrenia.

"The thing is, I'm sure they hold the answer to all this. To everything we've discovered here, perhaps. There *must* be some connection—mustn't there?

"If only I could get a handle on them. They cluster at the edges of my mind, but I can't grab them. Am I making sense?"

Her face was anguished, and he wanted to hold her close, and soothe her. But he just nodded again. "Yes. I think so."

She tapped her blonde head. When she had left Earth her hair had been cropped quite short, but she had allowed it to grow much longer than regulation length despite the occasional difficulty of tucking it inside her helmet, and she now looked much more as she had done back in the days of the Gas Giants. "It's all in here," she said. "And there must be a reason. I feel I shall never be at peace until I get at it. But how? *How?*"

"Have you ever thought of hypnosis?"

"Occasionally, yes. I don't believe it would work on me."

"I think it might. It's much more widely accepted by the medical establishment than it was even twenty or thirty years ago. As long as it's done by an expert, of course. It seems to be a way of reaching the subconscious, which may be just what you need. Come on—let's find out."

Without waiting for her to agree, he called: "Doc! Can you spare us a minute please?"

Lundquist looked up from the instrument case he was checking and reloading. "What's the problem? Not birth control?"

Beaumont and Aurora looked at other blankly, then burst out laughing. Such matters had been so far from their thoughts. "Oh, no—I've had my shots!" said Aurora. "I'm due for a booster soon though, as I expect you know."

Beaumont said: "Are you any good at hypnosis, Doc?"

"Hypnosis?" It was Lundquist's turn to look blank for a moment. They explained the situation.

"As a matter of fact I did dabble with it a bit when I was a student. Enough to know it can work, anyway. OK, I'm willing to give it a go, if you are. How about tonight? If you're going to come up with a revelation, it's best if every-one is around to hear, isn't it?"

"We-ell . . . "

Aurora looked doubtful, but finally agreed.

#

There was an air of expectancy as the team gathered in the Refectory that night. Out of deference to Aurora's wishes, Lundquist had started his attempt with only Aurora and her husband in the room. Beaumont had spent a little time briefing the doctor on what he knew of the key moments in her life, and had lent him his pendulum to use as a point of focus for Aurora's eyes.

It took only seconds of Lundquist's chanted litany—"You are feeling tired. Your eyes are tired and heavy. Tired and heavy. Heavy as lead . . . "—before Aurora was under.

Beaumont beckoned to Orlov, who was awaiting his cue, and the rest filed in quietly.

Lundquist seemed uncertain how to proceed. "What is your name?"

"I have no name. But I am known as Aurora."

"Where were you born, Aurora?"

"On the Second Home."

"What is the Second Home? Where is it?"

A pause. "I—don't know. It just is."

Robert abandoned that line of questioning. "Aurora, you are ten years old. Where are you?"

In a little-girl voice, Aurora said: "I'm at school at Nairn. We're going to see Granny Petrie on Sunday." Her face visibly paled. "I—don't want to think about that—"

Her eyelids flickered, and it seemed that she was about to wake up.

Hastily, Lundquist said: "That's all right, you don't have to. Aurora, it is June, 1972. You are on stage, playing in a concert with a group called the Gas Giants. What do you see?"

"Faces. A sea of faces. Swaying, like the waves. They are all looking at me. I am playing music, and they like it, they want to be part of it, part of me. We are all part of one. No, not all. Some are not able to be part of the whole; their minds are not open. That is sad."

Her voice changed, became deeper. "But now everyone is happy. It is the Music Festival, and everyone is always happy at the MusicFest. I see the Two Mountains. The people walk among trees and ferns, along the waterways. Everyone joins in the Music. Not all play an instrument. But I do. I am a Musician." She sounded proud.

Robert interrupted. "Aurora, where are you now?"

"Why, on the Second Home, of course. But my name is not Aurora. My name is . . . is . . .

"Father!"

Abruptly, her eyes opened wide, and a look of such incredible pain and loss suffused her face that the others had to look away, not wishing to intrude on her private grief. She hid her face in her hands and for some minutes her body was racked by sobs. Beaumont tried to put an arm about her and draw her to him, but she did not respond. The moment passed, but Aurora was now fully awake.

Refusing further hypnosis, at least for that night, she stumbled off to bed, white-faced. Her husband followed her, trying to speak reassuring nothings to her.

The others remained, talking among themselves.

Disruption

The next morning Aurora was depressed.

"I was a failure, wasn't I?" she said to Beaumont.

"Not at all," he replied. "That session was invaluable. We learnt things we didn't know. Like the fact that some of your memories—perhaps implanted memories?—are not yours but those of someone else, perhaps your own father's. Or was it a "Father" in the religious sense?"

"No. I don't think so. I felt better after I'd had a cry. But I know it's still in here." She tapped her temple in frustration. "How the hell are we going to get at it, Bryan?"

"I've had an idea about that. But I'll tell you about it later. I want to think on it a bit more."

Orlov came in from the comm desk. He did not look very pleased.

"Mission Control want us to go back to Camp One," he said without preamble. The other team-members raised their heads. "They say there's nothing more we can achieve here, with the equipment we have on hand, and we could do more harm than good if we continued to poke around. Oh, not in so many words did they say that, but it's what they meant. They'd like us to continue with our original scientific programme until it's time for us to return. Work on the alien ship will continue when the next team of so-called experts arrives. How do you become an expert on alien human life? That they could not answer me!

"It shows how much they know. They wanted us to take the Beacon back to Earth with us. I said, in the first place it seems locked in position inside the ship now, and in the second it appears to be essential for operating many of the mechanisms on the ship. That's not all. Only Aurora has been able to operate it. They've been putting out appeals on all the media, on every channel, every e-group, for anyone who resembles Aurora in physical appearance, or has had any kind of experience with "visions," or has healing or regenerative powers, to come forward.

"They've had to stop that. They're blaming me. Well, it's true I did suggest it—but they would have thought of it anyway, wouldn't they? Of course, every crank has been coming forward. Some bleached their hair. One even wore a long wig!

"They couldn't afford not to check any of them out, of course, just in case there is a genuine alien among them. But they have drawn a blank."

What Orlov said next surprised Aurora.

"How do you fancy staying here on Mars, Aurora? Or at least coming back here very soon?"

She turned a worried face towards him, not sure if he was joking or not.

Orlov did not seem to notice, but continued: "Robert, they want you to seal up the woman's body, making sure it's totally airtight, and one of the babies, complete in its capsule. We are to bring them back to Earth. It may mean taking fewer rock samples with us than the original plan demanded, but that's taking second place now, of course.

"They actually seem serious about a couple of us staying on the surface. They're looking into the logistics of it at the moment. They'll probably ask for volunteers, but . . . "

He turned to Aurora again.

"There will probably be a gap of only a month or so between us leaving and the next team arriving. Mars has a really high priority—at last. I'm afraid the military are in on the act—will they never learn?—but at least it means they are putting all their efforts into their new high-energy booster, and all our governments have high hopes for what they'll learn from the advanced technology we've got down here. Oh yes—Bryan, you'll probably be pleased to know that the next mission will make a stop-over on Phobos. It seems some scientists are taking seriously your idea—only they're calling it *their* idea, no surprises there—that Phobos might be the mother ship, a hollow asteroid ark left in a parking orbit.

"Well, I think that's about all. It's enough, isn't it? We have our orders. Start breaking camp."

#

Rover 1 was only half-an-hour from the landing site when an emergency signal blinked on its dashboard. It meant a message had come in from Earth which was so important that it needed attention at once and couldn't wait until they got back to base, so had been relayed to the rovers.

Orlov flipped a switch.

Aurora, who had been dozing as she bounced in her seat over the rocky ground, woke to hear Bill Emmart's voice begin talking, fast and urgently:

> *Mission Control to Orlov. You will need to act immediately; this message will be delayed reaching you because that duff relay satellite will be the one overhead to you when it arrives. I'll keep sending, so that one of the others will receive it.*
>
> *Our orbiting solar and X-ray telescopes have shown an increase in radiation levels from the Sun. Could mean an SPE. It might be nothing, but signs are it's gonna be a monster one, and the stream is heading your way. There's been a big group of sunspots building up for a while.*
>
> *Vitali, we suggest you start protecting the Hut the moment you get back. You know how. You'll have an hour at most before levels get dangerous—if they do. We'll be monitoring the situation, of course, and we'll send you regular updates.*
>
> *Good luck, guys! Over and out.*

"Roger, Bill, we got your message," said Orlov. "Bloody hell! What timing! Well there's nothing we can do until we get back—then we'll get right onto it. Keep us informed. Out."

The team was already feeling tired and sweaty after their long drive, but an SPE—a Solar Particle Event—was an ever-present danger on a long mission such as theirs.

Orlov contacted Rover 2 and said: "Did you all hear that message from Earth?"

They had, and had woken Lundquist, since as physician he was likely to be needed if the flare did indeed prove to be a bad one.

Verdet said: "I know we were all briefed before the mission, but what are our chances, Doc?"

"It depends on a lot of factors. The atmosphere will only shield us to a small extent, but as long as we can get under cover we *should* be OK. Otherwise, there's the risk of radiation sickness—bad sunburn, loss of hair—you all know the score . . . Plus a greater chance of getting cancer in future—the hazard of that is twice as high for you women. Sorry about sexual equality and all that, girls, but that's the way it is."

Nobody laughed.

At last the two rovers, separated by only a few hundred metres, came into view of Base Camp. The Sun was setting almost directly behind the conical Lander, and the two half-tanks which formed their living- and working-quarters glittered golden in the evening light. As the Sun sank, the glow leaked rapidly from the sky, whose colour passed through a sequence of amber, rose, magenta, ultramarine and finally near-black. Stars sprang into view as if flicked onto a dark canvas by an invisible brush.

When the Sun rose again, its light could well be accompanied by a hail of particles and electromagnetic radiation of all wavelengths as a shock-wave in the solar wind exploded in their direction.

As she stepped down from Rover 1, Aurora arched backward, hands on hips, trying to ease her cramped neck-muscles. As she did so, stars moved across her field of view, through the transparent faceplate. "I wonder which one it is?" she mused aloud. "Is it even in our universe at all?"

It took some time to unload all their equipment and surplus stores. The precious mylar tubes which contained the female astronaut and the dully gleaming cocoon holding the baby were taken into the stores section, where the temperature was kept uniformly low by the simple expedient of its having a silvered outer skin to reflect the light and heat from the Sun.

As decreed by the Mission Plan for such an emergency, the first thing they did to protect themselves was to unroll the Blimp and spread it out. Next, the big elevators—wings, effectively—which served as fins for steering in flight, and were separate compartments, had to be pumped full of water from the electrolysis plant. While they were away, this had filled a large tank and shut itself off automatically. The fins were then positioned, with difficulty, to where they would give the best shielding effect outside the Hut.

The next job was to drape the flaccid Blimp itself over the Hut. Its main job was done and it had been fully tested; now its silvery fabric would provide extra shielding. It was large enough to be folded back and forth several times, but they deliberately gathered it into horizontal pleats, using cords running through special loops, to create a highly crenulated appearance.

Both rovers were jacked up and their back wheels, with their thick metal-mesh tyres, were removed and replaced by a simple device: a sort of partially enclosed paddle-wheel with a movable, funnel-like spout near the top. Set spinning, these scooped up Martian regolith and showered it, like a snow-plough, over the Hut. Using shovels, the team helped make sure this was evenly distributed. A fold of airship material was lapped over each layer and taped into place, so that it retained the soil and prevented it from falling off. Orlov made sure that the Hut was covered by a sandwich over ten centimetres deep before they cut the motors.

"We'd better cover the Greenhouse, too," said Lundquist. "A dose of radiation could throw all our results out—or even kill our samples." The Greenhouse was his chief responsibility aside from his duties as physician. It consisted of a series of plastic domes which housed a variety of edible plants and vegetables growing in Martian soil to which controlled nutrients had been added, under a carefully monitored atmosphere. Future colonies would have to rely on agriculture for survival; also, certain plants had been selected for their ability to convert carbon dioxide into oxygen. An oasis of green would be psychologically uplifting, too.

Panting with exertion and streaming with sweat, at last they entered the Hut, which Lundquist had already brought up to full pressure. Tired as they were, they had to undergo the ritual of vacuuming their suits and belongings to remove as much of the insidious fins as they could leave in the airlock. A shower would have been better, but water was too precious.

Inside, and de-suited, some sank gratefully into seats, others went off to attend to personal matters. All obviously felt depressed that within a few days, their mission had slipped from high excitement into routine—and now into danger.

#

Next morning the Sun rose looking no different from usual, casting the webbed shadow of the big S-band antenna across their camp, the sand pocked with thousands of tiny dark craters: their footprints.

Orlov activated the Orbiter's instruments to transmit the telescopic image of the Sun down to them via the relay satellite currently overhead so that they could see it on the big screen.

There was no doubt about it now. A patch of the Sun's photosphere, normally at 6000EC, had heated to several million degrees. X-rays, ultraviolet light, cosmic rays, magnetic fields—all were way above norm. The speed of the stream of particles in the solar wind, normally up to four hundred kilometres per second, would now be doubling.

"This one could reach a thousand rem. Maybe even twice that," said Lundquist. "You realize we deliberately planned this mission during a period of low solar activity, to try to avoid this? It's damnably bad luck. But the Sun's no respecter of persons . . . "

"What would a dangerous dose be, again?" asked Verdet gloomily, like someone probing at a sore tooth.

"A maximum of six hundred rem is recommended. But, don't forget, that's the amount to be absorbed by your skin over your whole career in space. You may remember that one reason for the choice of a, well, mainly middle-aged crew was that none of us intended to have any more children."

Minako, as a meteorologist, seemed far too interested—indeed, excited—to be worried. "This will be affecting radio communications from Earth," she said. "If the flare was aimed at Earth they would be seeing the aurora at night, too." She looked round at Aurora. "Oh, yes! How appropriate."

Aurora smiled weakly. Minako continued: "But it's not, whereas *we* are in a direct line. I doubt if we'll get any aurorae here—the magnetic field is too weak. But it might be worth looking, all the same."

From the expressions on their faces, Aurora knew she was voicing a thought that had occurred to many of her colleagues. "You know, looking at this sight I can't help thinking of that alien 'movie.' That was speeded up, of course, but those sunspots, the bright faculae—those writhing prominences . . . " She tweaked the controls so that the glare of the solar disc was darkened but the beautiful foliation of the magenta-pink flames dominated the screen.

Orlov, who had been selected for his expertise as a pilot and engineer and had only basic training in astronomy, said, "I am sure this is stupid question, but is no way our Sun could become nova like one which destroyed that planet?"

From his suddenly assumed thick accent it was obvious that he was really talking to make conversation. Minako apparently took him seriously. "No. Our Sun will probably never become a nova. In five billion years' time it will expand into a Red Giant, and will swallow up the inner planets, including the Earth and Mars. But by then humanity will have changed out of all recognition—if it still exists at all—and will surely have found other homes out in the stars. If the Sun were ever to become a nova, it would be after the Red Giant stage. But current thinking is that it will become a planetary nebula for fifty thousand years, then a White Dwarf—and stay that way just about forever."

"Oh, good, so we can all breathe easy!" said Beaumont with an attempt at a grin. He obviously found her serious answer and earnest manner amusing.

Minako stared at him, reddening.

To change the subject, Verdet said, mopping his brow, "I'm not breathing so easily—is it me, or is it getting hot in here?"

"Yes, that is the problem with having to shield the living quarters. We can't use the normal temperature-control system on the outer skin," said Orlov. "We're shielded from sunlight, but we're all producing lots of watts inside. We've got the emergency air-conditioning unit working at full blast. I'm afraid we're just going to have to put up with this until the danger is past."

Now that the subject had been raised, everyone suddenly felt several degrees hotter, and some began to discard clothing.

"This could get interesting!" muttered Beaumont. Aurora glared at him good-naturedly.

The "incoming message" alarm sounded from the comm desk. Distorted by crackles and bleeps, and at times almost inaudible, the voice of Mission Control wanted to know if they were all safely under cover. Orlov reassured them that they had done all they could. While his message, repeated several times in case of communications problems, was on its way, another message came though:

We know you won't be able to act on this for a while, but here's an update on the analysis of the data you've been sending. At least it'll give you something to occupy your minds!

Nothing new on the appearance of the constellations. You'd have to travel at least a hundred light years to see noticeable changes in, say, the Big Dipper, and at that distance the Sun would be lost in a naked-eye view. You have to appreciate that we're not normally geared up to looking at this sort of problem—our space probes travel only light minutes, or light hours at most.

But another team has been looking at the geography and geology of the alien planet—as much as could be seen. And . . . well, are you ready for this?

They think it's Mars! *There are differences, apart from the obvious ones—the vegetation, the presence of the city and so on. And some geological features are not the same as they appear to us. But the experts say that the chances against those which do match up appearing in the same positions on another world are, well, astronomical.*

They say the figure-of-eight city encircles two of the smaller volcanoes on Tharsis: Uranius Tholus—that's the one in the foreground—and Ceraunius Tholus, the bigger one, looming behind it. That would make the city really vast; it would cover an area of hundreds of square kilometres.

Needless to say, not . . . [a burst of static] *. . . agrees with this analysis, but I* *have to say that it looks pretty convincing. The constellations wouldn't look any different than they would from Earth at the same period, as you well know. Present thinking is that there must have been a brief Martian civilization—or a colony from another star, maybe?—millions of years ago, and all trace of it has since been obliterated by volcanic activity, the flash floods, the erosion of dust storms, and so on. Only the main volcanoes are still in the same place. Oh, we think there's an impact crater missing on the flank of Ceraunius, though we might be seeing a lake there instead.*

All that doesn't bring us any closer to explaining the binary star, of course. We're still working on that . . .

Meanwhile, I'm putting my money on the next mission landing close to Uranius Tholus, with an archaeological team on board.

Good luck with the SPE, you guys. We're all rooting for you.

Mission Control, out.

This news did indeed give the team something else to distract them from the solar storm, and there was much discussion. Then Minako, who had been preoccupied with her meteorological monitor board, looked up and said: "It may be due to the solar flare, or it may not, but the weather on Mars is getting stirred up too. We've only been getting wind speeds of around ten metres per second lately, but that's going to rise to fifty, sixty—maybe even higher."

"Will that matter?" asked Lundquist.

"Probably not. If the speed is high enough it might cause "saltation"—you know? Sand grains skip across the surface and propel smaller ones into the atmosphere—which is why the sky is pink. We might be in a bit of a fog for a few days. Interesting!"

Her face was as animated as anyone had ever seen it.

As if on cue, the view on the big screen, which Aurora had flipped from the seething image of the Sun to an outside camera, showed a dust devil rising from the desert. Two or three others swirled into life, and together they marched in formation across the landscape, twisting and interlinking, like weird genies released from their bottles.

#

Three hours later, the view had been almost entirely obliterated, and, when the dust clouds did clear briefly, the landscape rocked as the camera was shaken on its mounting.

Something metallic flicked into view and vanished, but appeared again, and again.

"The Blimp! This stronger wind is getting under it and lifting it. I hope to God the gusts don't shake it right off," said Beaumont.

"Damn, damn! I should have anticipated this, and fastened guy ropes to anchor the Blimp," said Orlov angrily. "I was in such a hurry to get us under cover."

Now they could hear and feel the wind buffeting the Hut.

"I'm surprised at its power," said Aurora in a pacifying tone. "Oh, I've seen the numbers. But somehow you can't believe that such a thin atmosphere could have the strength to create this much effect, Well I can't, anyway."

"It has the strength to lift thousands of tonnes of fins high into the atmosphere," said Minako rather scathingly.

Suddenly from one edge of the screen there fountained a huge shower of red soil. A large area of metallized fabric appeared and began flapping like a pterosaur's wing. The airship was shaking loose, and minute by minute their shielding was being torn away.

Lift-off

"I'm going outside," said Aurora firmly.

"You can't possibly. I won't allow it. It would be sheer suicide," said Lundquist.

"I agree. I forbid it also," said Orlov, equally firmly. Beaumont was likewise shaking his head.

"Oh, fine, so we all get a heavy dose of radiation and contract cancer," said Aurora. "Very sensible. Very clever. Don't you see? I'm the only one who *can* go outside, because the chances are very good that my body will be able to counteract any adverse effects."

"You don't know that," argued Lundquist. "The effects of radiation are very different from those of bacteria, or injuries. I'm still against it." But his voice was becoming less confident.

"I don't see why. It seems that my body is able to protect me, period. Anyway, if I'm willing to take the risk and everyone is helped, who are you to stop me? I'm going."

Suiting actions to words, she marched into the airlock.

Orlov moved to stop her nevertheless, but Beaumont laid a hand on his shoulder.

"I'm afraid she's right. I'm the last one to want her to go into danger, but it's her decision, and it's probably the only hope for the rest of us. I think she has a good chance . . . "

Lundquist capitulated. "Even so, I'd better make sure you have this."

He held out a clip-on radiation meter, which Aurora took.

Two minutes later the monitor screen showed a spacesuited figure looming through the ruddy haze, head down and walking with stumbling steps.

#

The Sun glared balefully, a red eye in a blood-coloured dustbath. Aurora was still amazed, despite her scientific education and knowledge, at the apparent thickness of the dust being raised all around her. Above her, the sky pulsated with curdling billows of chocolate brown, of rust red, of burnt umber, while flickering shafts of sunlight—amber, gold, orange—spotlit her intermittently. Even at that stressful moment she experienced a brief flashback to the concert with the Gas Giants.

The wind tugged at her suit, and it was hard to walk. She trudged to the area where the Blimp was being torn free. Already quite a large section of shiny metal tank was exposed intermittently as the fabric flapped in the wind.

Almost weeping with the effort, she pushed one of the water-filled elevators back into place—a task which would have been impossible under Earth gravity and was difficult enough even here. Then she grabbed a corner of the main Blimp and pulled a whole layer, the length of the Hut, free. The wind snatched it viciously from her hands, but she caught it and managed to attach a length of nylon cord, taken from one of the rovers' lockers, to the exposed layer.

Lacking any pegs, she tied the cord around the biggest rock she could handle, then piled other rocks around and on top of it, building a small cairn. She repeated this process at other points, then got a shovel and began covering the Hut with regolith again. Finally, and feeling she might collapse at any moment—this job really needed at least two people—she folded the final layer of metallized plastic back over the top and secured it, so that hopefully it would hold the soil in place and prevent it being blown away.

Over the next few draining minutes, her consciousness occasionally seeming to dim, she fought her way right round the Hut, ensuring that everything was as secure as she could make it.

At last she staggered back to the airlock.

The inner door to the suiting-up chamber slid open after several eternities, and she almost fell through. She slumped into the nearest chair.

"OK. You were right. I should have stayed in here in comfort," she joked feebly, peering up through a deep red fog at Lundquist, who was standing over her looking concerned. He reached for her arm to take her pulse.

"Oh, go away, cool it, Bob. My mum always said "hard work never hurt anybody." Think how fit I'll be tomorrow after all that exercise."

Her eyes closed, and instantly she fell asleep.

When she awoke, with a jumbled dream-image of the usual gowned figures still in her head, she was in her own cot. She got up, feeling sore and stiff but otherwise well enough, and made her way to the tiny bathroom.

#

A little while later, as she entered the Refectory, heads looked towards her, then quickly away. Her fellows had obviously been deep in discussion.

"You've been dead to the world for over twelve hours!" said Lundquist. His face fell, and his voice was grave as he continued. "Sorry. I could have phrased that better. But you may as well know: I'm afraid you've absorbed over two thousand rem. That's a lethal dose, Aurora. I've given you an injection, and you certainly seem all right so far. The only thing we can do now is wait—wait, hope and pray."

"I *have* prayed for you," said Orlov, his face ashen. Then, obviously to take their minds off the subject, he added, "Things have been happening while you've been asleep. For one thing, the solar storm is over. And so is the one outside—though the air's still pretty hazy. But that was expected. What wasn't is that we're going to move on."

"What? Move where?"

"Yes. Mission Control has given us our marching orders. You can watch the recording if you want to, but in a nutshell they say they've been looking carefully at our reserves of consumables—propellant, food, oxygen—and that we have enough for a small hop. Care to guess where they want us to go?"

"Not Uranius?"

"Got it in one. Those two volcanoes are way up in the northern hemisphere, of course—too far to travel by rover, even if we had the fuel. Mission Control have picked out a landing site for us, just to the west of Uranius Tholus, on a smooth area just before the ground breaks up into the cracks and grooves of Ceraunius Fossae. They're having some problems with the launch vehicle for the next mission, and don't want to waste our last few weeks on Mars having us perform routine tasks when we could be taking a look at what might be the site of that double city. So, tomorrow we move. Today, we pack."

"We're leaving the Hut as it is, I suppose—and the Greenhouse and other experiments?" asked Aurora.

"Yes, we have no option. We can take a few of the smaller items with us, but that's all. We'll have to take the S-band antenna, of course. So let's get to work. Not you of course, Aurora, if you don't feel up to it."

"No, I'd rather help than laze around here."

Aurora started to get up, but then a wave of giddiness swept over her. She dropped back into her seat.

Lundquist was at her side in an instant.

"You stay here," he said, taking her wrist.

Aurora refused to go back to bed, but found herself confined to the Hut while the others packed up what portable equipment they could and loaded the Lander. She watched them on the monitor and kept in radio communication.

"I'm afraid we're going to have to leave most of our rock samples here," said Orlov.

This decision would affect Minako, Beaumont and Verdet as well as Aurora. "I'm sorry," he added apologetically, "but we've got to save weight wherever we can. We're taking the two bodies, of course. Fortunately, we were very economical on fuel when we landed—otherwise we wouldn't have enough to spare for this little jaunt."

He went into the *Lowell* with Beaumont to program their sub-orbital flight.

Lundquist came to check up on Aurora, who was dozing. "I'm a bit worried that you might not be able to take the strain of the launch," he said.

"Oh come on, Doc—I'll be fine. I'm just not used to all that physical work, that's all. I'm *tired*, for chrissake! But just give me another night's sleep . . . Anyway, it'll hardly be a high-gee launch, will it?"

"True. OK, we'll see how you feel tomorrow. It's an early start, by the way, so you'd better get back to bed right away."

#

At 07.00 next morning Aurora got up and folded her cot and duvet. She still felt weak and rather queasy, but, since she didn't want to be responsible for any delays in their plans, told Robert that she felt better. He seemed fairly satisfied with the readings on his diagnostic instruments.

The team took a last look around the interior of the Hut as they suited up. Orlov made a final check of the automatic instruments which would be left working, relaying their information to the Orbiter via the smaller satellites.

After ushering the others out he followed them, then closed the outer airlock.

#

The campsite was a wave-patterned beach of bright and dark in the early-morning light. The longest shadow was cast by the big, vaguely conical Lander, which crouched on its legs like some monstrous spider crab. Much smaller shadows, like parasites, crawled up its side and were swallowed by its open, red-glowing maw. Below, as always, Earth-people had left litter and pollution to mark their passing.

The ladder withdrew. The hatch swung closed. A wisp of pale vapour appeared near the base of the *Lowell* and became an expanding smoke-ring. Had anyone been standing on the sand to observe, they might have heard a thin roaring sound as, briefly, reddish flame flickered around the venturi. Only robot cameras watched, impassively, dutifully converting their electronic images into digital information to be reconverted and watched many minutes later by the waiting millions on Earth.

Dust and sand erupted from beneath the Lander. The legs flexed. The gap between them and their shadow widened. Within that gap the landscape wavered and distorted through a bluish haze, like a mirage.

For a long moment the spaceship hovered, balancing on a column of pale violet, diamond shockwaves, as though deciding whether to sink back down to the sand. Then, with startling rapidity, it shot upwards and arced across the bright orange sky, became a white star, and was lost to sight.

#

To Aurora, it seemed that no time passed before the view through the porthole of Arsia Mons was replaced by the much smaller cone of Uranius Tholus, with the larger Ceraunius Tholus directly to its south. The two volcanoes, she knew, lay to either side of the latitude line of twenty-five degrees north.

The motors whined, and the *Lowell* was dropping towards the plain. To their left appeared scores of long fractures running roughly north–south—tectonic patterns belonging to the crater of Alba Patera, already out of sight below their horizon to the northwest. The shadow-filled cracks, growing in detail as they drifted below, had an almost hypnotic effect, one replacing another but each successively growing larger, larger . . .

"Three hundred metres. Looks rough down there. Taking manual control." Orlov's face was strained as he tersely exchanged parameters with Beaumont. Beaumont had asked if he could make this landing himself, but Orlov had overruled him on the basis of his own greater experience. Aurora thought Beaumont had seemed relieved: they couldn't afford to take chances at this stage of the game.

Below, overlapping folds of lava were a highly uneven and not very promising landing field. Scattered boulders, some the size of a small house, were going to make the task even more difficult.

"Fifty metres. Impact crater down there. Right. Three forward. Twenty metres—damn! Right. *Right!* Ten metres."

"No, No—UP! There's a boulder right under our legs!"

"OK, OK. No! It has to be here or we're into reserves. Picking up dust. Five. Four—contact light—"

There was a grinding crunch and the craft tilted alarmingly. Then came a deafening screeching sound inside the cabin as they skidded horizontally in the moment that the landing pads touched the surface.

But only for that moment.

Then there was silence.

"Engines off."

"We're down!"

The silence actually wasn't a silence, Aurora discovered as her ears recuperated, but consisted of the dying whine of turbines, the ticking of cooling metal and many other sounds. The tilt of the cabin floor told her the steepness of the angle they had landed at. She hoped it would permit them to take off again safely. But Orlov, his face beaded with sweat, was grinning around at them through his beard.

"Congrats, Boss!" said Beaumont, pumping the Russian's arm. "For a minute back there you had me worried!"

"*Niet.* Piece of cake!" claimed Orlov.

Around them a miniature dust storm swirled. By the time it had almost cleared, the hatch was open and they began to emerge.

#

Feeling partly disgusted, partly relieved, Aurora found herself confined to her reclining couch in the Lander while the others unloaded stores and began to set up the Igloo on its new site. All she could do was watch them on the small monitor screen, and listen to them chat as they worked.

She still felt physically weak, but she was mentally active.

At least she could rotate the view from two cameras to cover 360 degrees. At first, she looked at the scene scientifically. Both craters were partially submerged under younger lavas, so, like rocky icebergs submerged in an ocean of solidified magma, much of them lay beneath the apparent surface.

Then she began to feel excited. The scene seemed . . . *familiar*—and not just from having seen the alien film, she was sure. She began to long to set her feet on the ground outside; already she seemed to feel the ancient planet calling to her.

If Earth was held in the protective hands of a caring goddess called Gaia, as some believed, who guided the destiny of Mars? In the minds of humanity, Mars had for centuries been associated with warfare and destruction. Even its tiny satellites were named Fear and Panic. But Aurora felt that men (yes, men—never women!) had for too long imposed their own subconscious fears and bellicose nature on this little world, just because of its supposed resemblance to the colours of blood and fire. No: she imagined an ancient, benign god, waiting patiently and trustingly to welcome life—even in the form of humanity—whenever at last it came. Or had it already come and gone? If so, gone where? Perhaps they were about to find out.

She hoped that humankind would not abuse the trust of the Martian god—that this time life would be welcome to stay as long as it wished.

But then again, she thought tiredly, perhaps she was just feverish.

She slept.

#

When she awoke, the lower slopes of Uranius were almost lost in purple-grey shadow, but its peak glowed a deceptively warm rose colour. Lundquist stood over her.

"If you feel up to it, you can move into the Igloo now," he said. "No problem if you'd rather not—you can stay here if you'd prefer."

"I'll move. I think I'm feeling a bit better. I'd feel better still with some company."

With his assistance she descended the ladder to the ground and picked her way over pillowy but crusty pahoehoe-type lava, reminding her again of Kilauea in Hawaii. The rocks sparkled in the light from the helmet lamps as though wet. Although huge, Uranius was tiny compared with Olympus Mons—a more manageable size for the human eye to encompass in its field of view. Only the tip of its peak, as the Sun set, still glowed a rusty magenta. The yellow lamp over the Hut's airlock entrance welcomed them in.

Inside, the team was preparing once more to watch the alien "movie"—such an inadequate description, thought Aurora. It was a holistic experience. Earth had sent enhancements and enlargements of certain sections, comments and suggestions, principally so that the team could explore and excavate various areas. Rather grudgingly, the experts on Earth had even suggested that Beaumont might care to dowse over various carefully marked spots.

He couldn't hide his delight. "At long last the scientific establishment has been forced to accept publicly that the human mind does possess powers that can't be duplicated by technology!" he pontificated gleefully.

Whether the public was aware of his claim or not, it had been enraptured by the pictures of the ship's launch from Arsia Base, as it was now known. During the initial landing only an expanding view of craters, rocks and sand had been visible. Earth's populace now waited with barely controlled anticipation for the discoveries they confidently expected to be forthcoming.

The big viewscreen came to life with the initial view of the double city. There was no mistaking the similarity with the landscape outside, but Aurora felt a sense of disappointment. This image was flat and colourless compared with the totally lifelike and all-encompassing reality of the version they had watched in the alien craft's cabin. She tried to concentrate on what her friends were saying.

" . . . and we're looking due south here," said Verdet. "See? There's Tharsis Tholus, and over to the right is Ascraeus Mons. But they're both blue and misty-looking in the picture, which is why we didn't recognize them before. And the impact craters of Uranius Patera and Fesenkov are almost hidden by vegetation. You can only see them when you know they're there."

"There's water in Fesenkov crater," pointed out Beaumont.

"Yes. It looks like a big lake."

Aurora found herself dozing again. She tried to pay attention to the discussion. Had someone just asked her a question? She didn't seem to have the energy to keep herself awake.

#

The rest of the team gazed over at her, and Robert shook his head. "It doesn't look good," he said softly.

A New Life

Once again, Aurora woke in her cot. She got up, feeling nauseous, and walked unsteadily to the bathroom. Only just in time. She vomited into the toilet bowl.

When she came out she saw Lundquist standing there with his eyes on her. "I want to give you a proper check-up." His voice was sombre.

"But I feel fine now. Really I do!" she said brightly.

"You've just thrown up, haven't you?"

"Damn these thin walls. Is there no privacy! Yes, I did. But I feel better for it."

"Come on, lie down. This won't take long."

But the examination was thorough, including a blood count, body scan and other tests. Throughout it, Aurora was watching his expression. It remained concerned, but after a while it became puzzled as well.

"I'll need a urine sample," he finally said.

"But . . . "

"I think I already know the result, though."

"It—it's the radiation, isn't it?"

"Radiation? Oh, no. That's a separate issue. You're pregnant," he said matter-of-factly.

Aurora gulped. Had he handed her a sentence of death from leukaemia she would have been much less shocked, in the circumstances.

"You—you *what*?"

"You heard me quite well the first time. You did say you'd had your Pregnil shots before you left, didn't you?"

"Yes. I did. I was due for a booster quite soon, though. I told you. But—how am I doing apart from that?"

"Oh, you're absolutely fine. Your blood-cell count is quite normal now, though it was down a couple of days ago. The problem seems to be that your body's self-protection system, however it works, seems to have objected to the intrusion of the birth-control hormone, too, and countered it. You've never been pregnant before?"

"No, of course not. I—never intended to be, ever."

To Aurora's surprise, he began to laugh.

"What the . . . ?" she began.

"Even if you weren't on Mars, and hadn't performed all those miracles already, you would make the news now," he said. "Seventy-eight-year-old woman to have baby! Can you imagine the field day they'd have?"

"Seventy-nine by the time I have it," said Aurora.

He sobered quickly. "You *can't* have it, of course."

"Oh yes, I can. And I'm going to."

"Now come on, Aurora. You must see that there's no way I could permit that."

"'Permit'? What are you going to do? Perform an abortion against my will?"

"Let's stop this, shall we? I don't want to fight with you. But you must see how impossible it would be. We'll talk about it again later, when you've had time to see reason."

"We can talk all you like. But I'm not going to change my mind. I may be a crazy old woman, but my first baby will have been conceived on Mars."

"Hmm. We'll see about that. Meanwhile, I suggest that we keep this between the two of us—right?"

"Sure."

The concertinaed curtain which served as a door to the comm desk parted, and Vitali Orlov strode in. "Sorry, but you said it yourself—the walls in this place are thin. And you were raising your voices rather. I couldn't help over-hearing."

His gaze as he looked directly at Aurora was grim. "The doctor is right. Of *course* you can't remain pregnant. It must be your hormones talking!"

"I don't see why it's such a problem," she hissed. "We're on Mars for another six weeks, right? Then there's a journey home of three months or so. So there'll be at least another three months after that before the baby is born. On Earth."

Lundquist snorted. "It's easy to see you've had no experience of babies. They don't keep to that sort of exact schedule, you know! Suppose it arrived early? How would you cope then? Would you be willing to trust it to the rigours of an Earth-landing?"

"Don't be so melodramatic, Bob! You know as well as I do that there's nothing particularly hazardous about transferring from the ship to a shuttle and landing on Earth. If anything went really wrong, whether the child was inside or outside my body would be the last of the worries."

Orlov said dryly: "There is the small matter of a spacesuit. We don't happen to have any in stock in junior sizes . . . "

"Now you're just making up objections. The combined science of Earth's nations isn't capable of solving a little problem like that?" She smiled. "Come to think of it, I've already solved it. If it did become necessary—and I really don't think it will; I have pretty good control over my body, as you've seen—we could use the baby's capsule from the alien ship. It's custom-made!"

"You've thought of everything, haven't you?" said Orlov sourly. She knew him well enough to understand that with his strong religious convictions he had probably been unhappy about the notion of her having an abortion, even while his intellect ruled that such a measure was necessary.

"Maybe. But in any case, I think the father should have some say in this, don't you? I'd like to talk to him tonight. Alone."

"OK. 'Til tonight then, Mum's the word!" said Robert.

#

Bryan's face lit up, then rapidly fell as he realized the implications and complications of this new situation. "No. You couldn't—I mean, *we* couldn't risk it," he said. "After all, we can always try again when we get back to Earth. Couldn't we?" he added hopefully, watching her face.

"I've already been through all the arguments with Bob and Vitali," she said determinedly. "You won't talk me out of it."

She explained about the time factor, and about the capsule.

"Our baby will have been conceived on Mars," she said again. "I never had any intention of having children, but this one I *am* going to have. And that's final."

And so, it seemed, it was. Verdet seemed pleased, and Minako did not seem to care one way or another. Was the woman jealous? wondered Aurora.

They then had to go through the whole routine with Mission Control, who were appalled by the idea. But there was not really much the people back on Earth could do at that distance except make noises.

Mission Control did insist, however, that this time the public not be told. Beaumont, red to the tips of his ears, agreed that he would not be an informant this time.

#

The Sun was still behind the bulk of Uranius when they set out in the rovers next morning. The volcano's long shadow stretched across the plain, a luminous blue-grey, but to north and south the lava fields glowed a warm orange. Also to the south, the striated slopes of Ceraunius reared above the horizon, the mountain's peak blazing in the early sunlight.

The going was rough, and the rovers had to weave their way around grotesquely shaped outcrops of lava or make wide detours to avoid deep crevasses. At last they found themselves on a relatively gentle incline as they climbed the flank of Uranius to reach the first site marked out for them by Mission Control.

"Time for a break, I think, before we start exploring," said Orlov over the intercom, his voice sounding in both cabins.

The tempting odours of coffee and soup filled the little cabins as the seals were broken on self-heating cans. By the time the gull's-wing hatches were swung upwards the edge of the Sun was peering over the lip of the caldera, and the spongy-looking lava flows around them were highlighted with gold. Below was a wasteland of iron–grey and rust, the conical shadow of their mountain clearly defined.

Robert had, to no one's real surprise, given Aurora, along with the rest of the team, a clean bill of health. Now they all spread out over the slopes, taking samples, drilling cores, setting up instruments and making measurements. It was arduous and exhausting work in their Mars suits, but they were all glad to be able to perform useful field work again.

Having completed his programme of "official" tasks, Beaumont produced his dowsing rods and began walking back and forth over a prepared area. After a while, having finished up her own allotted experiments, Aurora joined him, attaching the lead which enabled them to have a private conversation between suits without using the radio.

"Having any luck?"

"This is great!" he said enthusiastically. "I was thinking earlier how amazing it would be to work on Olympus Mons but, you know, this is better in a way. Uranius is more—familiar, somehow. Accessible, if you like. You can tell you're on a volcano, whereas on Olympus I'm sure you wouldn't be able to see the wood for the trees. It's too big. Know what I mean?"

"I do. I think we should try to reach the peak—where that sort of glass bubble, dome, was in the movie. If that really was Mars."

"You don't think it was?"

"I can't make up my mind. I mean, how *could* it be? I agree that the physical features seem to match up, and yet . . ." She shook her head in exasperation, her blonde hair swinging loosely inside her helmet. "I'm sure I should *know*. Anyway, how's the dowsing coming along?"

"It isn't. I had one false alarm—thought I'd found metal, but it seems to be only a nodule of iron oxide. There's nothing interesting down there. I'm sure of it."

"I'm afraid I think the same. I haven't found anything with my instruments either, other than what I'd expect, geologically. Disappointing, isn't it? We were so sure we'd find real archaeological evidence of that city. Or at least something to show it had been here."

"Never mind. We try a new site tomorrow."

"Yeah. S'pose so."

#

The atmosphere in the Igloo that evening was quiet, even somewhat depressed. None of the team had found anything of other than geological interest, and, while a few months ago that was all they would have expected, now it was a let-down.

"The lava is more fluid than I would have predicted," said Minako.

Beaumont and Aurora nodded bored agreement.

Verdet expressed their feelings when he burst out: "Goddamit! You would have thought we'd find *something* down there! Not near the surface, of course. But how could all that, that whole civilization, just vanish without trace?"

Lundquist found an opportunity to take Aurora aside. "I still wish you'd let me terminate your pregnancy while it's at an early stage," he said. "I accept your arguments for yourself—your health and so on—but I'm thinking of the baby. The fact remains that you took a dose of over two thousand rem, and even if *your* body could cope with that—well, whatever *you* are, the father is human. There's no knowing what sort of effect the radiation might have had on the genetic material of the foetus. And right at the most susceptible time, too."

"Whatever else I am, I'm human too. I'm pregnant by a human father. What more proof could you need? As a doctor, I'm sure you'd be the last person to believe those science fiction stories in which disguised alien lizards impregnate humans!"

"That doesn't alter my point."

"The point is that the baby is mine, it's inside my body and building itself from my tissues." Her face softened. "Bob, I do take your point, and I know you're only thinking of my interests. But it *will* be all right, you'll see. Trust me!

"Look, you'll be monitoring my progress, won't you?" she continued. "You could tell from a scan if there was any physical deformity, couldn't you? And I'm sure there are lots more tests you can do. If there's any sign of abnormality, we'll talk again. I promise."

Robert sighed. "I didn't come on this expedition geared up to hold a pre-natal clinic," he said. "But, yes, I expect I can modify some of my equipment. You win. As usual . . . "

Revelations

Spirits in the Igloo were low again next evening. Today's work had been as disappointing as yesterday's. There had been not the slightest indication that a great city might once have occupied the slopes of the volcano. Not so much as the smallest artefact.

As Lundquist had pointed out, neither had their research ever found any other trace of life of any kind—no algae or lichen, no microbes, no dormant spores; just a few of those supposed fossil bacteria. No life even in the canyons of Noctis Labyrinthus, where water had surely run millions of years ago. Mars seemed entirely barren, and gave every indication that it had always been so.

Beaumont and Aurora had climbed high on the slopes of Uranius, but had abandoned any idea of reaching the summit. It was difficult, though not impossible, yet it no longer seemed worth the effort. "If only we still had the Blimp!" Aurora had said. But Beaumont had pointed out that the air at the top of the volcano was so thin that even the airship would probably not have been able to reach the caldera.

Yet Aurora still felt the volcano, and its larger counterpart to the south, calling to her.

"If there is any place on Mars that I feel I had to come to, it is here," she told Beaumont. "I know that doesn't really make sense, but what *does* on this crazy expedition?"

He searched his brain for something to lift their spirits. His eyes lit upon his minisynth, left there after their wedding ceremony.

"Why don't you give us a tune, darling? Might cheer us all up a bit!" he said to Aurora.

She was at first almost as reluctant as she had been during her first public performance at the Grotto Club, but the others cheered and forced her to her feet. Finally she succumbed to their encouragement, and adjusted the tone settings on the instrument.

As always seemed to happen when she began to play, there was silence from her little audience within seconds. Beaumont had quite expected to recognize a melody from the Gas Giants' album, but this was something quite new.

He watched her face closely. It changed, became younger, yet—different.

Her eyes closed, and a trancelike expression took over her face . . .

#

The music was haunting, though not sad. Rather, it was calm, tranquil. It told, without words or the need for words but in clear images, of a world in which there was no war or strife, where weapons had been destroyed long ago and outlawed for centuries—but in which no one would anyway have wished to create or possess a method of destruction or cruelty. Indeed, there were few machines. But this was no static, sterile world, without change. Its people had simply forsaken non-essential technology, keeping only as much as they needed, turning instead to pursuits of the mind.

As Aurora played, the confined space of their pressure dome expanded and became a vast amphitheatre, its terraced slopes lined with seats full of people. In the centre, gowned musicians played instruments even smaller than her own, which they wore around their necks or as belts. The music they played augmented her own, swelling and soaring to incredible, spiritual heights.

It was night, yet everywhere a radiance shone from invisible sources. Foliage glowed vivid green . . .

Aurora swayed. The music faltered, the images wavered and shivered.

Lundquist moved towards her, but she shook her head.

The music passed through a series of violent chord-changes, calmed, shifted subtly into a minor key. When the images returned, the floor of the amphitheatre was cracked.

Somehow, there was an impression of heat. This was not right, an intrusion. Two suns, one large, one small, rose in a purple sky; but they were in different parts of the sky, not close, as they had been in the "movie." Clouds closed in rapidly, lightning flickered. A red glow pulsed on the underside of thick, turgescent clouds. The plants drooped and turned brown.

Orlov and Verdet mopped their brows. They were sweating visibly. The others looked uncomfortable too, except Minako, who seemed unaffected aside from a puzzled expression. Lundquist got up and checked the thermostat.

Bright rays of light streamed through cracks in the tattered clouds, which in places were ripped apart. The illumination became unbearable. Even the clouds themselves seemed to glow internally. Now, the other musicians having vanished, Aurora played alone, a plaintive threnody that rose and fell.

A bright spark rose from the horizon, then another. And another. At intervals they arced into the roiling clouds to be swallowed in a brief ripple of light. A few people remained in the amphitheatre, watching the ascending fleet. The music was a song of farewell. Soon Aurora and her friends would, likewise, be leaving their world.

The scene became indistinct, as though seen through a haze of smoke. She still played, but the music became faster—whirled, sizzled, grew discordant, dissonant, became a cacophony.

Verdet and Minako put their hands to their ears.

Beaumont's eyes were still on Aurora, half-knowing what to expect, and he caught her when she swayed and fell. He carried her into her compartment and laid her on her cot. Lundquist, following him through, pushed him aside, firmly though not roughly.

Aurora lay stiffly on the bed, her muscles rigid. "It's like catatonia," said Lundquist, seemingly to himself. Noticing Beaumont looking at him with worry and inquiry in his eyes, he added: "It's a state sometimes found in schizophrenics. But why? I can't understand it."

"Can't you *do* anything?"

"Not a lot, here. I think it's best to leave her. Knowing Aurora, she probably has her reasons and will find her own way out of this."

"But what about the baby? Will it be all right?"

Lundquist checked the instrument he held. "Aurora's vital signs are weak, but not dangerously so. All I can do is keep monitoring her condition."

He looked haggard. An expedition physician shouldn't be expected to have to cope with a patient like Aurora, his expression said.

#

She lay in a catatonic state all the next day, and the next. Worried, Lundquist explained the position to medical experts at Mission Control. They gave as much advice as they could from that distance.

He had attached a drip feed to Aurora's left arm. Her husband refused to leave her side. They brought Beaumont food and drink, but most of it went untouched.

On the third day, Aurora awoke, stretched, smiled beatifically, kissed Beaumont on the cheek, and made her way to the bathroom.

He went and woke Lundquist, who checked her over medically when she returned.

"You really will have to stop doing this sort of thing!" he said, his mock anger doing little to disguise obvious relief. "OK, you'll do. Go and get some decent food inside you." He removed the drip tube from her arm and put on a small bandage.

When he had left, Aurora kissed Beaumont more thoroughly, then said calmly: "I have it all now. I can get at it—at last. I have a full set of memories, just as I knew I should have had. But they aren't my *own* memories. They're my father's. He passed them to me moments before he died.

"In the middle of World War Two. The London Blitz."

Homecoming

Everyone had seen the same images, to a lesser or greater extent, except Minako. She had been moved by beautiful music but nothing more. She had seen no landscape, no people, had felt no rise in temperature.

Now Aurora sat in a chair, a video camera focused on her. After much discussion it had been decided that the best way for her to tell of her implanted and released memories was to do so in a single session, if it proved possible, to the whole world. So, now that she felt fit enough, not only her colleagues but everyone on the home planet was waiting avidly to hear her words. More people were believed to be watching and listening than for any other event in history.

"I want it to be just as if I'm telling a story—my own story," said Aurora by way of preamble. "To me, now, it's as if the memories were my own, anyway. But I need to explain that they are not only my father's memories but those of many other people too, some of whom lived hundreds or thousands of years earlier.

"They were able to access those huge unused portions of the brain which neurologists have known and wondered about for decades; and part of that use was to fill them with precious memories transferred from others. Their family, friends. It was a way of learning, too—instantly. But it tended to make books, tapes, computer data files—recordings of any type really—redundant. They had to rediscover the technology to make that 'movie' we saw.

"They didn't really expect the 'movie' ever to be seen. They hoped it would never be needed, because I had all the information—in here." She tapped her head. Then her face grew sad. "At least, my father and mother did. Yes. That woman astronaut we found in the desert was my mother.

"Her name was Anela."

For several seconds she could not speak. Then:

"My father passed on his memories to me as a final resort. But, as I was saying, the 'movie' was intended purely as a back-up—a fortunate back-up for us. It was also available as proof of my words, if needed. But it was never expected that we would find it on *Mars . . .* "

She paused to take a sip of water.

"I don't know why those memories were blocked from my conscious mind. Perhaps it was the trauma of my arrival on Earth, in the middle of an air raid on London by the Germans. Or of other traumatic events later in my life.

"Why did they return?

"Perhaps because I came to this magical place on Mars. Perhaps it's because I'm in love!"

She turned to Bryan with a smile.

"Or because of the baby, of changes in my bodily chemistry. Or a combination of all those things. I don't know. It doesn't really matter, does it?

"Music has always been the key, of course, and that is because of my father, who was a Musician—a highly respected position in his society. His name was Themor. Somehow, musical chords struck sympathetic chords deep in the recesses of my mind. Perhaps I just found the right note at last—struck the Lost Chord, as it were!"

Aurora drew another deep breath.

"Right. Here goes. You have to realize that I need to start by going back a long, long way; but what you don't know, unless you've managed to guess by now, is that to you it's not *back* at all. It's *forward*.

"It's all in your *future . . .* "

She took another drink of water. She looked nervous and very fragile—and young. Her image and the words she had spoken when she started speaking were still travelling towards the Earth at the speed of light.

"When I was born, the method of counting dates had changed—several times. I was born in your equivalent of the year 20,000AD."

There was a collective gasp from the people around her.

"So some of the earlier dates I give may not be completely accurate, but they are as close as I, we, can get. For reasons which you will see, many records were wiped out. Especially those that were kept on computers or used other electronic storage methods, and so were vulnerable to an electromagnetic pulse . . .

"We do have an accurate record of this: in the year 2069, there was—there will be? Look, I'm going to have to speak in the past tense. OK? In 2069 there was a series of devastating explosions that wiped out Baghdad and severely damaged Tel Aviv, Beirut, Tehran and other cities and towns in that area. Unfortunately they did not destroy all the secret underground command posts, or the nuclear missiles which had been stockpiled, contravening all those United Nations treaties. Or the people who then ruled that area, who instantly assumed it to be a nuclear attack on them.

"Here I am augmenting my "memories" with what I know of today's political situation, but you all know that, while the world seems to be progressing towards peace, the Middle East remains as ever a flashpoint for trouble, because of its oil. Which is not inexhaustible.

"The fireballs, complete with mushroom clouds, were certainly equivalent to several atomic or even hydrogen bombs, but were in fact caused by a portion of the head of a small, non-periodic comet. It came "out of the Sun," which is why it was not detected earlier, and it arrived in full daylight. Its arrival was preceded by a series of detonations high in the atmosphere, during which it broke into a number of smaller pieces. It originally weighed perhaps five thousand tonnes, and the main mass impacted in the Syrian Desert. It could as easily have landed on Washington, or Paris, or Moscow. The direct results would have been much the same. But it could hardly have happened at a worse place or time.

"Just to give you a bit of historical background, a similar object hit Central Siberia—only four thousand kilometres from Moscow—on the thirtieth of June, 1908. It flattened two thousand square kilometres of taiga forest. The name of the place where it fell was Tunguska.

"And in 1947 there was a similar event only four hundred kilometres from Vladivostok. As most of you will know, a comet is composed chiefly of ice, so almost all of it vaporises on impact, hitting the ground at perhaps thirty kilometres per second and leaving no solid traces. There is a crater over a kilometre in diameter in Arizona, but that was caused by a chunk of iron twenty-five metres across that struck twenty or thirty thousand years ago—"your" time. So such impacts as the ones in 2069 had not been unexpected. Organizations like Spaceguard had been warning of them for years, but governments had given little heed, even after a comet impacted Jupiter in 1994 and its effects were shown on TV worldwide.

"If I seem to be dwelling on this it's because it is one of the reasons I'm here.

To warn you of what is about to happen. I'm sorry, I don't even know if you can do anything about it. After all, to me, to my father's memories, it has already happened. But perhaps a timestream can be diverted? It is your—our—only hope."

Again she paused, placing the fingers of one hand to her brow for a few seconds. "I don't think I need to go into great detail about what happened next. The gaps can be filled in later—where I can. Other nations became involved. The world dissolved into war and chaos remarkably easily and quickly. Weapons appeared that were supposed to have been destroyed long ago.

"A nuclear winter descended upon the Earth, partly due to the amount of smoke and dust liberated by the initial cometary impact—after all, a similar impact may have caused the extinction of the dinosaurs, sixty-five million years ago—but exacerbated by the war, in which nuclear weapons were used. There were dark ages during which men and women had no time for anything but survival, when there was only suspicion, fear, brutality, hunger and disease, including radiation sickness . . .

"I would rather not dwell on this period, because it offends every fibre of my being. Suffice it to say that it was a hundred years or more before sanity regained control, and people began to cooperate and collaborate on building a new world. But there came other collapses—economic, political. Artificial upheavals which to my people seem, frankly, stupid and incomprehensible, but which I, as one of you, can of course understand—as much as any scientist can understand the workings of the Stock Market! I suppose I really have been schizophrenic, in a way, for I have had these other people locked away in my brain for nearly eighty years.

"Where was I? Oh yes. Gradually, a better world was built. It seems that sometime in the first half of this century the first scientifically tested and proven examples of the power of the mind appeared."

Beaumont's head, which had been bowed as he listened, jerked sharply upward.

"Of course, powers of ESP have been claimed for centuries, but it has always seemed impossible to prove the existence of such extrasensory powers—or to use them at will, in such a way that there could be no doubt of their effectiveness. If it was some sort of human mutation, it was a very elusive one. But, as I said, the first incontrovertible proof appeared—well, *will* appear—any time now."

She frowned. "Ah. I think I'm beginning to see a paradox."

This time she paused for so long that her audience began to wonder if she were feeling ill. Then she straightened. "I think I'd better get back to my 'future history.' It's safer ground.

"It seems that a portion of the human race has always possessed some type of psi talent. Could it be that some part of humanity is descended not from Cro-Magnon Man but from some other branch of the anthropoid family? I'm not qualified to say. Just maybe, many tens of thousands of years ago, we used these faculties much more widely, but with the advance of technology they became atrophied. However, some people still have them—my husband for one, with his dowsing ability." She looked over at him fondly, and again smiled, though with an obvious effort.

"The fact that some people don't have the slightest trace of these abilities may explain why, though always most of my audiences were affected by my musical performances, a few were not." She did not look at Minako. "Those who were affected received powerful mental images from my mind, released in this case by the music.

"Mental powers are not exactly as most people seemed to expect. And they re-developed very slowly. During the Black Ages I told you about they were suppressed almost completely, and when they did reappear it took literally thousands of years before they were fully understood and mature, so that it became possible to train children in their use as a commonplace part of education. Training is essential, by the way, for the abilities to be used consciously, and I was far too young ever to receive any—which is no doubt why my own talents are so . . . unpredictable.

"Reverting to my father's time, the future, talents like teleportation and telekinesis of actual objects are still very rare—and highly prized, and interbred. Oh, yes, I'll come to the genetic experiments later. Telepathy is common, but most mental powers are used almost exclusively for healing, therapeutics, the care and treatment of the body and mind. And for education. Medicine, as you know it, is almost unknown.

"My people have almost completely forsaken technology and science—again, as you know them. But this didn't come about because of some sort of conscious or even unconscious backlash against the forces which almost destroyed your—our—world. We use technology wherever it is essential—for transportation, for instance, by land or air, and occasionally by water. Oh, sometimes for pleasure too—people still enjoy flying, and sailing . . . And of course it's used for providing services such as electrical power and the pumping of water. Well, you can imagine others, I'm sure.

"But a form of telekinesis is commonly used on a submolecular level. The controls of the . . . vehicle we found in Noctis Labyrinthus operate mentally. The mind is able to operate submicroscopic switches and servos, and even affect power outputs directly. Again, even in the twentieth century limited experiments were carried out on influencing, with the mind alone, such tiny quantities as the particles in random radiation counts.

"In about two thousand years from today, science will concentrate on modifying the human body. This will be done partly by using mental powers, again at a microscopic level, but also by a form of what I suppose you'd call genetic engineering combined with nanotechnology, but using the most sophisticated and beautifully tuned microsurgical techniques, of which you have as yet barely an inkling. A type of—serum?—will also be developed. Actually it's a meld of drugs and hormones . . . No, that's not right. I don't think I can explain it now, but the information can probably be accessed . . . "

The child of two worlds took another sip of water. She was beginning to look wan.

"The end result will be that in my time the majority of humanity customarily live to an age of four or five hundred years, often even more. Virtual immortality is the ultimate aim, but seems elusive; some sort of entropy appears to be built into the human system, and degeneration occurs quite rapidly during the last few years of life. We have Old People's villages, where most elderly citizens end their days happily without reminding the rest of the populace of their *own* inevitable end. But this is quite voluntary; and most families, with their children, visit older members frequently and joyously.

"Most people, but not all, have automatic self-defences against almost every disease, bacterial or viral, and can regenerate limbs or organs when those are accidentally damaged. Those who cannot—and they seem to be the ones who themselves have little or no psi ability—can almost always be helped by mental physicians.

"You will have noticed that our toes have been allowed to atrophy. After all, we no longer need fingers on our feet! I'm sure, too, that you have all wondered—as I did myself—why the people of mine we have seen look so similar, especially in hair and eye colouring."

At this point Orlov, who was standing at the video camera, deliberately zoomed in on Aurora so that her dark oval face with its violet eyes, framed by long blonde hair, filled the screen dramatically.

Beaumont, noticing, grinned and nodded approvingly.

"I'm sorry," she continued, ignoring this, "but I don't know the answer. I'm not sure that anyone knows the answer, even in my day. Normally, the genes for light hair and pale eyes are recessive. Considering the amount of interbreeding between races that has taken place, one would expect darker features to predominate. But the genetic manipulation which took place around the year 4100—and it had nothing at all in common with Nazi-like schemes for an ideal race, I can assure you!—apparently reversed that, probably quite unintentionally. Although, as you have seen, our skin colour is actually quite dark; this isn't a suntan—it's been a very long time since I've had a chance to sunbathe, here on Mars!

She seemed pleased to be able to lighten her narrative with a small joke, and stretched a little, shifting position in her chair. But she still looked pale and strained, and Lundquist prepared to put a stop to the proceedings. She could continue at a later time. There was no need for her to put herself through what was obviously an exhausting ordeal any longer . . .

"About ten thousand years ago—or in as many years' time, it makes little difference which way I say it, there was another glacial period—another resurgence of the Ice Age—and it caused a great redistribution, and reduction, of the Earth's population. It was beyond the technology of the day to take much effective action; the power of ice is great. The survivors were often those who were not only physically fit but possessed the strongest mental and regenerative powers. So a sort of process of natural selection operated.

"But long before that happened, part of the human race had moved away.
"To Mars."

#

The transmission continued the next day, Lundquist and Beaumont having finally insisted that Aurora take a rest, despite her protestations that she was quite able to continue.

"Somewhere around the year 2500, humanity, which had once again started making tentative voyages into space—I'm sorry, guys, but most of *our* achievements on this mission seem to have become lost or forgotten!—took the decision to terraform Mars, to convert it into an Earthlike planet, habitable by humans. Having established that there was no indigenous life, and apparently never had been any, many people wanted to get away from Earth, with its blackened, ruined cities and radioactive wastelands, and start a new life with an entirely new lifestyle.

"Plenty of plans were considered. As you know, there are almost two thousand cubic kilometres of water locked inside the polar caps of Mars. That's enough to cover the planet with an ocean fifty centimetres deep. But most of Mars's water lies frozen deep below the crust.

"So the first method used was a rather crude one. Five ice asteroids, each ten to fifteen kilometres in diameter, were diverted from their orbits in the outer Solar System and steered carefully towards Mars so that they would impact in the basin of Hellas. That's already the lowest area on Mars, and was covered by an ocean millions of years ago. They made it an ocean once more. The impacts caused some disruption of the surface of Mars, but not as much as you might expect—Mars has a thick crust, or the asteroid which created Hellas in the first place would have gone right through that crust!

"You can imagine what a maelstrom it must have been, though, as the ice was converted almost instantly into plasma, then superheated steam, finally condensing into thick grey clouds which rose high into the atmosphere, perhaps even precipitating rain . . .

"Meanwhile, a mass-driver—an electromagnetic launcher—was set up on Phobos to eject the dark, carbonaceous material the moon's made of onto the Martian poles, increasing their absorption of infrared radiation—heat. This also increased the polar energy flux, but the process was accelerated by placing mirrors in orbit. Made of a very thin, metallized material similar to mylar, these reflected sunlight to warm the polar caps and release carbon dioxide, water vapour, oxygen and nitrogen from the crust. A greenhouse-effect cycle was started.

"Then, genetically engineered plant life was introduced into the system, forming a tundra-like landscape. Carbon dioxide was converted into oxygen. The temperature slowly rose, until it was above freezing point, and then to ten degrees Celsius. Can you imagine the transformation? The sky became deep blue. The Hellas Ocean was seeded with plankton which absorbed carbon dioxide. As it was fed by rivers and streams, the ocean grew in size. Another ocean grew in the northern lowlands—the Boreal Sea. Forests of evergreen trees spread from its borders.

"The crust of the planet contains all the essential elements for life. The ecology became self-sustaining; and, now that the atmosphere had been established, Mars had sufficient mass to retain it for tens of millions of years. It was generally known as the Second Home.

"The first real city—the planet's capital, if you like—was built on the

Tharsis Bulge, high above any water-line. The Two Mountains—the volcanoes of Ceraunius and Uranius—were chosen as its site, apparently mainly for aesthetic reasons. They were the right size, and their relative outlines, seen from above, were felt to mimic those of Earth and Mars. That "figure-of-eight symbol" has been significant to the inhabitants ever since. It was seen everywhere. You will even notice its echo in the shape of the device we found and called the Beacon, although actually it serves a number of purposes: remote control, transmitter, marker, key, confirmer of identity . . . One of our greatest strokes of luck on this expedition was that my genetic material is so similar to that of my parents, otherwise we might not have been able to enter the ship. Indeed, the Beacon, and that glowing light we first saw, might never have been triggered in the first place."

Aurora paused and looked down at some notes she had prepared so that she would not lose her thread.

"The psibot—the Beacon—had been buried for nearly eighty years, and after we'd discovered it it misbehaved at first. It was intended to project a . . . 'hologram' is as near as I can describe it, which would lead searchers to the ship. But the human shape took a while to . . . cohere. It's interesting that the Beacon was triggered by the airship on one occasion. Perhaps it confused the Blimp's shape with one of my people's craft?

"Anyway, the two civilizations, one on Earth and the other on Mars, became quite separate. The one on Earth became almost entirely pastoral. The cities were kept, along with all the machinery and technology they housed, as museums of humanity's past—and, to a large extent, of its follies. Science was not exactly banned, but it was excluded by common consent except where it was required for purely practical considerations, as I have already explained.

"The inhabitants turned to the Arts: to painting, sculpture, literature, poetry, music—to all pursuits of the mind, which they raised to incredible new heights. But they did not neglect the body, for all forms of dance were assimilated into the musical and visual arts, creating a whole new artform. I wish I could show you; perhaps I may even be able to give you some idea when I return to Earth and can communicate more directly. And gymnastics and sports, especially team sports—though less violent than, say, football—were also popular."

Aurora looked into the camera and smiled slightly. She shifted position yet again; sitting still so long for the video was arduous. "The life of the Martians, as they were of course known, followed a similar pattern, but certain types of scientific experimentation and development did continue—pursued mainly for their aesthetic value. Science and mathematics were seen as elegant, beautiful manifestations of Nature, and of human thought. There was rarely any sort of commercial end-product, though should one appear it would not necessarily be rejected.

"Life on both planets could be said to have approached as closely to that of a Utopia as could be imagined. But their inhabitants went about their pursuits sublimely unaware that a visitor was about disrupt their idyllic lives, never to allow them to return to their former perfection."

ACT FOUR
The Visitor

The Visitor

A star was drifting through space. Once, it had been a normal star and had waltzed in a stately dance with a partner, bound to it in the marriage of gravitation. But its mate had become greedy and demanding. It had stolen the outer, hydrogen layers of this star, leaving it stripped and naked, with only its helium core to glow against the eternal night of space.

Its consort had paid the penalty of its greed, though; had grown fat and bloated, and had finally disrupted. Its brightness increased three hundred million times as it disintegrated in a final cataclysmic blast of helium, carbon, oxygen, nitrogen . . .

A supernova.

Released from its unequal marriage partner, but greatly impoverished, the star had become a White Dwarf. It was hurled away from its former mate by the force of the explosion, and now sailed through interstellar space. The chances of it intercepting another body were remote; but a chance remained.

So it was that, after millions or billions of years of roaming alone, the star felt the faint tug of gravity from another sun. This was a commonplace yellow star, but it was surrounded by a retinue of planets, and, at a distance of fifty thousand astronomical units, by a vast cloud of a hundred billion insubstantial balls of ice and rock—comets.

The interloper disturbed the orbits of a few of these, which headed inward towards their own sun, to blaze briefly in the skies of the two inhabited worlds of this system like portents of doom. As well they might, for the star which had broken the peace and loneliness of the Oort Cloud was now also on its way towards the centre of their system, intent on wreaking a terrible revenge for its own maltreatment.

The white dwarf drifted in at a sharp angle to the ecliptic. The intruder had a diameter of only about 6500 kilometres, smaller even than the now red-and-green planet known as Mars. But the material of which it was made was so dense that its gravitational force was not far short of that of the Sun itself.

The visitor headed toward the Sun. It passed it at a distance of just over three million kilometres—and the Sun reached out a gravitational hand, spun it around and converted its headlong flight into an extended ellipse. Both stars were affected by the tidal friction as the latest member of the Solar System sped around its new partner and retreated once more into space, to prepare for another embrace in a thousand years' time.

But, while it remained close to the Sun, the star made certain that the inner planets became well aware of its passage. While just within the combined Roche Limit of the two stars—further inside and total tidal disruption would have occurred—it drew hydrogen gas from the surface of the Sun. This gas fell onto the white dwarf and exploded outward, causing a nova outburst.

This was but a pale echo of the supernova which had precipitated its own flight, but still it emitted more than ten thousand times more light than normal, and the star became wreathed in a halo of fluorescing gas as great jets and streamers of red-glowing hydrogen were torn from the tortured skin of the Sun, reaching out for the stranger like grasping fingers.

Mars was fortunate. It was on the far side of its orbit when the star approached the Sun, and, while its inhabitants saw everything, they felt only relatively minor ground tremors. The ozone layer which had been created high in the Martian atmosphere protected them from most of the brief burst of radiation.

Earth did not fare so well. The angle of the white dwarf's approach was such that it passed within a few million kilometres, and the tidal forces were fearsome. Earthquakes reduced buildings and whole cities to rubble; great cracks opened in the ground, belching flame and steam; ancient volcanoes came to life and blackened the sky with clouds of ash and dust, while pouring out rivers of red-glowing lava which devoured everything in their path.

Giant waves—tsunamis—reared up from the oceans and created more havoc, sweeping away buildings and trees and drowning many millions of people and animals. These were accompanied by the rush of mighty winds, bringing their own forms of destruction.

As if this were not enough, soon afterwards a blast of radiation from the nova outburst engulfed the Earth. The storm of particles lasted for well over the Biblical forty days and forty nights, until the visitor began to move away from the Sun and its brilliance diminished. It was, by cosmic standards, a modest outburst, but it held danger enough. Only the fact that, by the time the radiation arrived, Earth was almost completely shrouded in a thick blanket of cloud, smoke and dust prevented greater harm from being perpetrated.

The star retreated, gloating. It was watched by the Martians, who had not abandoned astronomy completely, though they now concentrated on the more esoteric aspects of cosmology and were engaged on a search for the answer to the great mystery of the origin and destiny of the Universe. A white dwarf would be invisible beyond a hundred light years even to their sensitive instruments; but such a tiny, insignificant object would never have interested them anyway, had they deigned to notice such a minuscule change in the normal star-patterns when it first became visible.

Communication between the two worlds had been rare in recent centuries. There was little to talk about. But the means for communication still existed. Once some semblance of normality had returned to Earth, its Council of Twelve (now reduced by casualties to seven, until its missing members could be replaced) contacted Mars, requesting asylum.

Before its transformation by terraforming, the surface area of Mars had been almost as great as that of the dry land on Earth. Even now that water occupied the lower portions of the terrain, the few millions living there had plenty to spare. Once upon a time its inhabitants might have held onto that land avariciously, but in this enlightened age they gladly welcomed their cousins from Earth. The spaceships which, thousands of years ago, had lifted their ancestors from the home planet were intact, cocooned in great hangars.

True, there was no one who knew how to pilot them, but records and implanted memories remained, and it was not difficult for young men and women to learn. Indeed, to them it was an exciting and unexpected challenge.

The ships, containing the pitiful remnants of Earth's great final civilization, crossed the abyss between the two worlds in a matter of weeks. The whole migration took many months. But at last the home planet was nearly empty of all but plant and animal life—and even some of the latter, unique to Earth, had been ferried to the new world. A few, mainly older, people chose to remain. They would die naturally long before the star's second coming, and preferred to live out their allotted spans in their own homes.

The people who left Earth took with them crystals on which were stored as much as remained of the home world's art and literature, and even some of its science. It was unlikely that they would ever return.

What remained behind them would be safe for centuries, for the white dwarf was still on its way into the depths of space, still at an angle which kept it clear of the outer planets. But its elliptical, cometlike orbit would bring it back to the inner system again and again. And each time it flung its invisible arms around the Sun and danced its deadly jig it would seize more material from the bigger star and hurl much of it into space. But much it would hug to its own chest, miserlike, growing more massive with each passage. As long as the output of light and radiation remained no more than one-fifth above normal, Earth would be scorched but Mars should escape.

Even so, Martian astronomers knew that each return would shorten the period before the next. One day in the far distant future, enough material would have been transferred from the Sun to the white dwarf that it would have absorbed more helium into its core than it could comfortably contain. It too would erupt in a supernova explosion—and the Sun, now itself nothing but a stripped helium core and so effectively itself a white dwarf, would be hurled away like a cast-off lover. Perhaps to wander one day, millions or billions of years hence, into some other unsuspecting star system . . .

The Martians, who over the years had assimilated the immigrant culture from Earth—both groups benefiting from the intermixture, and indeed the interbreeding—began to discuss very seriously the possibility of leaving the Solar System altogether in order to find a safer world orbiting another star. A few probes had been sent into interstellar space, millennia ago, but various historical disturbances had prevented further progress in that direction. Finally, the sending of probes had no longer seemed a necessity, or even particularly desirable. Instruments in space, or on the Moon, could provide all the information required.

Until now.

The brains of the Martian scientists were quite capable of designing theoretical drives that would produce speeds close to that of light. Some even wove dreams of there being tunnels through space, evading the need for such a finite and physical limitation. But the technological base, the industrial infrastructure, for the manufacture of starships no longer existed—especially ships capable of effecting the sort of massive evacuation which would be required. At last they rejected the idea of any massive exodus by mechanical means. Should a more elegant method of travelling to another star present itself—such as a matter transmitter—they would embrace it.

In the course of their researches, one scientist came across an ancient plan for another type of vehicle. A ship to cross not space but *time*.

The older and more entrenched scientists shook their heads in disbelief. Time had long been regarded as the one barrier that would never yield to humankind's probings. Yet . . . the theory behind this proposed machine did seem to be sound. It gave promise of being able to travel backward in time, though never forward, so anyone who attempted such a journey could never return, and those who sent that person would never know for certain whether he or she had succeeded.

Unless it proved possible to tamper with the past.

To change it.

The Journey

Themor and Anela laid their girlchild gently in her capsule. "We should have waited until after the Naming Ceremony," said Anela, not for the first time.

"It is better that she takes up a new identity in the twentieth century," he replied aloud. Sometimes a voice was comforting, if not necessary. "She will carry her name to her death, for she cannot return here. None of us can."

The timeship stood inside a low metal building surrounded in all directions by kilometres of sand—"in case of accidents," the Martian scientists had said. Its circular, domed shape gleamed dully in the sourceless lighting. The man and woman had arrived on Mars nearly two hundred years before in the mass exodus from Earth, and they hoped to return to their original world, but in a much earlier time.

In order for them to do so, the timeship had to be a spaceship also. For they would go back to arrive on their present world—Mars—as it had been twenty thousand years before: barren and lifeless. Then they would have to cross interplanetary space to the Earth, arriving in the year 1969 by the reckoning of that time. That year had been chosen because then, the year of humanity's first landing on the Moon, the world's consciousness had been attuned to the potentials and benefits of the exploration of space in a way that it would not be again for centuries. It also happened to be exactly a century before that first major agent of destruction—the comet—would arrive.

Or as close to that year as possible: travel through time was an unknown science. It was impossible to check results by any experimental or empirical method, only by theory and extrapolation, so calibration was difficult and guidance likely to be imprecise. They tried to ensure that any error would make their arrival early rather than late, because the date of 2069 was crucial; Earth had to be warned of the true nature of this particular coming calamity. Its inhabitants should know, too, of the natural catastrophes which were still thousands of years in the future, so that perhaps technology could be maintained at a level which could defeat these, or at least avoid them. An audiovisual projection had been prepared to help them to communicate the danger. Perhaps even the *human* errors could be avoided by forewarning—though the history to date of humankind made this seem unlikely . . .

And if the generations of the early twenty-first century were able to solve the problems, then perhaps the future could be changed. There lay the paradox. If the future had been changed, surely the time travellers would not be here to go back to an earlier time to alter it? Or were the strands of time somehow interconnected in such a way that the action and the result occurred "simultaneously"—in which case the future would change and no one would ever know that it had? Or did time constantly subdivide, so that one stream or branch would continue from a twentieth century in which mankind escaped the trials which destroyed them in another stream? The scientists and philosophers argued, but had no answer.

All that mattered was that they had to try.

A model could not be tested, because the vehicle that had been built was the smallest practicable size that could function. Some of the spaceships used in the evacuation of Earth had been cannibalized to help construct the timeship. Neither of its crew understood its workings. The scientists had tried to explain, simply, how a loop of cosmic string whirling inside the torus which surrounded the ship, and a mini black hole at its centre, would distort space so that the ship was forced to escape into the fourth dimension of time, but to the temponauts themselves it was meaningless. Just as long as it worked!

Thirty-six babies, aged between two and six months, had been chosen to make the journey along with the two adults. These were the children of parents who were among the most talented of the species, and who had the most powerful psi powers—many of them rare. There was no longer any official genetic program, but it was natural and logical for those with particular strengths to mate and breed. This was the only way currently known that might give their (perhaps even more talented) offspring a chance to live and continue their line.

The majority of the inhabitants of Mars accepted philosophically—even with resignation—the incontrovertible fact that their world would within a few millennia be vaporized by fire. Some hoped that a method might be discovered that would save them or move them to a new location; already, a faction was advocating a crash program to rediscover the means to build starships, using minerals from the relatively close asteroid belts.

Other scientists proposed the use of what might once have been called particle weapons: banks of gamma-ray lasers which could be fired into the white dwarf, literally bursting its heart. An Elder from Earth preached that the answer was not technological, but lay in freeing the mind, the ka, from the chains of the body. The spirit of humanity remained indomitable.

Anela and Themor had been chosen from many applicants, all of whom had children on the timeship. Of the thirty-six babies, their own child was the thirty-sixth to be sealed into its cocoon.

Only hours before, Anela had held the tiny girl and watched her as she in turn gazed and listened with obvious pleasure as her father and his fellow Musicians played a Concert of Leaving. They had tried to make it a joyous occasion, for her sake, but inevitably it was laden with sadness.

Whether they succeeded or failed, those who left in the timeship—if indeed it worked—would never be seen by their fellows again.

#

"There is nothing more to be done. Everything is prepared. All we can do now is activate the ship and hope. And pray," said Themor now. They had to be alone out here because of the possibility of danger from this untested machine. In fact, the scientists had said encouragingly, the most probable accident, in the unlikely event that any of the safety measures should fail, was that it would tunnel its way to the centre of the planet.

Both were already wearing close-fitting suits and skullcaps woven from a material that would protect them from the intense magnetic fields generated by the operation of the torus. The babies wore a similar material, although their cocoons should be protection enough. For the two adults, spacesuits and helmets could quickly be donned over these undersuits in an emergency.

They passed through the door into the control cabin, and Anela placed a palm on the tiny receptor which closed it. They seated themselves at the instrument console. Themor checked that the bubble canopy was in place, for it was so transparent that it was difficult to tell. He placed a hand on a darker panel, and mentally activated the sequence which should project them back in time. Both their faces were tense.

The black band which surrounded the upper sphere of the psibot glowed ruby red, showing that the mental pathways were clear. The crystals set in the control desk flickered briefly through a sequence of colours: violet, blue, yellow, magenta, green. All appeared to be well. Anela sent a telepathic message to the scientists at the laboratory five kilometres away, and received a mental green light.

"We cannot delay any longer," she said, and reached for Themor's hand.

He did not remove it from hers as he gave the command.

There was the faintest humming sound. The sequence of crystal lights changed rapidly, and then everything became insubstantial. The walls of the cabin were translucent, and through them could be seen the tiered rows of ovoid capsules containing their precious hope for the future.

Or their past. Which was it? They could no longer distinguish.

The torus which spun around the diameter of the ship glowed an impossible colour, unknown to any human spectrum. Then it, too, became almost transparent. Through it, the walls of their hangar were visible only briefly before they winked out of existence; then there was just desert outside, and beyond it the green-clad cone of the Lesser Mountain, blued by distance.

They watched as blue-green plant-growth retreated down the slopes and disappeared, leaving the volcano bare and stark. The sky changed from blue to violet. Clouds flickered briefly, and now the sky became orange-pink.

On one of two rectangular black readouts, white numbers flickered, too fast to read. On the other they moved more slowly, counting not years but centuries. Simultaneously, the crystals sparkled green. There was a wrenching, lurching sensation. The walls clouded, coalesced and became substantial.

But for a moment the numbers continued to flick, backwards:

1969 . . .

1960 . . .

1950 . . .

1945 . . .

1944 . . .

They slowed.

1943 . . .

1942 . . .

1941 . . .

1940.

They stopped.

#

For long minutes neither said a word. Then Anela spoke:

"We have arrived too early."

"Maybe not. We cannot be certain that the readout is accurate. The engineers tried to calibrate it by the method of dating used in this era, but who knows if they got it right? We might easily have arrived a decade or more on either side of that date. Well, we cannot go forward, and we cannot risk trying to travel further backward. We must hope that the people of 1940, if that's indeed where—when—we've arrived, are sufficiently advanced to understand and heed our warning. But, if they are not, we shall just have to bide our time.

"Time *is* on our side, after all!"

They both laughed, more in relief at being alive and obviously on an earlier Mars than at his attempted joke.

Then Themor frowned, and pointed out through the canopy.

Beyond was only a swirling ochre fog.

Anela put her hand to her mouth. "What is it? Where are we?"

Themor searched his extensive memory. "Don't worry. It seems that, before the planet was terraformed, dust storms were common on Mars. We must have arrived during one of those. If we wait, it may pass."

But it did not.

Once the clouds parted for long enough that they could see the Lesser Mountain, which had once been known as Uranius Tholus but in the time in which (they hoped) they had arrived was as yet unknown by human astronomers, as were any of the volcanoes of Mars. So at least they knew they were still in the area from which they had departed.

But the dust storm raged for day after day. They did not dare open the canopy, for the cabin would have filled with dust that even the automatic extractors could not have removed.

They checked their tiny passengers, who were still safely in a mentally induced state of sedation. Checking the ship itself was both unnecessary and pointless, for it was self-regulating and, while the necessary knowledge had been implanted in their minds, they could have done little in the case of a technical problem.

At last Themor said, "We shall have to risk leaving here for Earth. It should not be difficult, and if we can get above the dust storm we should be able to make visual observations. We must put our spacesuits on, though—in case of mishaps. You take the controls."

For a moment Anela looked about to argue. Then she placed her hand on the panel which controlled the spatial drive, her face set.

"Go!" she muttered.

Sluggishly the timeship lifted, hovering above the sand. Then it moved towards the east, as they had been instructed. In moments Anela knew they were lost.

Surely she was heading too far north? She swung the massive craft around.

Suddenly a flattened peak loomed grey through the canopy. She ordered the ship to rise. It did, but the base of the ship narrowly missed the volcanic peak. Which mountain was it? She tried to recall the map of Mars. But both their minds, once so brilliant and sharp, seemed dull, their thoughts turgid mud.

The canopy brightened and darkened, yellow and purple-brown. Anela tried to raise the ship, to send it streaking out into space, its true element. Its angle increased. Had she succeeded? Perhaps: ahead was darkness.

Too late, she realized that the darkness was the shadowed side of a mountain—perhaps the Great Mountain itself! Anela linked minds with Themor and together they willed the craft to rise above it. Almost, they succeeded. But there was a grating crash, and they were flung back and forth as the fluted underside of the craft scraped rock.

Anela wrestled with the controls and kept the craft upright, though it rocked from side to side.

"Get out!" she shouted in his mind. "Quickly. Take the scoutship. And—take our child!"

There was no time for hesitation. Themor left the control cabin and opened the cocoon which contained his baby daughter. He felt guilt at trying to save only his own child, but there would be no logic in taking any other in preference, and nor was there room for more—and he was only human. A hatch in the outer wall opened, and he walked—staggered—straight into a smaller version of their control cabin.

Housed in a special bay, a small scoutcraft had been provided which, despite its small size, should be able to cross the abyss between Earth and Mars—just once—and land. Or so it was hoped. It had been included mainly in case there might be a need for the timeship to remain in orbit while the scout made a reconnaissance below.

Or for an eventuality such as this.

There was nowhere to put the baby, so he laid her gently across his lap as he sat down and activated the outer door in the main ship. The lifeship shot out of its bay like a cork from a bottle just as the timeship flipped on end. He sent a message of hope, love and regret to his wife as he watched her ship, below him, flutter like a leaf in a gale and turn over so that it was flying upside down. It vanished into the dust storm.

His own ship sped into space.

#

Even as she fought to right the ship, some implanted memory in Anela's non-technical brain surfaced and told her that the air of this earlier Mars was much thinner than anyone had known—this was why the timeship had failed to gain lift. Hopefully, the little scout would fare better. It *must*.

Somehow she got her craft right-side-up and flying level again. In which direction, she did not know. Yes, of course she did, for an instrument had been provided for that purpose. Almost due south. Another instrument should tell her how high she was. That could not be right! It read "ZERO."

Sand spurted on all sides as she skidded across red desert, now below the dust cloud. If the land remained flat, she might just be able to come to a safe landing . . .

The ship rocked and juddered as it ploughed a furrow in the sand, grating on bedrock. It jerked almost to a stop. Then it tipped on end, bounced on rock several times, and began to fall. Down, down. Through the canopy, dimly seen through a shower of falling sand, was a canyon wall, passing rapidly upward. The altimeter showed negative numbers.

There was a rending crash, and Anela was thrown across the control board, unconscious.

#

When she came to, Anela heard a rumbling roar. The lower half of the canopy was obscured by reddish sand, and more was cascading down on the timeship in a landslide which she must have precipitated.

Quickly she left the control cabin and tried to activate the outer hatch. It would not open, no doubt because of the pressure of sand around it. She felt a wave of panic. Then she opened the door into the bay which had housed the scoutship. Air whistled out, but she was safe in her spacesuit. The babies were secure in their capsules.

The crash of the timeship had damaged this section most, and the edges of the bay were curled back and ragged. The teeth of rocks protruded into the ship. But at least this was a way out.

She dashed back into the cabin and removed the psibot from its recess. If the ship was buried, she would make sure that its Beacon would function, so she could find the ship and its precious cargo again. And so could any rescuers—though she knew how unlikely that was.

She pushed the psibot through the serrated gap and crawled through after it, even remembering to close the door behind her. The avalanche of sand was abating now, but it had left a delta-shaped slope leading up to the curved bite made by the craft in the rim of the canyon into which she had fallen. Through it, a single beam of amber sunlight pierced the retreating dust cloud and spotlit the almost-buried ship.

She placed the psibot on a flat rock that stood clear of the debris, extended its supports, and mentally activated it. Then she stood, hands on hips, staring around—and, finally, upwards.

Where was she going to go? Was there any point in going anywhere? Human survival characteristics had been passed down the millennia—and, so, perhaps, had wishful thinking. Anela searched her implanted memories.

They were scarce, and untrustworthy, for this period, but there was a record that for some tens of years a small colony had existed on this part of Mars, housed under domes. It was some decades ahead of her present time, if the readout in the timeship could be trusted. But suppose it had been wrong—wrong by only so much as a century? A century was a mere tick of the clock compared to the millennia they had travelled back.

She had to do all she could to save their uniquely talented children. And she would still be in time to warn the people of this age, should she find any, about the comet which was heading their way, perhaps only decades from now, should Themor fail in his own mission.

The whole affair seemed wholly misconceived and ill fated now, but still she had to try . . .

She climbed the slope of detritus, pausing frequently for breath. Physical activity of this sort was unknown to her, and the sensation and the smell of sweat—running down her face, dampening her hair, trickling down her neck inside her spacesuit—were new and unpleasant.

At last she reached the rim. The dust storm had diminished, and only a few twisting dust devils chased each other across the sands.

Which way to go? She searched for any sign of mental activity, but found none. She activated the unfamiliar controls of the black box on the chest of her suit—a receiver and transmitter of the radio waves believed to have been used in this primitive period.

There was no response.

She began to stumble along the long furrow made in the desert by the timeship as it had skidded towards the canyon. Twice she tripped and fell, once twisting awkwardly and hitting her backpack on a rock. There was a hissing sound somewhere inside her suit. A crystal flashed red inside her helmet.

Again she fell, and this time she did not get up.

She clutched at her throat, unable to breathe. Her mouth opened, gasping for air. Her eyes bulged. Her vision reddened.

The last object she saw before her sight failed forever was a bright, blue-white star, quite close to the Sun. It was a double star, for it had a close, grey companion.

Not a double star at all. A double *planet*.

Anela sent a final mental prayer towards the Earth.

Arrival

Themor felt a sense of failure. He had never imagined that he would arrive in such a nightmare world—could hardly believe that such a world even existed, that humans would voluntarily inflict such violence and suffering upon humans, and in which innocent old people and children suffered and died needlessly and in great pain.

He had hoped to be able to search for someone in authority, someone to warn. But in his small craft he had no power left to do more than hover over a small area of the night hemisphere. Still, old habits die hard, and he could not ignore the cries for help that he heard in his mind.

So he had aided the pilot of some kind of winged airship to reach the ground safely when his primitive safety mechanism—a billowing disc full of trapped air—was activated too late. He suspected that the man was one of the perpetrators of destruction on this city, but he had entered the man's mind and found it to be basically good.

To save the man he had used his most precious talents. First, teleportation to prevent the pilot from striking the ground. Then he had had to reach out and somnify the men who were about to attack them both when they landed. The hatred and fear in their minds had horrified and sickened him.

He had helped an incredibly ancient-looking woman in the only way he was able: to find the peace she desired, in her ruined home.

He was left exhausted. Worse, he had been hit by some jagged metal projectile while he was floating high above the ground. He had discarded his spacesuit so as not to draw attention to himself. He did not know if he had the strength to regenerate his damaged internal organs. He was about to move on when he saw more of the air-filled fabric domes descending. From each was suspended not a man but a canister of death.

Two exploded in the large building which he knew to be full of highly volatile and inflammable liquids. Another fell onto the roof of a house without exploding. It was closely followed by the toppling stack which had stood at one end of the large building. Adjusting his visor for night vision, he could see two figures—and a baby—inside the house and obviously in great danger.

He dropped over the blazing building, enveloping the flames with his ship's null-G field. Deprived of gravity, the fire quickly smothered itself in its own waste products. Then he drew up the deadly cylinder in the same field, took it inside the scoutship, and disarmed its primitive but—normally—effective mechanism.

He landed and entered the house. His senses were assailed by the unfamiliar smells and sounds of smoke and explosives. He found the woman and her son half-buried in rubble. He extricated them and performed routine first-aid on the boy. The baby girl he could not help, for she was dead.

A girl child . . .

His vision blurred, and he lurched. He would surely be condemning his daughter to death; yet she would die anyway if he took no action. He could read in the woman's mind that she was kind and, given a chance, would look after his daughter well. This was the last world he would have chosen in which to have her raised; but what else could he do? He had come on a mission, and in his daughter lay the final, despairing hope of passing on his message. The future of humanity was in the balance. He must not fail.

Themor returned to his ship, taking the tiny body of the dead child with him. His ship's power supply was almost spent. Minutes later, he was back in the wrecked room. He set his own child—the changeling—in place of the dead infant, laying her tenderly on the chair. But not before he had implanted as many of his own memories as he could into his daughter's brain—a matter of moments.

He tried to halt the process before reaching the most recent memories, of horror and destruction and hatred. But he was weak, and unable to stop.

Too late.

He wept.

The memories of this hell of human barbarism might well cripple her mind forever.

There was no way of erasing those memories again, but . . .

Desperately, he tried to set up a mental block, so that her mind could remain whole.

He did his best. He thought he had succeeded, but couldn't be sure. No time to check . . .

He stood for a moment, looking down at his newly awakened daughter, and bade her goodbye with a blessing. It was all he could do for her now.

Footsteps were approaching.

He left, silently.

#

Themor looked down on the shattered remnants of what had once been a great city, and felt a great sadness. There was a sense of lost opportunities as he took his last view of the city—a shimmering red glow, seen through shifting clouds of smoke.

Then he activated the self-destruct button which would vaporize his ship; warning the species was one thing, but it would be an unforgivable crime to allow the people of this era to lay their hands on such futuristic technology—especially since, on the current evidence, it seemed they would incapable of turning it to anything but warlike ends.

With a soundless blue flash, the man from the future and his ship vanished.

Below, in a ruined house, a hungry baby cried.

EPILOGUE

Aurora and Bryan Beaumont stood on a hill overlooking the Space Centre. The evening sky was a luminous turquoise, brightening to lemon at the horizon. A pale crescent Moon followed the Sun to rest. High above it a ruddy star glowed steadily.

Mars.

Had they really been there?

Aurora proudly held their child—a healthy, robust boy with red hair and pale violet eyes.

Three kilometres away, across the sand, a battery of floodlights suddenly burst into life, starkly exposing the winged shape of the shuttle being readied for launch. It carried the crew of the third Mars mission.

"The technology learned from the crashed timeship we found is already proving invaluable," said Beaumont. "And perhaps—just perhaps—humankind's now ready to use it in a way of which its makers might have approved. What do you think, darling?"

"Only time will tell," said Aurora, then neatly evaded a nudge in the ribs from her husband. It was impossible to make a remark like that now without it seeming a pun. "At least it seems there will definitely be a Mars colony very soon. And there's talk of starting to terraform the planet in a few years' time. So the future—or is it the past?—has been changed already, it seems."

"And they're talking about using a version of that ion-drive to go out to Jupiter's moons Ganymede and Europa—maybe even Titan," mused Beaumont. "I doubt they'll ever figure out the time-travel aspect though— or the antigravity. It's like giving Galileo a TV set and expecting him to build one."

"I'm not sure I'd want them to make a time machine, ever," said Aurora. She suppressed a shudder.

Little Themor, too, shivered, but in his case it was because a cool breeze had riffled his fine, curly hair.

"Yes, it's getting late," said Aurora, wrapping him tighter. "Nearly your bedtime."

Beaumont frowned in concentration. "You know, I can't get my head around this time business," he remarked. "You said just now that it looks as if the past of your people has been changed. If so, they don't know it, because you're still here. You didn't suddenly vanish when your mission was accomplished. Thank God!" He squeezed her waist, now slim again.

Aurora looked sad for a moment. "I know. I wish there was some way of telling if I've really accomplished anything. I must have, mustn't I? The rulers in the Middle East now know that their cities will be destroyed in 2069, and that it will be a natural disaster, not an act of war. In fact, I hear they are already starting to evacuate them, and build new cities in safe locations."

"And we're looking at the possibility of detecting that comet nucleus while it's still millions of kilometres away and deflecting it—maybe even destroying it—using some of those missiles and warheads that governments around the world weren't supposed to have."

"Well, just as long as that's *all* they use them for . . . "

"So we can only hope that the other time theory is right. That the timestream *we* are in will continue, and that those unwanted visitors from space won't have the terrible effects that your memories say they did. I wouldn't put it past the technology of a few thousands of years hence to be able to destroy that white dwarf."

Arm in arm, they started to walk slowly back down to their apartment. Aurora was still having to act as a guinea pig, for the scientists wanted to know as much as they could about her longevity and her regenerative capability—not to mention her psi abilities. She sighed. It would be a long time before they were allowed to live as a normal family. It was a penalty she was glad to pay. And yet, sometimes . . .

Her husband was talking, and she brought back her concentration.

"There's something I've been wanting to ask you. When you were telling us—and the whole world—about the memories that had returned, you seemed about to . . . well, you said something about sensing a paradox," he said. "I've thought about that a lot since, and I think I know what you were going to say."

"Oh, Bryan, your poor head!" She smiled, and then her face grew serious again. "Go on."

"You said that the first conclusive signs of psi powers appeared just about now—as far as you could tell. Now, you were out in that radiation storm on Mars, and Robert said it was almost bound to have affected the genes of our child. He's healthy, thank Heaven—all the tests show that. But, even if the child of a woman from the future and a man from today wouldn't necessarily have, well, 'unusual' powers, it must be possible that the flare caused some sort of mutation. Mustn't it? And it's not just you: you said yourself that I have some sort of psi ability; well, I've proved it, haven't I?

"A lot of people seem to think that "mutant" means some kind of monster. *You're* not a little monster, are you? Well, only sometimes." He tickled Themor under the chin. The baby chuckled indulgently, then went back to watching a model aircraft that was buzzing high overhead. "They've just seen too many bad movies, I guess. Mutations can often be beneficial—or at the very least . . . different. And there are more and more men and women going out into space. It's inevitable that they'll receive doses of radiation above the norm. For that matter, the people living in space stations have already been affected to some extent. You see what I'm getting at?"

"I saw it the moment you opened your mouth," said Aurora. She was not yet sure exactly what active psi talents she possessed herself, other than healing and—well, she was still awaiting an opportunity to tell him how, since soon after her memories had returned, she had often been able to "read" his thoughts. She regretted her lack of training and guidance.

She continued, "At first you thought that *we* would start—had started—this whole psi ball rolling, by getting together. That if I hadn't come back in time, psi would still be a random and unpredictable power . . . OK, I admit it: yes, that was going through my mind, too, back on Mars when I made that broadcast.

"But then you just defeated your own argument by suggesting that it's the radiation from solar flares and living in space that have caused psi powers to appear.

"I shouldn't worry about it if I were you. You'll hurt your brain!"

Little Themor certainly wasn't worrying about it. He was too busy making the model airplane loop the loop.

About the Author

David A. Hardy is internationally renowned as one of the world's leading astronomical, space and science-fiction artists. His cover illustrations have appeared on most major science-fiction magazines, including *Analog*, *The Magazine of Fantasy & Science Fiction* and *Interzone*, and he has done countless interior illustrations for magazines and books, as well as much advertising work. A retrospective of his art, with text by Chris Morgan, appeared in 2001 as *Hardyware*.

Nonfiction books written and illustrated by Hardy include *Challenge of the Stars* (with Patrick Moore), *Galactic Tours* (with Bob Shaw), *Atlas of the Solar System*, and *Visions of Space*. His short stories and factual articles have appeared in numerous magazines and newspapers, including *New Scientist* and *Astronomy Now*. A second novel is in progress.

He is a Fellow, Board Member and former President of the International Association of Astronomical Artists (IAAA), a Fellow of the British Interplanetary Society, and a recipient of the Lucien Rudaux Memorial Award. In 2003 an asteroid was named after him.

His website is at **http://www.astroart.org**

Printed in the United Kingdom
by Lightning Source UK Ltd.
9703400001BA/7-18